W

by

KATE BENEDICT

CHIMERA

Wages of Sin first published in 2000 by
Chimera Publishing Ltd
PO Box 152
Waterlooville
Hants
PO8 9FS

Printed and bound in Great Britain by
Caledonian International Book Manufacturing Ltd
Glasgow

WAGES OF SIN

Kate Benedict

Chapter One

'Faster, Alex! Faster!' urged Jane, thwacking his flanks smartly with the short quirt in her hand. The hot, silken muscles clenched and flexed between her thighs, sending quivers of excitement spiralling through her body, and the horse surged forward in response to the small heels drumming against his sides. She laughed with exhilaration and crouched down on his neck, her long auburn hair streaming backwards as they thundered over the long sweep of grass beside the coppice.

She should be at home, like a dutiful daughter, helping her mother supervise the servants as they swept the winter's accumulation of stale rushes from the floor and replaced them with the fresh, sweet-smelling ones the carter had delivered yesterday. Her nose wrinkled at the thought. The whole place stank of smoke, dogs, and the ancient food – and God alone knew what else! – that had been carelessly dropped to rot underfoot over the long dark nights.

It had been a matter of moments to make up her mind and tiptoe out of the hall like a sneak thief, only breathing once she'd reached the safety of the stables. She laughed again as she thought of the expression of outraged respectability on the young groom's face as she'd swung up on to Alex's back without benefit of saddle or bridle. Well-born young ladies were expected to ride sedately side-saddle, accompanied by an equally sedate maid, not behave like hoydens. Ignoring his protests, she'd grinned at him mischievously and, with a final jaunty wave, wheeled out of the yard – to freedom.

Alex was slowing now, his first energy spent. Jane allowed him to drop to a canter, enjoying the fresh green morning. Sun dappled the grass and she inhaled the still, cool air, savouring the signs of spring. White flowers studded the branches of the hawthorn and bluebells covered the ground beneath the trees like a sweet-scented tide.

Guilt washed over her at the thought of her poor mother, stuck at home in the middle of all the muddle and stench – and no doubt wringing her hands with worry, lest her stepfather, Thomas, find fault with her housekeeping. Jane's face darkened. The man was a braggart and a bully, taking a sadistic delight in terrorising his unfortunate wife. Nothing was ever to his satisfaction: the beer was too thin; the meat either over or underdone; the servants too well-fed, pert and idle. In a thousand little ways he made her mother's life a misery, as if to make up for his lower birth by proving himself her master in every other way.

Jane sighed again. There was nothing she could do about it. Women were chattels to be given in marriage wherever their fathers – or in this case, His Majesty, King Henry VIII – deemed fit. Her mother had been handed over in reward, as easily and as thoughtlessly as some cheap gewgaw at Saint Audrey's Fair. You want a well-off widow with her own estate? Here! Take her – and welcome!

Her lips tightened. The only thing Thomas – she could never think of him as 'father' – was generous with was his fists. A slap for a maidservant too slow with the serving. A buffet for the manservant who spilt the wine. And though her mother never said anything, Jane could draw her own conclusions from the dark fingerprints that sometimes appeared on the white skin of her arm, or the puffy lips that were swollen from more than overenthusiastic kisses. The secrets of her mother's bedchamber were not happy ones, going by their consequences.

She brightened. She might not be able to change her mother's life, but at least she could bring a little taste of pleasure into it. She would pluck an armful of bluebells and carry them home to her as both gift and apology. Tugging Alex's mane, she brought him to a halt beside the coppice. The grass was sweet and fresh. Even without a halter, he would remain, gently cropping until she returned.

The ground was soft underfoot and the scent of flowers dizzying in the morning sunlight as she wove her way into the coppice in search of the prettiest ones. Reaching a small clearing, she flung herself down on the smooth grass with a sigh of contentment, her green dress blending with her surroundings and giving her a sense of invulnerability. She smiled, remembering how when she was younger, she and the other children would put fern seed in their shoes to make themselves invisible and how her mother would pretend not to see her as she danced around the bedchamber pretending to be one of the Little People.

Lying on her back she stared dreamily up at the birds flitting in and out of the canopy of trees above her. Spring was the time for mating – and in a month's time she would be mated too. The dressmaker had already finished her gown of cloth-of-silver and she would walk down the aisle of the tiny church, her wild red hair streaming down her back, to show that she came proudly virgin to her husband. She smiled. She was luckier than most. She had been betrothed to Ralph since she was four.

She sighed. Handsome Ralph with his dark hair, his warm brown eyes and merry smile. They had known each other since they were children and loved each other almost as long. Hers would be no loveless match of convenience, followed by an unwilling bedding. Their marriage might be designed to link their two families and join the estates but, on her wedding night, she would give her young body to his with joy and pleasure.

At the thought, a pang of excitement ran through her. The private place between her thighs, which still throbbed from her wild ride, moistened, and her breath came thicker in her throat. Her nipples stood out hard against the rough cloth of her bodice and she pulled it down to release her breasts, one hand idly stroking them as she thought of Ralph's eager lips against her warm flesh. The night before she had stood naked in front of her mirror, trying to see herself through his eyes, admiring the way her white body looked in the candlelight: the sweet fullness of her breasts, with their rose-coloured tips; the soft curve of her hips, and the way her red maidenhair blazed like a flame at the juncture of her slender thighs.

The throbbing between those thighs was more demanding now. Glancing round to ensure she was still alone, she pulled her skirts up to her waist, spreading her legs on the cool grass. The warm sunshine lit her auburn hair like a bonfire, and its warmth tantalised her already overheated skin. Tentatively at first, she stroked the soft cleft, shuddering at her own touch. She knew it was a sin to pleasure herself and her impure act would have to be atoned for at her next confession – but it was such a sweet sin, and the sensations radiating out from her exploring fingers swept her doubts away.

She gasped as she slid one finger inside herself, feeling the hot wetness grip it. She moved it gently in and out, her thumb stroking the hard nub which had sprung erect at her touch, and the craving grew. Her hand moved faster and another finger joined the first, widening the moist opening. Even that, however, was not enough to satisfy the hunger that tormented her.

Eyes closed, she groped around for the quirt she had dropped when she first lay down. Her fingers closed over the thick smooth handle. Parting herself with one hand, she pressed it against her eager cleft, moaning at the sweet ache of her body's resistance. She arched her back, there was a sudden, swift pain, then it slid smoothly and easily inside and she groaned with pleasure as its hard length filled her. This was how Ralph would feel on their wedding night.

Her hand moved faster now, pushing the quirt in and out, her hips pumping in time to the thrusts, while the other fondled her swollen nipples. She writhed and whimpered as one final stroke brought her blessed release and she sagged back against the warm earth.

The sound of a laugh brought her bolt upright with shock, frantically tugging her clothing back into place. Heart beating, she looked round with frightened eyes, then relaxed slowly. There was no one there. It must have been a bird calling. Even so, she flushed scarlet at the thought that someone might have seen her brazenly caressing her own body and she scrambled to her feet, smoothing down her skirts. Perhaps it was time to go home after all. She quickly gathered a bunch of bluebells and wended her way back through the coppice to the place where she had left Alex.

He was still there, peacefully cropping the spring grass – and none too pleased to be recalled to his duties, either. She was forced to use her quirt, its handle still sticky from its earlier service, to remind him of his manners. Cradling her flowers in one arm, she urged the horse on and they jogged sedately home again, the rosy glow on Jane's cheeks the only reminder of her wanton behaviour in the woods. She would creep back as quietly as she had crept out – and no one would be the wiser.

She was wrong.

'Mistress Jane! Mistress Jane! Where have you been?' gasped old Alice, panting up as fast as her bulk would allow her. 'We've been looking everywhere for you. Your lady mother is frantic and as for your father–' her eyes rolled round fearfully, in case he was in the vicinity '–he is quite beside himself with rage.'

'Much as usual then,' Jane said ruefully. 'Though, the Blessed Virgin knows, one of him is quite enough to be going on with.' She smiled at the elderly woman who had been her nurse and was now her lady's maid. 'Calm yourself, Alice. I am here now. No doubt it is all a storm in a cup. I'm sure the rushes were laid just as well without me.'

'It isn't that,' began Alice, wringing her hands. 'It's—'

'God's blood girl, where have you been?' demanded her stepfather, striding up, his heavy features mottled red with fury. 'The entire household has been hunting you this hour past.' His eyes ranked over her, taking in her shabby green gown, with its damp hem and grass-stained skirts. 'Sir Harry is in the solar with your mother and you're gallivanting round the countryside looking like a kitchen slut! Get to your chamber and make yourself presentable.' He stamped off again, almost knocking Alice over.

Jane's lips curved in a happy smile. Sir Harry! Ralph's father – and no doubt, Ralph with him. She slid lightly from Alex's back and patted Alice's withered cheek. 'Well, woman? What are you waiting for?' she demanded. 'Come and help me into my best gown.'

Grinning happily, Alice puffed after her young mistress.

'There, my lovely, what do you think?' Alice beamed, holding the hand mirror up to show Jane the back of her head. Jane nodded in satisfaction. Her wild locks had been tamed, smoothed into thick coils and entwined with strings of freshwater pearls that sat like dewdrops on the shimmering hair.

'Beautiful,' she replied. 'Thank you.' She got to her feet in a rustle of petticoats and walked across to the long mirror to see the full effect. She smiled at her reflection. The rich amber velvet of her gown complemented her auburn hair and swung like a heavy flower with every step. The wooden corset that Alice had laced as tightly as she could manage thrust her breasts into prominence over the low-cut, square neckline, and the embroidered stomacher emphasised the neatness of her waist. The long sleeves belled out gracefully, concealing her hands so only the fingertips showed beneath them. The very latest fashion, according to her dressmaker, who had her news directly from a cousin who served at court.

'Set by Mistress Boleyn,' the woman had said proudly. She had lowered her voice then and glanced around before continuing. 'Though some say 'tis to disguise a deformity of the hand and that she's a witch.' Her eyes widened with a mixture of horror and delight. 'Using her black arts to entice His Majesty away from good Queen Catherine.'

Jane smiled again and twirled in front of the mirror. Black arts or no black arts, it was a pretty style and she was sure Ralph would appreciate it. She bit her lips and pinched her cheeks to bring colour to them, then turned and dropped smoothly into an exaggerated curtsy. 'There,' she said, smiling at Alice. 'Will I do?'

'Beautiful, lovey. Just beautiful,' beamed Alice, one gnarled hand fondly stroking Jane's russet hair. 'But be quick now. They're waiting for you.'

With a final smile at her old nurse, Jane hurried along the gallery and into the solar.

Her mother's anxious expression disappeared as soon as Jane entered the solar, the worry-wrinkles smoothing out of her pale face, to be replaced by a proud smile. Sir Harry was standing by the window that overlooked the great park, talking earnestly with her stepfather. They both looked up at her entrance and she sank into another curtsey, smiling at them demurely from beneath her lashes. The wild girl who'd lain pleasuring herself on the woodland sward might never have existed.

'Ah, Jane,' smiled Sir Harry, revealing a mouthful of rotting teeth. 'As pretty as ever.' He bussed her on both cheeks and she was hard put not to recoil from the revolting stench of his breath. She forced a smile, her eyes searching the room. Where was Ralph? Hunting? Hawking? Surely not. Even with their wedding so close at hand and the rest of their lives in front of them, he wouldn't have missed a chance of seeing her. Perhaps he was indisposed.

'You are well, my lord?' she asked. He nodded. 'And Ralph?' she went on eagerly. 'He is well too?'

His expression darkened. 'Ralph's dead,' he said bluntly. 'Damned boy.' He snorted. 'Always was a weakling. Took after his late mother.'

For a moment the room went dark and she thought she was going to faint.

Ralph? Dead? Impossible. How could he be dead? He was but seventeen, with his whole life before him. Their whole lives before them. She stared at him, her green eyes huge in her white face. 'Dead?' she whispered.

'Sweating sickness,' grunted Sir Harry. 'A sennight since.'

A wave of nausea swept over her. Dead a week and she

hadn't even known. His warm lips cold and his sweet body already mouldering in the grave. She bit her knuckles to suppress the sobs that threatened to overcome her.

'Never fear, sweeting,' chuckled Sir Harry. 'Your finery won't be wasted. You'll still have your wedding.'

She stared at him in disbelief. What did he mean? How could she still have her wedding when her betrothed was dead and buried? The man was mad. The loss of his son must have turned his brain.

Oblivious of her thoughts, he continued. 'Your father and I have been talking,' he said cheerfully. 'There's no reason why our estates should not still be joined. If you cannot have the son – why, then you shall have the father!' He chuckled jovially, his protuberant eyes running over her, lingering hungrily on the swell of her bosom. 'And between us we'll soon beget another heir.'

She gaped at him in horror. What was he talking about? He was older than her own mother and had seen two wives into the grave already. Did he seriously imagine that she was eager to be the third?

Her eyes took in Sir Harry's thick-lipped, purple face and balding head with its few remaining tufts of greying hair. Despite his bereavement he was dressed in his best: a richly coloured doublet and hose, with an exaggerated codpiece flaunting his manhood. His potbelly bulged out over his spindly shanks, making him look like a jaunty old cockerel crowing on a dung-heap.

Bile rose in the back of her throat at the thought of sharing a bed with this wizened old man, instead of her beloved Ralph. Marry Sir Harry? Never!

She spun on her heel and stalked towards the door, her skirts swishing angrily. 'Wed that filthy old lecher,' she spat over her shoulder. 'I'd rather die!'

Chapter Two

'What is it, my lamb?' asked Alice anxiously as Jane marched into her bedchamber and flung herself on the bed. She dropped the armful of clothes she'd been tidying away and sat down beside the girl, laying a comforting hand on the quivering shoulders. 'What's upset you?'

'I'm to be married,' said Jane brokenly.

Alice smiled. Was that all? Most girls got a touch of the greensickness at the thought of leaving their mothers. Time remedied all. Why, this time next year Mistress Jane could be a mother herself and all this pother forgotten. 'There, there,' she soothed, patting her shaking charge. ''Tis nothing to fret about. Master Ralph is a fine boy. He'll treat you properly, you mark my words.'

Jane sat up, her eyes red with weeping. 'You don't understand,' she cried. 'Ralph's dead! They want to marry me off to his stinking old father instead!'

Alice's mouth fell open. Her pretty young Jane, still barely out of childhood, wed to that old popinjay? She sighed and shook her head. The child would have no say in the matter. If her stepfather said she would be married, then married she'd be, no matter how she felt about it. And as the old country saying had it, 'What can't be cured must be endured'.

Still, she did her best to console the girl. 'It won't be too bad,' she soothed. 'He's an old man. How long can he last? A few years? Then you'll be mistress of his estate and your parents too, when the time comes.' She smiled slyly. 'And a rich widow can pick and choose to please herself.' She thought of Jane's mother and a frown creased her brow. 'Mostly,' she added honestly.

Jane shuddered. 'I can't,' she whispered. 'How can I share a bed with him and – and do *that*? She closed her eyes, shivering with disgust.

Alice could imagine her thoughts: those clammy, age-spotted hands crawling over Jane's innocent body; those bony knees forcing themselves between her thighs and…

Jane shook her head. 'I just can't,' she repeated desperately.

'Maybe you won't have to,' smiled Alice. 'If your parents know how strongly you feel.' She did not have much faith in that idea, but Jane was prepared to cling to any straw.

'Do you think so?' she asked eagerly. 'Maybe you're right.' Hope gave her more confidence and she corrected herself. 'Of course you're right!' She laughed contemptuously. 'They can't force me into his bed, can they?' She shuddered as though she was suppressing a wave of sorrow. Alice was not surprised. A lady did not weep and wail in public like a serving maid. No doubt Jane would mourn for Ralph later, in the privacy of her bed, when the candles were blown out and the darkness hid her tears, but for now she was putting on a brave face.

'Undress me,' Jane ordered. 'There is no point to this finery now. My green gown is good enough for everyday wear.'

Muttering, Alice did as she was told, lifting the heavy amber velvet over her charge's head and smoothing the full skirts before going to hang it in the garderobe.

Dressed in her shift, Jane sat down at her tiny mirror and impatiently began to untwine the pearls from her hair.

'Wha-!' she exclaimed as the door of her bedchamber

banged open. She looked up with startled eyes to see her stepfather standing in the doorway. He strode in and seized her arm in an iron grip, spinning her round to face him. She opened her mouth to protest at this rough treatment, but before she could utter a word his open hand slapped her face hard. She recoiled, holding her injured cheek.

'How dare you shame me before Sir Harry?' he hissed.

'You shame yourself,' spat Jane. 'Behaving like some gypsy horse-trader! Selling me off like a brood mare to the highest bidder.' Her lips tightened and she flung her head back, haughty despite the white finger marks on her cheek. 'I will not marry him,' she said insolently. 'No matter what you do.' Her lips curled in contempt as she looked at his face, swollen with ill-temper and frustrated ambition. 'You may carry me to the altar kicking and screaming, but even you cannot make me say "Yes" once I get there.'

He controlled himself with difficulty and a cruel smile twisted his mouth. 'Do you really think I can be bested by a slip of a girl?' he grinned. 'We'll see how strong that will of yours is after a few days on bread and water – and a little taste of what's to come if you continue in your headstrong ways.'

Wrenching her to her feet, he bent her over his knee and his hand rose and fell as he chastised her like a child. As she struggled futilely to escape her flimsy linen shift rode up, revealing the soft white thighs and rounded buttocks beneath. She squealed in pain and outrage as his palm, rough and calloused from riding, smacked against her tender flesh, making the globes of her bottom quiver and redden with every blow, the marks of his fingers standing out white against the flushed skin. He grunted with a mixture of fury, excitement and effort as she writhed against him, her legs kicking frantically in the air. Finally he stood up and flung her from him. She stood with her back to her chamber wall, panting with rage and humiliation.

He grinned at her mockingly. 'Not so proud now, are you, my lady?' he sneered.

She flinched at the way his eyes ran over her body, barely concealed by the thin shift, lingering on her firm young breasts as they heaved with her outrage.

The grin became a leer. 'If Sir Harry could see you now he would forgo your dowry entirely.' His lascivious chuckle made her blood run cold. 'I envy him the taking of your maidenhead,' he whispered lewdly. 'There's nothing quite so sweet as a fresh young virgin, ripe for the plucking.'

With a final leer he sauntered out, leaving Jane staring after him in dismay.

Her eyes popped open as an outrageous idea flashed into her mind. Her stepfather would have her married, even if he had to beat and starve her into submission, but there might be a way out after all.

Sir Harry was looking forward to taking her maidenhead, was he? Her lips curved into a wicked smile. Then perhaps he wouldn't be quite so keen to marry her if there was no maidenhead to take!

Chapter Three

'Where are you going?' quavered Alice, wringing her hands as Jane pushed past her. 'Your father has given orders that you are to be kept in your room. He will beat me if I disobey him.'

'He's not my father,' said Jane hotly. She regained her temper and smiled slyly. 'And how could any blame be laid at your door, when I was already gone when you returned?'

Alice stared at her in bewilderment for a moment, then an answering smile crossed her face. 'That's right,' she agreed, practising the lie. 'By the time I came back the bird had already flown.' A frown creased her wrinkled forehead. 'But what if...?'

It was too late. Jane had gone.

Holding her breath, she tiptoed along the musicians' gallery that overlooked the great hall. Her stepfather was there, taking out his temper by berating an unfortunate manservant for some imagined fault, and Jane silently blessed the poor man for distracting him. It was a matter of moments to sidle down the servants' staircase and out through the kitchens.

Lifting her skirts free of the dung in the courtyard she fled towards the stables, hoping against hope that her stepfather's orders had not yet reached the outdoor servants. If they had her bid for freedom would end right here, and she would be escorted ignominiously back to her chamber. She crossed her fingers as she approached the young groom.

'Goodmorrow again, Robin,' she smiled – and breathed a sigh of relief as he looked up from brushing Alex with nothing more than an appreciative grin.

'Goodmorrow, mistress,' he nodded, patting Alex's smooth flanks. 'He's been watered and fed. Haven't you, lad?' He smiled as the horse tossed its head and whinnied in agreement. 'I was just going to put him back in his stable.'

'No,' ordered Jane imperiously. 'Saddle him. I would ride again.' She paused, running her eyes over the handsome young groom. Yes, Robin would do. Robin would do very nicely. She smiled at him. 'And saddle Geraint, too. I wish you to accompany me.'

For a moment the guileless brown eyes clouded, then they cleared again. Robin shrugged. Jane smiled with satisfaction. She was the daughter of the house, and the servants knew her orders were to be obeyed as much as those of the master.

Whistling, Robin went off to do as he was told.

As he saddled the horses Jane stood, glancing over her shoulder and tapping her foot, impatient to be off before they noticed she was missing and raised the hue and cry. In the distance she could still hear her stepfather's hectoring voice and she relaxed a little and turned her attention back to Robin. The homespun jerkin failed to disguise the breadth of his shoulders and she admired his long muscular legs and taut buttocks in the threadbare hose as he bent to buckle the girth. Unruly brown hair tumbled over his brow and he swept it back with a tanned forearm as he turned to face her.

'There, mistress,' he said. 'Ready.' He looked at her enquiringly. 'Shall I lead Alex to the mounting block?'

'No need,' said Jane, smiling coquettishly. 'If you would be so kind?'

He bent and she placed her foot in his linked hands and leapt lightly on to Alex's back, allowing her skirts to fall back to reveal a neatly turned ankle. A flush stained his cheekbones and she suppressed a grin. He swung himself on to Geraint and followed her as she turned Alex's head and walked him sedately towards the gate of the courtyard. It wouldn't do to be caught at the last moment.

As soon as they were clear she bent forward and kicked Alex's flanks, urging him forward. With a snort he took off, thundering across the greensward, his hooves digging into the smooth turf. Robin gave a startled exclamation and followed suit as Geraint pounded after his stablemate.

Laughing with excitement Jane led them a merry dance along the bridle-path, ducking her head to avoid the whipping branches that threatened to tangle in her flying hair. Finally she pulled Alex to a halt and waited for Robin to catch up.

'A fair ride, Robin,' she smiled. 'And a pretty morning.'

'Aye, mistress,' he grinned, admiring her flushed cheeks and bright eyes. 'But we'd best not tarry too long. I've work to do and the master's quick to complain if it's not done swiftly enough.'

'A plague upon the master,' pouted Jane. 'You must wait upon the mistress for a change – and 'tis my desire to take the spring air. I will walk a little.' She gazed at him imperiously. 'And you will accompany me.'

'As you wish, mistress,' he agreed, swinging down from Geraint and tethering him to a nearby tree. Jane sat waiting until he walked across and stood beside Alex, then dismounted, sliding down into his waiting arms. Pretending to stumble, she laughed up into his startled face and allowed her body to lean against his for a long moment, relishing its ready response.

'My lady,' he said stiffly, stepping back as soon as she

was steady on her feet. His face turned scarlet as he attempted to tug down his jerkin to hide the evidence of his excitement. His swollen manhood bulged against the thin hose and she deliberately held his eyes as she reached forward and fondled him, feeling the thick length of his shaft stir and swell even more beneath her questing fingers. His breath came harder as she ran her thumb over the smooth curve of its head; then, with a laugh, she whirled away, lifted her skirts and ran towards the woods.

His control broke and with a wild whoop of excitement he took after her, no longer a deferential servant but a primitive male in pursuit of a willing female. Panting with a mixture of fear and excitement, she ran on, ignoring the thorns and briars that caught at her hair and clothing, the leaves that tangled in her hair. Finally she could run no further and she turned to face her pursuer, like a deer at bay.

He was on her in a moment, his mouth pressing down on hers, his hands pulling the clothing from her body. When she was naked he scooped her up and laid her on a bed of wild thyme, her body like a white flame against the green. Smiling, he stood astride her and tore off his own clothing.

She stared up at him in awe. Beads of sweat stood out on his tanned chest, catching in the thatch of curly brown hair that narrowed to a thin line running down over his firm belly. His broad shoulders tapered down to a neat waist and hips and brown, muscular legs. He was like some pagan woodland god.

But it was his manhood that made her gasp. Thick and long, it jutted from the base of his belly like a club, its swollen head as big as a baby's fist. A pang of terror ran through her. He would split her in half! She whimpered and tried to wriggle away, her eyes wide with fear.

It was too late. With a groan he flung himself down beside her, his hands reaching for her. One cupped the nape of her neck and her head tilted back as his tongue forced into her mouth. The other ran over the smooth curve of her breasts, his fingers finding her nipples, kneading and twisting first one and then the other.

When she tried to twist away he crooned low in his throat, soothing her as if she was a frightened horse. The exploring hand became gentle, stroking her flanks until she began to relax, then returning to her breasts. His thumb made small circles round her nipples until they rose hard against his touch. She moaned softly as she began to moisten, the taut muscles of her thighs slowly relaxing, allowing them to part.

He lifted his mouth from hers and smiled down again. 'Easy, girl, easy,' he murmured, then his lips were on her breasts, shocking in their insistence. She moaned again, this time with rising excitement, feeling his lips curve in a smile against her as his tongue delicately teased the soft flesh.

His other hand was between her thighs now, his fingers parting her cleft, seeking the hot wetness inside. It was his turn to groan as she raised her hips in welcome and they slid inside her silken softness. She could feel his manhood pressing against her and her own hand slipped down to explore him. He groaned again as she gripped it, feeling the hot blood pulsing through it.

He rolled on top of her, his knee parting her thighs even further – and she felt the huge head of his organ pushing against the lips of her sex. She whimpered again with fear and pleasure as his hips moved and he began to force his way inside her, tearing her maidenhead apart, then she gave a shrill scream of pain as he thrust his entire length inside her.

For a moment he lay still and she could feel his hot thickness filling her, then he began to move slowly, pulling back before plunging forward again. She whined in the back of her throat as every stroke stoked the fire burning inside her. Her hips arched to meet each thrust, her legs twining round him, pulling him even deeper. He moved faster and the tormenting sensations in the pit of her stomach built to an unbearable pitch. Finally he bucked and spasmed and a scream of animal pleasure burst from her throat as she sagged back in relief and satisfaction.

They must have slept then, curled up against one another like a pair of healthy young animals, because when Jane became conscious of time again the sun was already high in the sky. With an exclamation of dismay she sat up, disturbing Robin, who stretched, yawned hugely, then gaped in horror as the realisation of what he'd done struck home.

'Mistress Jane, I...'

She laid a finger against his lips. 'Hush, sweet Robin,' she smiled. 'You did no more than I wished you to.' Her forehead creased in a worried frown. 'But if my stepfather ever found out your life would not be worth a farthing.' Her face cleared. 'They must be looking for me by this time. You must ride back alonc and say you searched but could not find me.' He opened his mouth to protest, but she silenced him with a final kiss. A servant could not afford to be chivalrous and she had no desire to see the body that had given her so much pleasure whipped and broken.

'Go,' she ordered. Reluctantly, he pulled his clothes on and did as he was bid.

It was mid-afternoon before she returned to the house, her belly quivering with hunger and nerves. Concealing her unease with an innocent smile, she rode back into the stable yard and swung down from Alex's back. Robin cast a quick, sympathetic glance in her direction, then bent his head over the lame leg of the horse he was working on. Angry footsteps clattered on the cobbles behind her and a hard hand gripped her upper arm and swung her round.

'How dare you disobey me?' snarled her stepfather, spittle spraying from his lips with rage. He lifted his other hand to strike her but her mother caught his wrist in frantic hands.

'Please, Thomas, please,' she begged. 'She's only a girl,' she searched for an argument more likely to appeal to his sense of propriety, 'and the servants are watching.'

He shook her off, but his first rage was blunted. Jane threw her a quick smile of gratitude.

'Get to your chamber,' he hissed. 'I shall speak to you in private.' She stalked off, head held high and he followed her. Her mother watched, wringing her hands with anxiety.

'Well?' he demanded as the door banged shut behind him.

Jane stared at him defiantly. 'Well what?' she taunted.

'You know very well,' he snarled. 'Have you come to your senses yet?' He forced a smile. 'Come girl,' he muttered gruffly, 'cease this damned foolishness and marry Sir Harry. He won't wait forever.'

'If Sir Harry wants a virgin bride he may wait till hell freezes over,' she jeered maliciously. 'He's too late.'

The colour drained from her stepfather's face. 'What do you mean?' he said stiffly, his lips white.

'I mean, dear stepfather,' she smiled, 'that if he planned on deflowering me, he's going to be disappointed. That pleasure has gone to another.'

The blow nearly knocked her from her feet. She staggered and fell against the wall. White-faced, she pulled herself erect, then recoiled from the hatred in his eyes.

'You'd better be lying, you little bitch,' he said softly, in a tone that was somehow more terrifying than any rage could have been. He walked away, opened her chamber door and smiled coldly over his shoulder. 'Or you'll regret it for the rest of your days.'

A pang of terror ran through her and she buried her face in her hands. For the first time she was truly afraid of what she might have let herself in for.

Chapter Four

Sunlight was already glinting through the narrow leaded window of her chamber when she woke, dull and heavy-headed. She had spent the night tossing and turning, her mind racing like a rat in a trap as she tried to see a way out of her difficulties. She had finally fallen into a thick sleep when the sky was turning from black to grey and the birds were beginning their dawn chorus. Even then she had been troubled by evil dreams where she pursued Ralph down endless woodland trails, never managing to reach him – while in the distance she heard hoof beats behind her, getting closer and closer no matter how hard she ran.

She shook herself and swung her legs out of bed, biting her lip at the pain in her buttocks from her stepfather's beating. Despite her aching muscles, her usual early-morning ride would blow the cobwebs away and let her think more clearly.

The water in her ewer was cold but she welcomed its icy sting against her warm skin. Washing herself quickly, she slipped into her ancient green riding-dress, tiptoed towards the door and turned the handle.

It refused to open. She pulled harder, a flicker of fear gripping her insides. It was locked! Taking a deep breath to control her rising panic, she beat upon it with the flat of her hand. 'Alice!' she called. 'Alice! Open this door immediately. I command you!'

She stopped to listen and heard the shuffle of Alice's feet as she hurried along the corridor. 'Open this door!'

she ordered again, forcing her voice to sound confident and imperious. 'Or I shall have you beaten.'

There was a faint moan; Jane could imagine Alice standing on the other side of the door, wringing her hands in dismay. She softened her voice. 'Please, Alice,' she wheedled. 'Unlock the door.'

'I daren't, my lady,' whimpered Alice. 'It's more than my life's worth. Your father has ordered that you be confined to your chamber until the midwife arrives.'

Jane paused in bewilderment. Midwife? Why should he need a midwife? She was not with child. The colour drained from her face as realisation dawned. He was going to have her examined to find out if she had been lying. She groaned in dismay. He had been outraged at the very thought that her maidenhead was gone. What would he be like when he found out the truth? With leaden feet she retraced her steps and curled up in a small ball on her bed, wrapping her arms round herself for comfort.

How long she lay there for, she didn't know. The only sign of time passing was the sunlight creeping slowly across her chamber floor. Finally she heard the clatter of hooves in the courtyard and got stiffly to her feet.

From her window she could see the woman descending from her donkey. She removed a leather script from the pommel before the animal was led away. Her mother stood, wringing her hands in the background, while her stepfather, gesticulating fiercely, his face purple with anger and embarrassment, was obviously explaining the reason why she had been called. The woman nodded and the unlikely procession began to make its way towards the house.

Jane fled to the safety of her bed again, pulling the covers up to her chin.

All too soon she heard footsteps in the passage and the

sound of the key being fumbled in the lock. The door swung open and the woman was ushered in.

Jane stared at her with frightened eyes. She was tall and her plain but well-made garments showed how successful she was in her profession. Rings – no doubt the gifts of her more well-born clients – glinted on her fingers as advertisement of her talents. When many women failed to survive childbirth, a good midwife could mean the difference between life and death. Jane suppressed a bitter smile. No mumbling, toothless old granny for her. Her stepfather had spared no expense to check on her maidenhead.

'There she is,' he spat, indicating Jane with a disgusted wave of a hand towards the bed, where she lay shrinking. Her mother fluttered uselessly in the background, her face twisted as she plucked nervously at her dress and tried to suppress her tears. He stood with his hands on his hips. 'Well, woman,' he ordered, 'be about your work.'

Jane cringed. He surely wasn't going to watch? She closed her eyes, her humiliation complete.

The midwife was made of sterner stuff, however. She stared back at him coolly until he flushed and his eyes fell. With a grunt he strode out, banging the door behind him. Only then did she turn towards Jane.

'If my lady would raise her shift,' she said, laying the leather bag on the chest beneath the window, 'we can begin the examination.'

Scarlet, Jane did as she was bid, pulling the thin material above her hips. The woman carefully removed her rings, took a pot of sweet butter from her bag and began to oil her hands. When she was finished she approached the bed. Jane clenched her thighs in anticipation of the hated violation.

'You must part your legs, my lady,' said the woman

briskly. 'If you resist me it will only make it more painful.'

Gritting her teeth, Jane reluctantly let her knees fall apart. She stared at the ceiling, trying to wish herself away, wincing as deft hands parted the lips of her vulva and invaded her body. The midwife's face remained blank as she examined Jane, her questing fingers finding no resistance to their entry, but a small sigh escaped her lips as she withdrew again, shaking her head a little at the pity of it. The fate of a well-born girl who lost her virginity before marriage was not a pleasant one.

Jane's mother swayed, her face turning white. Panic lent wings to her feet and she was across the chamber in a heartbeat. 'Please,' she begged, tugging at the rings on her hands and thrusting them towards the woman. 'Please. Who would know? I will give you anything. Anything.'

The woman shook her head as she continued stolidly washing the sweet butter from her hands. 'I am sorry, my lady,' she said in a low voice. 'If it were found out I should be ruined – or worse. His lordship is not a forgiving man.' She glanced towards the bed, her expression a mixture of fear for her own plight and sympathy for Jane's. 'If I did as you ask, and he found out, who's to say I wouldn't meet with an unfortunate "accident" one of these dark nights? Or be raped and robbed and left to die in a ditch?' She laughed harshly. 'There are evil men abroad.'

Lady Agnes let her hands fall to her sides. It was the truth – and one of those men was her husband. Who knew better than she what Sir Thomas was capable of? The man was a devil. She jumped as the door quivered under a barrage of heavy blows.

'Aren't you finished yet?' Sir Thomas demanded.

'Yes, my lord,' said the woman. The door burst open and he strode in.

'Well? Is she still virgin?' he demanded. She shook her

head reluctantly and his lips curled in a snarl. He fumbled at his belt, pulling out a bag of coins which he flung at her viciously. It hit her shoulder and fell to the floor, clinking. 'Get out,' he spat, 'and take your foul baggage with you before I have you burned as a witch.'

One glance at the rage suffusing his face and even the midwife's formidable composure broke. Stooping for her wages, she seized her bag and scuttled for the door.

He stalked over to the bed and Jane cowered back against the pillows. 'As for you, you little whore,' he said icily, spitting out each word as if it was poisonous, 'mark my words, you'll pay for bringing shame on me. My God, but you'll pay!'

He seized her mother's arm and dragged her towards the door. It banged shut, the key turned with an ominous click and Jane was alone with her terror.

The next few days dragged unmercifully. Confined to her room, Jane grew pale with lack of exercise and poor food. She watched wistfully from her casement as the business of the house went on without her. Boredom made even the smallest event – from the cook pursuing a recalcitrant chicken round the yard to the gatekeeper's daughter playing in the dust – something to be savoured to while the weary hours away. Robin flung longing glances towards her window each time he passed, but she withdrew, lest she bring retribution on his innocent head as well as her own.

She wandered over to her mirror and smiled wanly at her reflection. At least there was one consolation; time also seemed to have tempered her stepfather's rage. Despite his threats he had not been near her chamber since the dreadful confrontation with the midwife. Three times her mother had ventured in to see her, unlocking the door with care and glancing over her shoulder before slipping through, but her nervousness and the fresh bruises on her skin had only served to intensify Jane's guilt. She sighed. Better to suffer alone than see the suffering her impulsive behaviour had brought on others.

The sound of laughter and chattering outside in the courtyard brought her back to the window and she stared down in amazement at the crowd of servants thronging their way towards the gate. They were dressed in their best, even the lowliest kitchen maid flaunting a fragment of ragged ribbon in her hair. Behind the common throng rode her mother and her attendants, a splash of vivid colour in a sea of grey and brown and green. What was going on?

Realisation dawned. Of course! It was the Mayday Fair. The maids would have already been out at dawn to wash their faces in the May dew and now everyone from the oldest to the youngest would be off to join in the revelry on the common green.

A wistful sigh escaped her lips as she thought of what she was missing. The striped maypole, set up in the centre of the green. The brightly coloured stalls and booths scattered round the edge of the common, their wares spread out to tempt hoarded coins from greasy purses. Gypsy fortune-tellers promising luck, love and fortune to anyone gullible enough to cross their palms with silver. Hucksters and pickpockets and sweetmeat sellers. Lovers holding hands oblivious to everything but each other. Old men and women remembering their youth as they carefully nursed their ale and watched with bright beady eyes, storing up gossip for months to come.

Last year there had been a dancing bear and the year before that a bull-baiting – though she hadn't enjoyed that. She shivered at the memory of the excited faces and greedy eyes watching eagerly as the dogs were tossed into the air to lie twitching and bleeding in the dust. Still, even that was better than being shut up inside while everyone else was off enjoying themselves. Depression descended like a grey cloud as the empty house settled round her, enveloping her in silence. She hadn't realised how much she took the usual hustle and bustle for granted: voices calling from the courtyard; the sound of feet pattering along the corridors as maids fetched and carried; the normal comings and goings of a busy household which were simply an accepted part of life. It was only once they were gone that you missed them. She shivered. It felt as if she was the only person left alive.

A faint scratching noise made her gasp as all the forbidden ghost stories Alice had whispered to her when she was a child rushed back into her mind. She pressed one hand to her breast to still the pounding of her heart, laughed breathlessly and scolded herself for her own stupidity. Now she was being ridiculous. It was nothing but a mouse scuttling behind the wainscot.

She paused, feeling suddenly cold. There was something! She held her breath and strained her ears to listen. This was no figment of her overheated imagination. She was alone in the house yet she could hear the sound of heavy footsteps echoing along the deserted corridor – and they were coming towards her room! She whimpered with fright as they grew nearer, her eyes focused on the thick door that was the only barrier between her and whatever horror stalked the long gallery.

The key grated in the lock; she cowered back as the doorknob turned slowly and the door yawned open to reveal – her stepfather!

Relief made her smile, until she saw the expression on his face. All thoughts of ghosts and bogles evaporated before the terrifying reality of what she read in his eyes. Face white, she began to back away.

For a moment he stood on the threshold, his lips twisting with pleasure as he savoured her terror, then he advanced into the room, kicking the door shut behind him.

'Ready, my pretty little whore?' he whispered. 'It's time to pay the piper.'

Chapter Five

'Wh-what do you want?' she managed through numb lips, as she scrambled away from him.

'What do I want?' he jeered mockingly. 'You thick-witted slut! What do you think I want? I want what you've already given away to every Tom, Dick and Harry.'

For a moment she stared at him. What was he talking about? Then it dawned on her and her already pale face drained of all remaining colour. No! He couldn't mean that...?

'I... I don't know what you mean,' she stammered, playing for time as her mind raced, looking for an escape from this monstrous situation.

'Oh, yes, you do,' he hissed, his hands reaching for the buckle on his belt and beginning to fumble it free. 'If you can play the whore for any passing stranger, then you can play the whore for me.

'Who was it took your fancy?' he sneered. 'Some glib-tongued gypsy rogue? Some sturdy beggar with a strong body beneath his rags? Or a pilgrim perhaps, who stopped to pay his respects to Venus instead of Our Lady?' He snorted, his smile becoming lascivious. 'What does it matter who he was? He had you. And now I shall have you too.'

'You would not dare!' she gasped. 'It is against all the laws of man and God! You are my father!'

'Stepfather,' he reminded, grinning. 'As you are so fond of pointing out, I am merely your mother's husband.' His cold eyes ran over her cringing body in an assessing fashion. 'And why should I content myself with the scrawny old hen when the plump young pullet is so ripe for the plucking?'

'I shall scream,' she warned, taking a step backwards.

'Scream away. There's no one to hear you. Everyone's at the fair, except for old Tom and he's as deaf as a post. You could scream loud enough to wake the dead and he'd still not hear you.' He chuckled as he stepped towards her. 'There's no knight in shining armour coming to save the fair maiden this time. It's just you and me.'

Backing away from him she bumped against her toilet table. One hand groped behind and her fingers closed on the carved wooden box that held her few jewels. As he stepped towards her she lifted it and swung it towards his head. He grunted as the corner caught his temple and the lid flew off, scattering her baubles over the floor. For a moment he staggered and she made a dart for the door – and freedom.

She squealed in pain as a cruel hand caught her upper arm and dragged her back. He whirled her round, his face, swollen with rage, scant inches from hers, his breath hot against her cheek. Blood trickled down from the wound above his eye. 'You little bitch,' he snarled, slapping her with his open palm.

Her head spun, but she still managed to raise her other hand to claw at his cheek. He grinned as he caught it, forcing it behind her back to join its twin. He had both wrists trapped in his left hand now and she writhed against him in a futile effort to break free. He twisted viciously and she arched her back, trying to escape the pain in her shoulders.

'Nice… very nice,' he said, grinning as the movement thrust her heaving breasts against him. He tugged at the neck of her thin shift so that it tore away, revealing the soft rosy-tipped mounds quivering beneath. He took a ragged breath, his mouth becoming slack with lust. Even beneath the codpiece she could feel him swelling and cold fear ran through her.

His free hand began to fumble at her dress and she squealed with pain and terror as his fingers dug into her skin, leaving red imprints as he fondled her roughly. Then he seized her nipples, twisting and pulling until they hardened beneath his attentions. He bent his head and took one in his mouth, rasping his tongue over the soft flesh, his teeth closing round it. She froze, waiting for the moment of agony when he bit down.

But it didn't come. Instead his mouth moved upward over her throat, leaving a snail trail of saliva behind. Gripping her hair he pulled her head back and forced his mouth down on hers, thrusting his thick tongue between her lips. Jane responded by biting down, hard.

With a muffled curse he threw her from him. She sprawled on the bed. As she fell her head banged against the head-post. There was a moment of sick dizziness, then everything went black.

When she came to she was naked, face down amongst her pillows, her arms stretched out above her head and tied to the head-post with the remains of the shift he'd torn from her back. She tugged frantically at the twisted cloth, but it held as strongly as any rope. She was helpless.

'Not so clever now, are you, madam?' he taunted, his voice thick. Blood stained the spittle on his lips. 'Let's see how you enjoy this little game.'

She strained to turn her head, then wished she hadn't. He was standing, legs apart, his hands on his hips – and the belt which had been round his waist was now hanging from his hand, the end trailing on the floor. As she watched in horror, he raised his arm. The lash flickered through the air, landing on her smooth white buttocks with a crack. Her whole body stiffened as pain exploded through her, but she bit her lip, determined not to give him the satisfaction of a response. He paused, breathing heavily, and licked his lips as he watched the rich colour stain the plump white cheeks of her bottom, still quivering beneath his blow. He raised his arm again.

This time she did scream. The blow landed in the same place, curling lovingly round the curve of her hips and leaving a broad white line before the blood rushed back in a crimson tide. She clenched her buttocks and writhed against the coverlets, her body trying to escape the intensity of the hurt that flooded it. Another blow followed, then another; each one more agonising than the last. Finally she broke.

'No more,' she whimpered. 'Please, no more! I'll do anything you want. Just stop, I beg of you!'

'That's better,' he said, with satisfaction. 'A whore should be obedient to her master.' His tone became threatening. 'Shouldn't she?'

'Yes... *yes*,' Jane moaned.

'Good,' he said. 'You've learned your place at last, my fine lady.' His breath came faster. 'Now roll on your back like the bitch you are,' he ordered.

Arms still tied, she struggled to do as she was told, the material biting even more tightly into her wrists as she twisted round. She winced as her tender bottom came in contact with the harsh brocade of the coverlet, but the pain was nothing compared to the shame she felt, exposed to his lustful gaze. She closed her eyes in humiliation as he gloated over her naked body.

His eyes glazed as he gazed down at her. 'Spread your legs, slut,' he ordered thickly. She shuddered and pressed her thighs tightly together, trying to protect the last tatters of her modesty. It was useless. With a curse he wrenched her legs roughly apart, leaving her open and vulnerable, her vulva parting like the soft petals of a flower to reveal its moist pink centre. Smiling ruthlessly, he used the remains of her shift to pinion her ankles to the posts at the bottom of the bed, leaving her spreadeagled helplessly before him.

'That's better,' he said, with satisfaction. Licking his lips, he took in the enticing picture before him. Her auburn hair, spread out over the coverlet like a burning tide; the proud swell of her breasts; the narrow waist, leading into the soft curve of her belly and the gateway to paradise that lay beneath, guarded by its crest of fiery fleece, waiting for him to enter.

He leaned closer and ran his hands over her as if he was assessing a piece of horseflesh. He lingered on her breasts, kneading and squeezing, then turned his attention lower. His fingers bit into the soft flesh of her inner thighs, then he thrust two fingers inside her, smiling as she squealed at the sudden pain.

She groaned in humiliation at the reaction of her treacherous body. Despite her fear and loathing, tendrils of excitement began to spiral through her and she felt herself moisten beneath his exploring hand. Heat from her beaten bottom radiated through her lower body, intensifying every tiny sensation. She moaned again, this time in reluctant pleasure.

'Whore,' he murmured. 'Randy as a bitch in heat, aren't you?' Eyes fixed on her face, he began to move his hand, sliding his fingers in and out, revelling in the hot silky wetness beneath them.

It was all too much to bear. With a groan he withdrew his fingers, slick with her juices, and began to untie the points of his hose, letting them fall to his ankles. Jane's eyes widened with horror at the size of his male member. It jutted, long and thick, its head the size and colour of a ripe plum, a bead of moisture leaking from its swollen red eye. She writhed in a futile attempt to free herself, her head turning from side to side in denial of what was to come.

He knelt between her legs, one hand gripping his member, then snorted with dissatisfaction. Pulling a pillow from the head of the bed he thrust it beneath her hips, raising her up so that her sex gaped even wider, offering easier access. He leaned forward, pushing his rampant cock against it, and she whimpered as it thrust into her, splitting her open. There was a moment of agony as the last vestiges of her maidenhead were torn away, then his weight crushed down on her and he slid completely inside her, his hot length filling her. It was like being impaled on a bar of molten steel.

Grunting like a rooting pig, he began to thrust himself in and out of her helpless body. Her breasts bounced and quivered with every jerk of his hips, their hard points rubbing against the coarse material of his doublet. She groaned again and, only partially against her will, her hips thrust upwards to meet him. He grinned savagely down at her, his buttocks clenching as he redoubled his efforts, and she could feel the unbearable tension mounting in her loins.

Finally he gasped and shuddered his release, his prick jerking and spasming inside her, and she shrieked aloud as it brought her own climax with it. He collapsed on top of her, crushing her with his weight. She felt his member shrivelling and leaking against her thigh and a shiver of revulsion ran through her. She hated him – and hated herself even more for her animal response to his attentions.

He raised his head and grinned into her eyes. 'Well, slut. Are you satisfied?'

She gathered the bitter saliva in her mouth and spat straight in his face.

He jerked away from her, spittle running down his cheek. 'You little bitch,' he hissed, raising his hand. 'You'll pay for that.'

She cringed to avoid the blow, then froze. What was that? A slow smile crossed her face as she recognised the sound of hooves clattering in the courtyard below. Rescue at last!

'I believe we have visitors, sir,' she said, laughing triumphantly up at him. Her expression became bitter. 'And even your poor reputation would suffer, were you to be discovered forcing yourself upon your stepdaughter.'

With a snarl he flung himself away from the bed, frantically pulling up his hose. 'I'll be back,' he muttered over his shoulder as he hurried from the room, still tying his points and tugging down his doublet.

She stretched her tortured limbs, trying to ease her bindings. He might be back, but with someone else in the house he would have no option but to set her free. She grimaced, feeling his cold dribblings on her thighs. And once she was free, he would pay for his wicked violation.

The minutes lengthened and anxiety began to set in again. What was taking him so long? He should have been back by this time. Her hands and feet were beginning to lose all sensation, becoming heavy and lifeless. Where was he?

She sighed with relief as she heard the sound of footsteps coming along the gallery towards her room. At last!

But her relief turned to dismay as she saw him lounging against the door, an expression of satisfaction on his face. Her mouth went dry with fear as he smiled at her maliciously.

'Are you ready to receive guests, my dear?' he purred, raising one eyebrow in a quizzical expression. 'We have a visitor.'

With difficulty she lifted her head and stared past him, then let it fall back with a hopeless moan as she saw the figure standing behind him. Sir Harry, Ralph's father! The man she had scorned to take as her husband. As he took in her naked body, spreadeagled across the bed, his beady eyes almost popped out of his head. Then a slow, lascivious smile crossed his lips. As a potential wife he would have had to treat her with the respect befitting her position – at least until they were married. Now, a proven slut, she was fair game.

'Come now, mistress,' chided her stepfather mockingly. 'You are remiss in your duties. You must entertain your guest. A glass of wine and a little refreshment, perhaps? Or a tune upon the lute, to lighten the weary hour?' He strode across the room and leered down at her. 'Or perhaps we could find another way to amuse our visitor and pass the time?'

He bent over and took her breasts in his hands, squeezing and kneading as if he was judging fruit. 'A pert whore,' he said conversationally to Sir Harry. He trailed a hand over her shrinking flesh until he reached her open vulva and thrust his fingers rudely inside her, then held them up, glistening. 'And a juicy one, too. Would you care to sample her wares?'

Sir Harry nodded eagerly, already fumbling at his clothing. Divested of his doublet and hose, he was not a pretty sight. His chest was scrawny, apart from a pair of hairy tits bigger than her own, and his belly curved out like that of a woman eight months gone with child. Beneath it his male member dangled flaccidly against his balls.

The whole sorry edifice was supported by a pair of skinny legs that would have done credit to a chicken. Jane was unable to prevent herself from giggling hysterically. It was a mistake.

'So you find me amusing, do you, madam?' he snarled, his lips white with temper. 'First you refuse me as a husband and now you have the temerity to laugh at me. Perhaps you need a lesson in manners.' He turned to her stepfather, his face vicious. 'Untie the wench so that I may teach her.'

Hands fumbled with the knots at her wrists and ankles and she gasped as the blood rushed back. Ignoring it, she grasped the coverlet and tried to conceal herself, wriggling to the far corner of the bed as far away as possible from her tormentors.

It was useless. Sir Harry leaned over and wrenched her back. He was stronger than she expected and, despite her frantic struggles, he pulled her over his knee and held her in a grip of iron. Beneath her writhing body she felt the first stirrings in his member and froze, frightened to move in case she roused him more. He raised a hand and brought it down with a crack that made her gasp. The smooth skin, already flushed from her previous beating, turned scarlet immediately and she writhed again.

'Not so saucy now, wench, eh?' Sir Harry panted, his hand rising and falling, each blow making her squirm with pain. She moaned, tears staining her cheeks as she felt his cock, rigid now, pressing into the soft flesh of her belly. Would this torture never end? She closed her eyes against the picture of her stepfather, lounging comfortably on the window-seat, avidly watching her humiliation.

At last Sir Harry flung her from him. She whimpered as he stood over her, legs spread, his straining prick peeking out from beneath the mound of his belly. 'And now, madam, unless you wish to feel the weight of my palm again, you will pleasure me, like the whore you are.'

In front of her horrified eyes, he stretched himself out on her bed and pointed to his rampant cock, jutting upwards from the folds of flesh at the base of his belly. It was the same angry red as the wattles of the cockerel that strutted round the courtyard, but this time she felt no desire to laugh.

'Well, girl?' he leered, indicating it with a wave of his hand. 'To your work. Put those sweet cherry lips of yours to better use than insulting your betters.'

She staggered to her feet and stared at him blankly. What was she supposed to do?

'Get on with it,' he snarled impatiently. 'Suck it, wench! Suck it!'

She recoiled in disgust, shaking her head in denial, but a hard push from behind propelled her forward and she fell on her knees on the bed, her face coming into contact with Sir Harry's sweaty belly. With a groan of satisfaction he grabbed her hair and thrust her face into his groin, the swollen head of his prick pushing against her tightly closed lips. He grunted impatiently and gave a warning jerk that almost pulled the hair from her scalp. Reluctantly, she opened her lips.

With a moan he raised his hips and his cock slid into the soft warmth of her mouth. She gagged as the thick rank flesh filled it, the bulbous head touching the back of her throat. Guided by his hand tugging her hair, she began to bob her head up and down, sliding her mouth the length of his swollen shaft and running her tongue round the rim, while his free hand toyed with her breasts, rolling each of her nipples in turn between his thumb and forefinger.

A movement behind her made her freeze, and a wave

of sick horror washed over her.

Her stepfather, excited beyond endurance by the sight of her sucking Sir Harry's cock, was ready again. She heard his heavy breathing and felt his hands pawing at her bottom and between her thighs. She struggled to break free, but Sir Harry pulled her back down, grunting as his member moved faster between her lips.

The hot weight of her stepfather's prick pressed against the soft crease of her bottom and she flinched as it slid down until it was nudging against the tight pucker of her anus. Her eyes widened in terrified disbelief as she grasped his intention. She tried to resist, unable to believe he wished to take her there. Pain jabbed through her as he pushed harder, the tip of his penis beginning inexorably to penetrate her most dark and secret place. She moaned as, inch by slow inch, he forced himself inside her. His hips jerked and his full length sank into place.

She parted her lips to scream as he thrust, but her shriek was muffled as Sir Harry's cock slid even further into her mouth. He was gasping now, bucking like a stranded fish as he watched his friend take her up the arse while she was forced to suck him off. With a final groan he exploded, making her gag again as he flooded her mouth with the salty taste of his come. For a few moments more her stepfather thrust and groaned. To her horror she felt her treacherous body react to the relentless pounding with excitement of her own, then he, too, spasmed, his hot seed spurting into the forbidden recesses of her body, and he withdrew, leaving her humiliated as she gasped with frustrated desire.

Released from the grip of her abusers, Jane collapsed whimpering on the bed, her eyes closed in a vain attempt to blot out what had just happened. She felt the bed move as Sir Harry rose, and listened to their cruel laughter as they dressed again after their merry 'sport'. At last she found the strength to raise her head and glare her hatred at them.

'I shall tell the priest,' she spat, calling on the ultimate sanction.

Her stepfather was on her in a moment. 'I wouldn't do that,' he hissed, pulling her head back by the hair and snarling into her face. 'Not unless you wish your lady mother to pay for it.'

She groaned. It was no empty threat – and how could she condemn her mother to suffer even more? Her head fell. He had won. There was nothing she could do.

'Get dressed,' he ordered, 'while I decide what to do with you.'

Apathetically, she did as she was told. Once she was clothed again she stood, head drooping, in front of the two men, waiting to hear her fate.

'A pity we can't keep her,' said Sir Harry. 'She makes a pretty little whore.'

'True,' agreed Sir Thomas, 'but she is a lady, and even if she does not tell the priest, there are always those who will. It is too dangerous. Your namesake, King Harry, has a conscience, even if it is a convenient one. And what he gave he can just as easily take away.' He thought for a moment, then grinned and snapped his fingers. 'I have it,' he crowed, smirking, 'and a merry jest it is, too. Where's the best place for a whore?'

Sir Harry looked at him. 'A brothel?' he ventured.

'No,' chuckled Thomas. 'A convent! We'll send her to repent her sins.'

They were still chuckling as they left.

Jane pulled the coverlet from the bed and crawled beneath the sheets, curling into a ball as the slow tears trickled down her cheeks. She dashed them away, angry at her weakness. A convent wasn't such a bad place, when she thought about it. The nuns would be kind and highborn ladies could live almost as well in a nunnery as they did at home.

Laughter in the courtyard below told her that her mother and the servants were returning from the fair. She began to drift into a healing sleep, secure in the knowledge that her stepfather would not dare return now. Her last conscious thought was that at least in a convent she would be safe.

Chapter Six

The rain beat down, turning the highway to a mass of treacherous mud. Spring had retreated under the last dying onslaught of winter and even the jaunty new buds were cowed and beaten. The villages they had passed through had been rain-swept and shuttered, with scarce a person venturing out to brave the unseasonable storms.

The weather reflected Jane's misery as the little procession plodded along, Alexander's muffled snorting protesting the dreary slowness of the journey. Her cloak was sodden and her long skirts were so heavy with water they clung to her legs, chilling her to the bone. Her hair stuck to her face in lank rats' tails and her only consolation was that the raindrops disguised the tears trickling slowly down her cheeks.

Behind her trailed old Alice, bewailing everything from the weather and her aching limbs to the stubbornness of the donkey she rode and the impending loss of her 'sweet baby'.

'But why send you away?' Alice had moaned, when Jane told her of her fate, and the reason for it. Alice had greeted her words with a rueful smile. Not that she'd had to be told. Thomas's uncontrolled ranting after the midwife had gone let the whole household know her secret.

'Who's to know your maidenhead's gone, if we don't tell them?' Alice had continued. 'There's no child on the way to shout your shame to the world.' A cunning smile creased her old face and she tapped the side of her nose. 'A little phial of chicken blood tucked beneath the pillow on your wedding night and you're a virgin still, with the stain on the marriage sheets to prove it!' Crossing her arms on her formidable bosom, she had nodded with satisfaction at her own cleverness. 'You wouldn't be the first to fool a jealous husband. Nor the last.'

'It is my stepfather's order,' Jane had replied dully. 'And who's to gainsay him? My mother?' She laughed bitterly. 'I don't think so. He beat her into submission years ago. She may love me, but she fears him more. And who could blame her?' Jane bit her lip, remembering what her own defiance had led to. 'Not I. I shall get me to a nunnery and repent my sins as he has ordered. No doubt, when this has blown over, he will come round in time and call me home again.

'After all,' she had continued, forcing a smile. 'I have my uses. A daughter is a good bargaining tool for an ambitious man. What better way to seal an agreement than by a judicious marriage?' She had patted Alice's trembling hand. 'Mark my words,' she said bravely, 'a few months and I shall be safely home again and all this pother forgotten.'

She did not feel quite so brave now. Thankfully her stepfather had not insisted on escorting her, but Fletcher and Cooper, the servants he'd chosen to send with her, were his men through and through. They did not have the bearing of servants. They were hard men, scarred and ruthless, who had fought with him in France and, had he not employed them in his household, would no doubt be picking their living off the bodies of unwary – and unlucky – travellers.

She shivered again, and this time it was not from the icy rain that trickled from her hood. She had seen the way the two men looked at her from the corners of their eyes, with a kind of cunning greed. It reminded her of nothing more than the way a hungry dog looks at a bone, assessing his chances of stealing it. Did they know why she was being sent away? They had spoken to her respectfully enough, but beneath that surface respect was there a lurking contempt? She closed her eyes and shook her head. Of course not. Her fevered imagination was causing her to see things that were not there. No matter what she'd done, whatever her shame, she was still the daughter of the manor. Far above the common ruck. Untouchable. She laughed softly at her silly fears. What on earth was she thinking of? She was jumping at shadows like a green girl.

Her thoughts were interrupted by a relieved shout from old Alice. 'Mistress! Mistress! See, we are almost at Sanford.'

Jane looked, just in time to see the small town nestling beneath them in the valley, before the rain swept in again, obscuring the view.

'Thanks be to our Lady for another day's safe journey,' Alice went on, crossing herself piously. 'And let's hope this inn doesn't have as many fleas as the last one. I was near bit to death!' Spurred on by the thought of a dry bed, regardless of bloodthirsty occupants, she kicked her unfortunate donkey into renewed effort.

Jane suppressed a smile at the sudden descent from the pious to the practical. Still, any haven from the storm was welcome and the thought of a hot meal and a tankard of mulled ale put fresh heart in her, too. She kicked Alexander's flanks and he broke into a canter.

Half an hour later they were comfortably ensconced in front of the inn fire, their wet clothes steaming. The smell of roast meats made Jane's mouth water and even old Alice had ceased her eternal complaints and was ordering the innkeeper about with her usual briskness. A warming-pan, filled with hot coals from the kitchen fire, was already toasting the bed they would share – and hopefully banishing any livestock which was still lurking in the straw of the mattress.

Much to her relief, her two escorts had left Alice and herself to go about their own business, seeing to the horses and making arrangements to bed down in the stable – and afterwards no doubt, to find a bottle, a card game or a woman or two, willing to bed them in return for a few coppers. The latter thought made her shiver. God go with them, whoever they were. She didn't envy them.

'Dinner, my lady,' the innkeeper announced, interrupting these unpleasant thoughts. 'It is a poor one, I am afraid. Only four courses. Roast beef, a goose, a turbot and some sweetmeats. I hope it will not prove too unsatisfactory.' He smiled anxiously, eager to please his highborn guest.

'I am sure it will be excellent,' said Jane, handing him a coin and smiling graciously. He bridled with pleasure as he led them through to a small room, where they could eat in private. Not that it was necessary. They had the entire inn to themselves, no one else being foolhardy – or desperate – enough to travel in such harsh weather.

'That was delicious, thank you,' Jane said as the maid cleared away the ruins of the meal. A full tummy, a few glasses of red wine and a warm fire had restored her natural optimism. She sat contentedly cracking nuts with her white teeth, laughing as Alice tried in vain to do the same with her few remaining ones. 'Here,' she said, offering one she'd already cracked. 'Poor creature. I would not see you starve.' She stopped short with a stricken look on her face and Alice gazed at her in alarm.'

'What is it, my lovely?' she asked anxiously. 'The bellyache? A chill? The beginning of the ague?' She cursed. 'This damned cold. Your stepfather – God rot him – had no right to send you abroad in weather like this, the selfish swine.'

'No, I'm the selfish one,' said Jane contritely. 'Sitting here on my backside, stuffing myself. I forgot to look to Alexander. Fine thanks for his faithfulness, that is. He was just as wet and cold as we were. I must go to the stables and see that he was rubbed down before he was fed and watered. And see that they gave him oats as well as straw.'

Pushing her chair back she got to her feet, picked an apple from the fruit bowl and went through to collect her cloak from the hook beside the fire. She grimaced as she put it on; it was still damp despite the roaring flames. She debated calling the innkeeper to fetch a lantern, then decided against it. The stables lay only a little distance away and there was light enough left yet in the sky to see by. Hoisting her skirts against the mud, she stepped out.

She regretted it almost immediately. Rain lashed down and a gust of wind caught her hood and blew it off. Tugging it up again she raced across the yard, splashing through the puddles.

The stable was dark, redolent with the comforting warmth of horseflesh and the dusty scent of straw. Breathless, she threw off her hood and shook the raindrops from her hair. Alexander snorted a greeting and she walked across to stroke his soft nose. He nuzzled her impatiently, searching for the apple he could smell in her pocket.

Pulling it out she took her pocket-knife and cut it into neat sections, laying each one on the palm of her hand. He took them daintily, rolling an appreciative eye as he ate. When they were gone he nuzzled her again, hoping for more.

'All gone,' she smiled, showing him her empty hands.

'And have you been looked after properly?' she asked, patting his neck. 'Had your water? Had your oats?' There was a snigger from the darkness and she spun round. A figure stepped out of the shadows, quickly followed by another.

'He's had his oats,' said a mocking voice, 'but we haven't.'

She suddenly became very aware that she was alone with the two men. Old Alice was comfortably settled and probably dozing by the fire by this time. The innkeeper, busy about his tasks, wouldn't even miss her. She gulped. 'Fletcher?' she quavered, peering into the darkness.

'At your service,' he grinned, stepping forward. Cooper sniggered again in the background. Leaning against the side of the stall, Fletcher raked her from head to foot, his eyes glinting. She shivered.

'Thank you,' she said, pretending she hadn't noticed anything untoward in his behaviour. 'But I require no service.' She waved a hand. 'I have seen for myself that Alexander has been cared for. There is no more to be done here. I shall return to the inn now. You are dismissed.' Concealing her fear, she moved towards the door.

He stepped in front of her, blocking her escape.

'How dare you, sirrah!' she snapped. 'Get out of my way. I told you: you are dismissed.'

'Oh no, my lady,' he hissed. 'You don't get away so easily. Your horse has had its oats. Now it's our turn.'

She whirled, to find that Cooper had moved behind her. She was trapped!

'My stepfather shall hear of this!' she snarled. 'He will have you beaten.'

Cooper's scarred face twisted in a leering grin. 'I think not, madam. Sir Thomas is a generous man, particularly where old comrades are concerned. He'd not begrudge us our share, eh, Fletch?' Fletcher licked his lips and nodded in agreement.

Jane felt sick. The thought of their grimy hands pawing at her was unbearable. She fumbled at the waist of her gown and felt the hard shape of the pocket-knife she'd used to cut up Alex's apple. Her fingers folded round it with relief and she freed it surreptitiously.

When Fletcher made his move she was ready. She lashed out and the thin blade sliced down his cheek. He swore foully and stepped back, glaring at her, a hand to his wounded face. Blood leaked out from between his fingers. 'You little bitch,' he snarled, knocking the knife from her hand. 'You've narked me!' He reached for his own dagger and brought it out. It glinted wickedly in the dull light. 'You won't be so pretty once I've finished with you,' he hissed.

Jane closed her eyes and waited for the blade to bite into her flesh.

It was Cooper who saved her. 'Hold fast, Fletch,' he muttered, seizing his friend's wrist. 'She's still Sir Thomas's stepdaughter. 'Do you want to hang?'

Still breathing hard, Fletcher slid the dagger back into its sheath. 'No,' he replied. He smiled at Jane, eyes cold. 'But if I can't have my revenge one way, I'll have it another.' He reached for a thick quirt that hung on the stable wall and flexed it between his hands. 'Take her,' he ordered.

Before she knew what was happening, Cooper had seized her, twisting her round to face him. She beat her fists futilely against his chest as his wet mouth slobbered down on hers, one hand groping at her breasts. She pulled her head back, gagging at the taste of stale beer, then everything went black as Fletcher scooped up the hem of her skirts and pulled them up over her head, revealing her pale buttocks and muffling her weak cries beneath the heavy cloth.

A bolt of pain hit her and she screamed as Fletcher brought the plaited leather of the quirt down on her exposed bottom, leaving a thin red line on the white skin. Her struggles redoubled as she tried to break free, but it was useless. She was helpless, trussed up as neatly as a pig in a sack. Another blow followed the first, then another, reducing her shrieks to moans.

But worse was to follow. Even through the heavy material she could hear Fletcher's lascivious chuckle. 'Not so frisky now, are you, madam?' he sneered. She felt his rampant cock press against her aching bottom and whimpered at what was to come. She began to struggle again, but all that did was push her body harder against Cooper's, exciting him, too.

Hands wrenched at her thighs, pulling them apart, then there was a moment of fierce pain as he thrust himself into her, stretching the soft flesh. Hot and rigid, he pushed inside her, grunting as he rammed his prick as deep as it would go. Knees bent, fingers digging viciously into her hips, he jerked and thrust, his cock sliding in and out, faster and faster. She moaned again as each movement pushed her against Cooper, her tender breasts scraping against his coarse leather jerkin, even through the material of her skirts.

Fletcher gave one last heave and she whimpered as his hot seed spurted inside her. Then, with a grunt of satisfaction he slowly withdrew.

But her ordeal wasn't over yet.

'My turn now,' panted Cooper. She staggered away from him as he released her, but her freedom was illusory. A push sent her spinning and she stumbled backwards and fell amongst the hay, the harsh stems pricking her tender skin. She tried to free her arms and pull her skirts from round her head, but he fell on her like a ravening beast.

Grabbing her ankles he hauled her towards him, and pulled her legs over his shoulders, leaving her body open and vulnerable to the harsh fingers that plundered her. For a few moments he savoured the hot wetness of her, still dripping with Fletcher's seed, then he took his swollen cock in hand and guided it into her, his buttocks pumping as he took her furiously, groaning with pleasure. For the second time she was ravaged, her world reduced to blackness and revulsion as his unwashed body pounded hers.

He spent himself, shuddering and moaning and his heavy weight rolled off her. She lay there, used and beaten, waiting for what might come next.

Whatever they chose to do, she could not stop them. Hopeless tears leaked from her eyes.

Then the sudden noise of hooves, clattering in the inn yard, broke the spell and she heard Fletcher and Cooper swear beneath their breath. There was the brief sound of feet as they melted back into the night and then she was alone.

Stiffly she sat up, freed herself from her tangled skirts and pulled them down to hide her aching, welted body. Holding on to the side of Alexander's stall, she pulled herself to her feet and stood there swaying as the door to the stables was pushed open and the innkeeper came in, leading the horse of some traveller who had been delayed on his journey by the foul weather.

He took one look at her and dropped the reins. 'My lady,' he gasped. 'Are you all right? What happened?'

She stared at him dully. What was the point of telling him the truth? What could he do? Fletcher and Cooper would never have dared to treat her as they had, had they not been sanctioned by her stepfather. Sir Thomas had bested her again.

'I stumbled and fell,' she lied. 'I must have hit my head against the stall, but I am fine now.' She forced a smile. 'A glass of your excellent wine and I shall be fully recovered.'

'Here, take my arm, my lady,' he insisted. 'Lest you stumble again.'

She allowed him to help her back to the inn, grateful for his assistance, her thighs still weak from the savagery of the treatment she had received. At least tomorrow she would reach the safety of the convent and she need never see Fletcher or Cooper again.

Hatred washed through her. Her stepfather had called her a whore, and that was exactly how she'd been treated. She smiled bitterly. No, that was not quite true, was it? They had treated her worse than any whore. At least a whore got paid!

Chapter Seven

'Wake up, my pet,' said Alice, shaking Jane's shoulder. 'This is no time to lie abed. We must break our fast and be off. We have another day's ride ahead of us.' Certain that her charge was now awake, she bustled off to see to the ordering of food and drink.

Jane sat up, groggily wiping the sleep from her eyes. It had been a bad night. As Alice snored beside her she had lain awake, her body aching with unfulfilled desire, staring into the darkness, starting at every sound, terrified that Fletcher and Cooper would return to drag her from her bed and repeat their foul attack upon her.

When she had slept it was only to dream about what they had done. Dreadful nightmares in which she gloried in their base attentions, urging them on to further excesses, shamelessly revelling in the sinful pleasures of the flesh. She flushed as she remembered the explosion of heat that suffused her loins in her dreams, bringing both humiliation and satisfaction before, sated, she had finally fallen into dreamless oblivion. She shuddered. Perhaps her stepfather had been correct in his assessment of her, for surely only a slut could have such perverse feelings?

'Still not up?' demanded Alice, bustling back again. 'Come now, slugabed! Rise and dress yourself before the day is any further gone.'

Reluctantly, Jane rose, pulling her night rail about her to hide the dark marks on her breasts, where the soft flesh had been bruised by demanding fingers. There was an ache between her thighs that tormented her as she moved;

a strange mixture of pain and pleasure. She bit her lip and moaned inwardly. It was true. She was a whore!

Sharp-eyed Alice caught the slight wince of pain. 'What ails you, girl?' she demanded. 'You walk as stiff as some old gammer with the bone-sickness.'

Jane forced a smile. 'And so should you, old woman,' she said lightly, 'sleeping on such an ill mattress. I think I preferred the fleas to this poxy damp.' She turned her back and began to dress quickly.

'There now,' she said, once fully clothed. 'Satisfied? Now, let us go and eat. My aches and pains will vanish once we begin to ride again.'

'And mine will return,' grumbled Alice. 'Damned donkey! All bones and bad temper.'

'Just like you,' teased Jane. 'But I love you anyway.' Mollified, Alice grinned and led the way downstairs.

Fortified by bread and cheese, washed down with a tankard of small beer, Jane braced herself to face her tormentors, and was relieved to find that, the false bravado of drink having worn off, it was they who avoided her eyes as they busied themselves about the tasks of saddling the horses and packing the bundles. Fear of the consequences of their actions had instilled caution. There was much respectful nodding as they handed her into the saddle – and if there was the occasional lecherous sideways smirk between them, then she didn't see it. Gazing straight ahead, she ignored their clumsy attempts to ingratiate themselves and the small company set off.

Thankfully the rain had stopped and the countryside was green and fresh in the early morning sunshine. Alice ceased her interminable complaints and jogged along in companionable silence, enjoying the warmth, and even the donkey seemed less fractious.

As they passed, workers planting in the fields stopped

what they were doing to watch and touch their bonnets in respect. There was even the occasional feeble cheer. Jane smiled and nodded back, thinking that this must be how King Henry himself must feel when he went on procession. For a few hours she could forget their destination and the fact that she was to be incarcerated for God knew how long in some bleak convent and simply give herself up to the enjoyment of the moment, the countryside spread in front of her like a tapestry. Yet all too soon the sunny hours passed. As evening began to fall, the sky darkened and the drizzle began again.

That was how she saw the convent first: a dark shape against a rain-swept horizon, its grey stones as cold and ominous as the cloudy sky behind it. A shiver of premonition ran through her. It might have been a house of God, but her first impression was one of unholy evil. A miasma of darkness seemed to cling to it, chilling her to the very soul.

Alice, however, was oblivious. She sighed in relief. 'At last. I swear my stomach thinks my throat's been cut. At least we shall be fed.' She chuckled. 'You never see a scrawny priest, do you? No doubt the nuns will eat well, too.'

'God's blood, old woman,' said Jane in disgust. 'Do you never think of anything but your guts? You'd think you were glad to be here and see the back of me.'

'Oh, no,' protested Alice. 'Never that, my sweet. But you won't be here forever. A few months and it'll all be by.' She shook her head. 'If I thought not eating would make it pass the sooner, a bite would never pass my lips till you were safely home. But since it won't, we might as well eat and keep our strength up.'

Jane sighed and smiled ruefully. Perhaps she had a point, but her own appetite had deserted her. The closer they got, the worse she felt. It was as if the wings of some great bird of prey had swept over her. The watery sun was setting, and the shadows cast by the convent seemed to stretch towards her like dark, grasping fingers. She shivered again.

As they clattered into the small courtyard and halted, silence enfolded them. The huge wooden door remained shut and there was none of the usual hustle and bustle of a normal household – just a hushed, expectant quiet. They looked at one another nervously.

'Should we knock?' said Alice, so quietly that Jane could barely make out what she was saying. 'Or do you think the nuns are at prayer?'

'What are you whispering for?' Jane demanded. 'My stepfather's clerk wrote to say we were coming. We should be expected.'

She stopped as the door creaked open, pushed by two nuns. They scuttled back inside and a tall woman, dressed in an immaculate habit, stepped onto the threshold. 'I bid you welcome,' she said, smiling humbly – but her eyes belied her words. They were as cold and grey as the stones of the convent and the smile on her lips did not reach them. High cheekbones in a face as white and cool as marble, and the arrogance barely concealed behind the humility, reminded Jane again of some monstrous bird of prey. A hawk, perhaps. Or a peregrine falcon, its threat hooded for the moment, but there beneath the surface.

'Thank you,' she muttered through stiff lips. 'We are weary after our long journey.'

'Then you must eat and refresh yourselves,' the woman said. 'Your men may sleep in the stables and feed at the kitchen door.' She nodded her head graciously. 'I am Ursula, Mother Superior here. You may call me Mother Ursula.' She turned away and they followed her reluctantly inside.

Despite the cold exterior the inside was not as frightening as Jane had imagined. Once they had availed themselves of the privy they were led into the refectory and found themselves seated at a long polished table. Broth was put in front of them and mulled wine and, once they had finished that, a pasty stuffed with meat was brought in. Alice fell to with a will, but Jane barely picked at hers. The nuns ate in silence, casting curious sideways glances at them when they thought Mother Ursula's attention was elsewhere.

It was a relief to escape finally to the guest dormitory. A warm fire burned in the hearth and the mattress was soft and well packed with straw. Alice bounced on it cheerfully. 'See,' she said in a consoling tone of voice, 'it's not as bad as you expected. You'll be comfortable enough, for all the time you'll be stopping here.'

Despite all these assurances Jane was awake long after Alice was snoring, a feeling of dread gnawing at her stomach.

It was worse the following morning, when she had to bid goodbye to Alice. For all her fine words her old nurse dissolved in tears at the thought of parting with her ward. Jane was forced to put on a brave front, but she felt so heartsick that even Cooper and Fletcher seemed the lesser of the two evils. 'There, there,' she said, patting Alice's heaving shoulders. 'Dry your tears. I shall be back soon.'

She stopped as Fletcher led Alexander past and tied him to the back of his own horse. 'Where are you taking Alex?' she demanded. 'I shall need him here.'

'I think not,' said Mother Ursula coolly. 'The convent has stabling only for its guests. We do not have the resources to keep such a great beast, eating us out of house and home.' She clapped her hands and Jane watched in dismay as Fletcher tested the fastening, to make sure it was secure.

After one last tearful hug, Alice mounted her hated donkey and the small procession began to move out of the courtyard. Jane waved goodbye, tears blinding her eyes as she strained to watch them growing slowly smaller in the distance.

'Right,' said Mother Ursula briskly. 'Now that your escort has left, you will take your cell in the block with the other novices.'

Jane stared at her in shock. 'Novices?' she gasped. 'I am no novice. I am merely here to make a retreat. I have no vocation for the religious life.'

'That is not what your father said,' smiled Mother Ursula. 'Once you have passed your noviciate, you will take your vows and join our order.' She clapped her hands again and four nuns scurried to obey her.

As the heavy courtyard gates swung shut, cutting off her last contact with the outside world, a horrifying realisation dawned on Jane. She was effectively a prisoner.

Chapter Eight

For a moment she stood there, rooted to the spot, then she took to her heels and ran towards the gates, her hair billowing out behind her like a copper banner. Shrieking, she banged her fists against the unyielding wood until she realised the hopelessness of her task. Like an animal at bay, she turned and faced her captors.

Mother Ursula had made no move to follow her. She stood watching the tearful girl with a cool smile on her lips. Some of the nuns regarded Jane with frightened, sympathetic eyes, while others tittered behind their hands, exulting over her misery. Either way there was no help forthcoming. Jane's shoulders sagged.

'Have you quite finished your tantrum?' enquired Mother Ursula sarcastically. Jane nodded dully and the woman's lips twisted in a cruel smile. 'Good,' she said. 'Then perhaps you will do as you are told without any more of this foolishness.' She clicked her fingers. 'Sister Marie, Sister Michael. Take our young novice to the dorter,' her eyes ran disparagingly over the rich fabric of Jane's dress, 'and see that she is more suitably clothed.'

The spirit of generations of ancestors who had fought on every English battlefield since William first came from Normandy came to her rescue. Suppressing her panic, Jane straightened her shoulders and stared coldly back at Mother Ursula.

'I will not go,' she said, forcing herself to speak with a calm she did not feel. 'I have told you already. There has been some mistake. I will return to the guesthouse and remain there until it has been rectified.' Ignoring them all, she turned and, head held high, began to walk towards the grey stone building.

She had barely gone four steps before a hand seized her hair and she was jerked to a halt. She twisted round, screaming as flares of pain jolted through her skull. Mother Ursula's face, distorted with rage, was scant inches from her own.

'I think not, mistress,' she hissed, and Jane could feel the woman's hot breath against her cheeks. 'You are no longer some spoilt miss, giving orders to your servants. I am in charge here and you will do as I say.' The hand holding the fistful of hair jerked again and Jane whimpered with pain, then staggered back as she was released. Mother Ursula looked at her and dusted her hands with distaste. 'And if you will not go of your own accord, then you must be aided.' She nodded to the two nuns. 'Take her.'

Sister Michael stepped forward, smiling. She was well named. Tall and gaunt, she looked more like a man than a woman, her loose habit barely disguising the flat chest and scrawny body beneath. Her bony fingers dug into the soft skin of Jane's upper arm. Her companion, Sister Marie, fluttered round her ineffectually, her round face pink with distress.

'Don't struggle, it will only make things worse,' she whispered, her lips barely moving. Her frightened eyes darted sideways towards Mother Ursula. 'She likes it when you struggle.'

Jane caught the triumphant expression in Mother Ursula's eyes and made herself relax. Her lips tightened. She wouldn't give the vile woman the satisfaction. As the watching nuns dispersed about their tasks she allowed herself to be half-marched, half-carried towards the novices' wing, Sister Michael holding her firmly while

Sister Marie pattered along at her side. Mother Ursula glided along behind.

When they reached the novices' dorter, Jane's resolution deserted her. The windowless cell was more like a prison. It was tiny and completely featureless apart from a crucifix on one wall. A narrow cot, with a thin rolled-up straw mattress and threadbare blanket, took up more than half the space. Crumpled at the foot of the cot lay a stained grey shift that looked as if it was made out of old sacking. A pair of down-at-heel shoes, patched, worn and at least two sizes too big for Jane's dainty feet, sat beneath.

'Your novice's habit,' said Mother Ursula, indicating the grimy cast-offs. 'You will remove your worldly garments and put it on.'

'Oh no, I won't!' spat Jane. She picked up the coarse shift and held it between two fingers. 'It isn't even clean.' She flung it down and glared at Mother Ursula. 'You cannot make me put it on.'

The woman's lips curled in a cruel smile. 'Oh, I think I can, my dear,' she purred. 'Sister Michael?'

Bony fingers seized the neck of Jane's velvet gown and pulled viciously. There was a rending sound as the seam gave way and the dress fell to the floor, dragged down by its own weight. Jane gasped and crossed her arms protectively across her chest. Sister Marie gasped, her hands held to her face in dismay. Mother Ursula gave the plump nun one scathing glance and dismissed her contemptuously, then turned back to enjoy the spectacle before her.

Grinning, Sister Michael grabbed Jane's wrists and twisted her arms behind her back, trapping them in one enormous hand. With the other she gripped Jane's flimsy shift and tore that away as well, then pushed her on to the narrow cot and deftly peeled off her shoes and stockings, leaving her naked and defenceless.

To Jane's horror the woman's hands seemed to linger for a moment on the soft flesh of her thighs before she stepped back and stood waiting for Mother Ursula's next order. She shook herself. She had imagined the caress. Of course she had. No matter how unfeminine, Sister Michael was still a woman, after all. She glared up at her tormentors and a defiant smile touched her lips. 'I'd rather stay naked as God made me than put on that foul garment,' she said defiantly.

Mother Ursula shrugged. 'As you wish,' she said. 'But perhaps you will feel differently when the cold begins to bite.' She ran her eyes over Jane's shrinking body and smiled. 'Vanity is a sin. 'And we must try and wash our sins away, must we not?' She nodded at Sister Michael again and Jane found herself wrenched to her feet and propelled naked out of the cell and along the cold corridor.

The next room she found herself in was larger, but just as bare, except for the wooden tub in the centre of the floor. It was filled with water – but, unlike her bathtub at home, there were no comforting tendrils of steam rising from the surface, no hot towels waiting to be wrapped round her afterwards, no fire to toast herself in front of as she sipped a warm glass of mulled wine and nibbled comfits. Nothing but the tub itself, waiting ominously.

She halted on the threshold and attempted to back away, but Sister Michael was right behind her. With a grunt of satisfaction she scooped Jane up, carried her across to the tub, held her above it – and let her drop.

The icy water closed above her head. For a moment the shock was so intense she could not breathe, then she gasped and spluttered as her head broke the surface and air flooded back into her lungs. Her feet scrabbled for purchase and she forced herself to stand, gasping and shivering. Her hair was almost black, plastered against the whiteness of her body in long tendrils, from which rivulets coursed down her quivering thighs. Her nipples, tightly puckered with the cold, stood out from the soft globes of her breasts as if they had a life of their own. Sister Michael's eyes lingered on them, then turned towards Mother Ursula, hopefully seeking permission.

Mother Ursula smiled. 'We must mortify the flesh, must we not?' She nodded to Sister Michael. 'Perhaps you will be kind enough to teach our young novice her first lesson? Help her scrub away the temptations that beset the unwary sinner.'

The next quarter of an hour was one of the worst of Jane's life. She flinched as sadistic fingers pinched and poked her tender body, invading its secret places under the masquerade of 'cleansing' her. She gasped as the harsh scrubbing-brush scoured her back, leaving a mass of thin lines as Sister Michael drew it down with exquisite slowness, revelling in the way Jane writhed and whimpered as her fine alabaster skin reddened in its wake.

But most of all, what scoured her soul as well as her body was the humiliation, and the frightening knowledge that here was a kind of calculated wickedness she'd never faced before. She shuddered. Even her stepfather and Sir Harry – even Fletcher and Cooper – had been *natural* compared to this.

Beneath her mask of piety and her claims that she was 'mortifying the flesh', Jane could sense that Mother Ursula was looking on, taking an unholy pleasure in the way her perverted puppet was abusing her. There was a faint hint of colour in her marble cheeks and her breath was coming quicker through slightly parted lips as she watched Sister Michael twisting and kneading Jane's pale breasts.

At last it was over. Mother Ursula clapped her hands,

the expression on her face leaving Jane in no doubt that the pleasure the woman was taking from the scene was sexual in its nature. 'Enough,' she ordered. 'Take her back to her cell.'

Reluctantly, Sister Michael withdrew and allowed Jane to stand up and climb slowly and painfully from the tub. Jane stood there for a moment, shivering and sobbing, then began to limp along the corridor to her cell, her arms huddled round her for comfort, the deathly chill in her body matched only by the chill in her soul.

Without a word she gratefully put on the shift she had refused to wear earlier, feeling its coarse fibres scratch her already tender skin.

'Good,' smiled Mother Ursula. 'Already you have learnt two parts of the rule: poverty and obedience. Perhaps we shall make a nun of you yet.' She bent and picked up a length of material that had been hidden beneath the sacking dress. 'Here,' she ordered, flinging it at Jane. 'Cover that blasphemous red hair of yours.' Her lip curled. 'When you take your vows it will be shaved off. Until then, we'll have none of Satan's temptations here.'

Dumb with misery, Jane did as she was told, winding the rough material round her head. Mother Ursula seemed to regard the shabby figure before her with pleasure, satisfied there was now nothing left of the wilful young miss who had tried to defy her.

'You may remain here and think about your many sins, until you find repentance,' she said. Gliding out of the cell she closed the door firmly behind her, and Jane heard the key turn in the lock. For a moment she stood staring at it, then collapsed on the narrow cot, giving herself up to her misery.

On the other side of the door Ursula listened to the muffled sobbing, a smile of relish on her lips. Not such a cocky young madam now. Her smile widened. Not that this abasement would last, she was certain of that. She could recognise a fighter when she saw one. Give the girl time to recover and she'd try to stand up for herself again.

The smile became lascivious and Ursula licked her lips as a familiar heat surged through her loins. When that time came she'd be ready and waiting. Miss High-and-mighty might think she had done her worst – but she had only just begun!

Chapter Nine

'Bless you, mistress,' muttered the toothless old woman, accepting the ladle of slops that Jane tipped into the wooden bowl she held out in her palsied hands. Jane shivered. Even with nothing but a sacking apron tied over her threadbare shift and the broken shoes that had already raised blisters on her tender feet, she was better dressed than the pathetic bundles of rags who queued patiently outside the gate for whatever poor meats the convent doled out.

She sighed. The slop bucket was almost empty, yet the pitiful line still stretched out, waiting to be fed. Dull eyes stared at her hopelessly as the ladle scraped the bottom of the bucket and came out empty.

'Isn't there anything else?' demanded Jane. 'We can't just leave them hungry.'

'No,' whispered Sister Marie. 'This is all Mother Ursula allows.'

'There's got to be something,' said Jane indignantly. Her lips twisted in scorn. She might be deficient in kindness and Christian charity, but the one thing Mother Ursula did not stint on was food. There had to be more left over. 'I'm going to look in the kitchens,' she announced.

'You mustn't,' whimpered Sister Marie. 'If Mother Ursula finds out...' Her voice trailed off, then she swallowed and tried again. 'You don't know what she's like.'

Sister Marie was wrong. Jane knew exactly – and for a

moment she paused as she remembered the icy ducking she'd had to endure at the hands of Sister Michael and the way those same hands had crawled over her helpless body. Then she took another look at the scrawny children huddling into their desperate mothers, the old and the weak and the crippled, all waiting with the dumb patience of brute beasts. Her heart smote her. She couldn't turn them away starving.

'I don't care,' she said defiantly. 'I won't be long.' She spun on her heel and headed towards the convent kitchen as fast as her blistered feet would allow.

Inside, the warmth of the ovens and fires hit her like a blow after the cool air outside. The kitchen was a hive of industry. A great joint of meat was already dripping its grease on to the flames as the spit-dog wearily turned in its treadmill. Two enormous trays of fresh bread sat cooling from the ovens. The fat nun who was in charge wiped sweat from her forehead as she supervised several hefty lay sisters who sat, heavy thighs splayed wide, scraping the vegetables.

Jane's eyes searched the steamy room and finally lit on two covered buckets standing beside the long table. She darted across, lifted the lids and smiled as she saw the contents. They were piled high with broken crusts, scraps of meat and squashed vegetables. Admittedly they were still leavings, but compared to the thin slops she'd just been doling out this was a banquet fit for King Henry. Grasping a handle in each hand, she staggered towards the door.

'And just where do you think you're going with those?' demanded the fat nun, stepping in front of her, clutching a broom.

'To feed the poor,' said Jane, edging sideways. 'Isn't that what we're supposed to do?'

'Not with that you're not,' replied the cook smugly. 'That's for the pigs. Mother Ursula wants them fattened up in time for Father Peter's visit.'

For a moment Jane was stunned. Hungry people were waiting at the gate and Mother Ursula was letting them starve while she fattened up pigs? Her mouth set in a grim line. Well, not today she wasn't.

One of the heavy buckets collided with the cook's shin and she suddenly lost all interest in preventing Jane's passage. 'Sorry,' Jane apologised as she pushed past the wincing woman, the buckets still swinging dangerously. She was aware of every person in the kitchen watching her in astonishment, mouths open, and was suddenly overwhelmed by the desire to giggle. As she passed the tray of bread she paused, put down one of the buckets and helped herself to a couple of loaves, tucking them under her arms before retrieving the bucket again.

She shrugged as best she could under the circumstances. 'Might as well be hung for a sheep as a lamb,' she announced cheerfully to her stunned audience before fleeing the kitchens as fast as her burdens would permit.

Sister Marie's eyes widened as she saw Jane's booty. 'Where did you get that?' she whispered.

'Don't ask,' muttered Jane. 'The less you know, the better. Right, who's next?' she called, brandishing her ladle. The little crowd surged forward with renewed hope and for the next ten minutes there was no time to think as she dished out the life-giving food. Finally the last scraps had been devoured in a mutter of grateful blessings and, with full bellies for once, the supplicants dispersed.

Jane smiled grimly as she watched them go. No doubt she would pay for her temerity in defying Mother Ursula, but whatever happened to her it would be worth it if she'd managed to make the harsh lives of these poor unfortunates just a tiny bit easier.

She smiled ruefully at Sister Marie. 'Well,' she said, lifting the empty buckets, 'time to face the music.'

Mother Ursula was waiting, almost incandescent with anger. Her thin lips were nothing more than a tight line in her gaunt face and her eyes glowed with suppressed rage. 'So,' she hissed, 'you dare to defy me yet again.'

'Why no, Reverend Mother,' said Jane, bowing meekly. 'I was merely acting from Christian charity. Didn't our Lord teach us to feed the poor and hungry?'

In two quick strides Mother Ursula was standing in front of her. A hand lashed out so fast that Jane didn't even see it. She bit her lip to keep from crying out as her head rocked on her shoulders and a white handprint appeared on the side of her face where the other woman had struck her. As the blood flowed back the print turned from white to scarlet, as if the mark of Cain had been branded on her cheek.

'Go to your cell and pray for humility,' ordered Mother Ursula, her voice shaking. She controlled herself and smiled coldly. 'And since you have shown such concern for the poor and hungry, you will not mind going without yourself, as penance for your disobedience. Your meat can go to the pigs.' She whirled on Sister Marie, who cringed back like a rabbit in the glare of a stoat. 'And as for you...'

Jane stepped forward. 'The fault was mine and mine alone, Reverend Mother,' she protested. 'Sister Marie did her best to dissuade me. I would not listen.'

'Headstrong as well as disobedient,' purred Ursula. 'Is there no end to your sinfulness, girl?' A smile touched her lips. 'And since you are so well versed in the words of the Good Book, you may remember another quotation from it. "Spare the rod and spoil the child". You may think on that as well, while you are in your cell.' She turned to Sister Michael and Jane's insides shrivelled. 'Take her there – and lock the door.'

Jane spun on her heel before the woman could put her foul hands on her and stalked down the grey corridor with her head held high. Sister Michael strode behind her, the skirts of her habit rustling, and it took all Jane's courage not to begin running to get away from her. It seemed an age until she reached the sanctuary of her cell. Once inside, she backed against the wall and waited for whatever was coming next.

To her relief Sister Michael did not follow her inside. For a moment she stood on the threshold and leered at the panting girl, then the door swung slowly closed, shutting out the light, and Jane heard the key turning in the lock. She breathed a sigh of relief at getting off so lightly and flung herself down on the narrow cot.

With nothing to do but think, the minutes seemed to drag like hours. With no window to see the passing of daylight she had no way of telling how long she lay there. The walls of the cell seemed to close in upon her in the darkness, the air thickening in her throat. To pass the time she thought of escape. The village was only two miles away. If she could reach it, would someone there hide her?

She dismissed the thought as quickly as it had come. Last year's poor harvest had brought the villagers close to ruin. She remembered the number of supplicants at the gate that morning. They were unable to feed themselves, let alone a runaway. Besides, she thought bitterly, the convent provided their only source of help in a hard and unforgiving world. If they aided her, Mother Ursula would have no compunction in punishing them too, and without the food and medicines the nuns dispensed, no matter how grudgingly, how would the very young and the very old survive? She shook her head. There was no help to be found there.

Her stomach rumbled and hunger pangs gnawed at her insides. She'd had no time to break her fast this morning and now even the thought of the scraps she'd doled out made her salivate. She rolled over and curled up beneath the thin blanket. If only she could sleep she could forget her hunger.

A sound made her freeze, her eyes staring into the darkness, searching for its source.

She forced herself to relax. Perhaps it was just a rat. She smiled ruefully. If it was, then it was on a fool's errand; there was nothing to eat here.

Her smile vanished as she heard it again. That was no rat – or if it was, it was the human kind. A thin line of light flickered beneath the ill-fitting door and she cringed back as she heard the key turn surreptitiously in the lock. Holding the blanket to her breasts, she watched as the door quietly creaked open.

For a moment, so used to the darkness, she could see nothing. Then, as her eyes adjusted, she drew in a shuddering breath. The scene before her was one from her worst nightmares. Six shadowy figures stood there, each with a candle in its hand, the flickering light distorting their faces into masks of evil. She cowered back against the wall.

'Ah, not quite so defiant now.' It was Mother Ursula. Her voice whispered back from the stone walls like the hiss of a snake.

Fear settled on Jane like an icy blanket. 'Wh-what do you want?' she stammered.

Mother Ursula laughed coldly. 'Did you think you had escaped your punishment? No one defies me and gets away with it. Oh no, my dear. You must learn your lesson – and we are here to teach you.'

Cold hands grasped Jane and tore her from the safety of the cot. The bare stones struck cold on her feet as she was dragged along the corridors, the candles streaming in the draught and casting monstrous shadows on the walls. The only sounds were their footsteps and Jane's desperate panting as she struggled to break free. Her thoughts raced as they stopped before a carved wooden door. It was the chapel. What were they doing here? The door swung open and she was thrust through. For a moment her mind refused to grasp what it was seeing.

The roof soared away into nothingness, and the chapel itself was a mass of shifting pools of blackness, apart from the altar, which was surrounded by hundreds of candles. But this was no celebration of Christianity. This was something older and darker. A scarlet cloth embroidered with gold covered the altar and at its head – Jane swallowed – lay thin ropes, coiled and waiting like poisonous serpents.

She whimpered and tried to back away, her bare feet slipping on the polished floor. It was useless. Like a sacrificial lamb she was dragged towards the waiting table. Flickers of light illuminated the faces of the holy statues, which seemed to peer down at her in pity.

All too soon she stood before the altar. 'Strip her and bind her,' ordered Mother Ursula. Eager hands pulled the ragged shift from her body, using this as an excuse to fondle the shrinking flesh beneath. Her russet hair spilled down her back as the rough linen binding was tugged off, emphasising her pale beauty, then she was pushed face down on the altar and her hands were seized and bound above her head. She moaned as she was hauled into position and the coarse embroidery rubbed against her tender breasts.

Mother Ursula smiled down at the smooth white body that lay stretched out before her like an offering, the proud globes of Jane's buttocks quivering in the candlelight. She withdrew her hands from the concealing robes and there was a greedy intake of breath at the sight of the thin leather whip she held. Jane twisted her head and gasped. She closed her eyes and waited for her punishment to begin.

She didn't have to wait long. Mother Ursula raised her arm and the lash whistled through the chilled air to cut into Jane's tender bottom, leaving a thin red line against the milk-white skin. She stiffened as a wave of agony gripped her. She bit back a scream, determined not to give in – but Ursula had only just begun.

The whip rose and fell, rose and fell again, until Jane was sobbing helplessly, her bottom scarlet and glowing. Eventually it was over and she sagged with relief... but it was short-lived.

'Turn her over,' ordered Mother Ursula. Willing hands seized Jane again and she whimpered as her bruised flesh met the rough cloth beneath her. She gazed up with frightened eyes and gasped as Mother Ursula ran the whip gently over her breasts, teasing the soft flesh of her nipples until they rose into tight pink buds. Smiling, her tormentor trailed the lash down her body and over the curve of her stomach to the secret place hidden by her clenched thighs. Jane's muscles tightened convulsively as she tried to protect herself. 'Why don't you beg?' said Mother Ursula softly. 'I would like to hear you beg.'

Jane stared at her defiantly. 'Never!' she spat.

'Dear, oh dear.' Mother Ursula sighed, shaking her head with mock regret. 'So young and yet so sinful. Perhaps

Sister Michael can teach you better than I can.' She nodded and the woman stepped forward, smiling evilly. Jane shuddered as she slipped off her habit to reveal her bony body, the chest almost as flat as a man's, a tuft of wiry grey hair at the juncture of her scrawny thighs. Jane closed her eyes to shut out the sight. No matter how much the woman beat her, she would never give in. She braced herself for more pain.

Instead, humid wetness enveloped one nipple, while fingers twisted and squeezed the other. Her eyes shot open and she gasped in horror. This unnatural act was worse than any pain. She gazed at Mother Ursula, pleadingly. 'No! Please, no!' she begged.

'Too late now.' Mother Ursula was smirking. 'You brought it upon yourself.'

Jane moaned and tried to twist away, but Sister Michael continued her tormenting attentions. Her tongue circled and teased the trapped nipple, her fingers kneading and pulling its twin until they were both pulsing and swollen. Jane gasped in dismay as the heat in her buttocks began to radiate through the rest of her body, changing from pain to a kind of twisted pleasure. She felt herself moisten and groaned again, this time in horror at her own reaction.

The tormenting tongue began to drift lower, leaving a hot wet trail behind it. Jane's belly quivered as it reached the juncture of her thighs. She brought her knees up, twisting sideways.

'Oh no,' said Mother Ursula. 'It's not that easy, my dear.' She clapped her hands and Jane's legs were seized and pulled apart to reveal the glistening pink opening crowned with flame-red hair. She whimpered as Sister Michael bent her attention to the swollen knob of her clitoris, lapping and circling it until Jane thought she would go mad. The tongue darted into the soft wet centre of Jane's body, slithering in and out like a hot snake.

'Please, *please*,' she moaned, no longer sure whether she was begging for her torment to stop or continue. Her hips jerked convulsively, forcing the muscular tongue deeper inside herself.

'Enough,' ordered Ursula. Reluctantly Sister Michael withdrew, and Jane stared up, her eyes glazed with unsatisfied lust. Then she realised what Ursula was holding and moaned with fear.

The church candle was two inches in diameter and almost ten inches long. Smiling, Ursula watched as Jane tried frantically to twist away from what was coming next, but the cruel hands held her in place as Ursula advanced.

Jane whimpered as she felt the thick candle pressing against the vulnerable opening of her body. There was a moment of resistance then, inch by irresistible inch, Ursula pressed it home, smiling as most of the length disappeared from sight. Jane's eyes flickered shut and she whined with a mixture of pain and pleasure as it filled her completely. Mother Ursula began to move it slowly in and out. It slid smoothly, faster and faster, lubricated by Jane's juices, and she forgot everything but the wild sensations spiralling through her. And when other hands took their pleasure from her writhing body she didn't even notice as she screamed her satisfaction and release.

For a moment she lay there, warm and sated, then reality broke in again and she burst into tears of humiliation. Unbearable shame washed over her. These perverted women had used her for their own satisfaction, reducing her to nothing but a hungry animal, willing to do anything to satisfy its basest appetites. And she had let them do it!

Lost in her own misery she barely even noticed the lewd comments or the stumbling return to her cell.

Once there, she curled into a protective ball and huddled

beneath the thin blanket, shivering. Her last thought before she fell into a sleep haunted by nightmares was that Mother Ursula was no bride of Christ.

She was a bride of Satan!

Chapter Ten

At the head of the refectory table Mother Ursula sat with a small, triumphant smile on her lips as she regarded the results of her handiwork.

Exhausted by a night of sleeplessness, Jane had dragged herself through the day avoiding everyone. Now she kept her head bowed low over the early evening meal – not through piety but through mortification. Her eyes darted sideways, surreptitiously surveying the nuns as they ate. Which of these chattering women had witnessed her shame of the night before? Mother Ursula, certainly, and Sister Michael – but who were the other four? She closed her eyes and shuddered.

The leering faces, hidden by the veils and coifs and distorted by the flickering candlelight, had been hideously anonymous. How could she look any of them in the eye, not knowing if the pious expressions they wore hid the secret knowledge of her shame? That when they looked at her they were gloating over the memory of her base, animal writhings? She pushed her plate away, sickened.

How could such evil exist in a place dedicated to God?

Mother Ursula's mocking voice floated over the chatter, stilling it immediately. Jane flushed as every eye turned towards her. 'Not hungry, my dear? What a pity. I wonder what has caused your loss of appetite? Still, waste not want not. What doesn't fatten you will fatten the pigs. And since you are so fond of feeding the hungry, I think we shall give that task to you. I am sure you will do it very well.' She put down her spoon, daintily dabbed the corners of her mouth with her napkin, and rose. 'You will begin immediately,' she ordered.

Jane opened her mouth to protest, then thought better of it, fearful of risking another punishment. 'Yes, Reverend Mother,' she replied meekly, writhing inwardly at her own cowardice and the knowledge that those poor unfortunates would go hungry because of it. But what could she do? Rebellion would solve nothing. It would only provide another excuse for Mother Ursula to torment her, while people still starved. She stared after Mother Ursula, hatred in her eyes as the woman left the refectory.

One by one the others finished their meal and drifted off to their evening prayers, leaving Jane alone. With a sigh she went to the kitchen and returned with the half-filled slop buckets to begin the distasteful task of scraping the slimy remains of the food into them.

With another sigh she rolled up her sleeves, seized one of the overflowing buckets and staggered out of the refectory and across the back court to the tumbledown lean-to which housed the pigs. Her entrance was greeted with grunts and snorts as the two animals jostled each other in their eagerness to reach the food. She tipped it into the trough, spilling it over her shift. The odour of stale food and sour milk drifted up to her and she smiled ruefully. Now she would smell as bad as the pigs did.

Returning to the refectory she collected the second bucket. On her return to the sty she passed a stout lay sister, sweat stains under her arms, working in the convent garden in the last of the daylight. Glad of the diversion the woman stopped her weeding, leaned on her hoe and gave Jane a cheerful grin from which the two front teeth were missing.

'The Last Supper, eh?' she chuckled. Jane stared at her blankly. 'The Last Supper,' the woman repeated, annoyed that her wit had gone unrecognised. 'The pigs.' She rolled her eyes at Jane's stupidity. 'Not long for this world,' she explained patiently. 'Father Peter's visiting next week. The pig-sticker's coming at first light tomorrow morning, so this'll be their last supper.'

'Oh, I see,' said Jane. She forced an answering chuckle. 'The last supper. A clever jest.'

Mollified, the woman continued. 'Just you wait. There will be no stinting when he's here.' She grinned and smacked her lips. 'Roast pork. Boiled ham. Sweetmeats. Wine with every meal. Nothing but the best for Father Peter and his company.' Cheered by the thought, she returned to her weeding with fresh vigour, leaving Jane to continue to the pigsty.

The second bucket of slops was greeted with as much enthusiasm as the first.

'Enjoy your meal,' said Jane sadly, leaning over to scratch behind a floppy pink ear, eliciting a grunt of pleasure. 'Poor beasts. It will be your last.'

She sighed. It was hardly the pigs' fault if they fed well at the expense of others. Though they could not know it, they would soon pay dearly for the privilege. It was a hard world.

She slept badly again that night and was woken by an unholy shrieking. For a moment she thought she had died and gone to hell, then she realised what it was. She moaned and rolled over in her narrow cot, covering her ears to shut out the sounds of the pigs being slaughtered. There was a final squeal of terror, then silence.

Then the door of her cell banged open. 'Get up, you lazy slugabed,' ordered Sister Michael, jerking the thin blanket from her naked body. 'Lying there like a lady when there's work to be done!' For a moment she stood watching as Jane slid wearily out of bed and into her stained shift, then, satisfied that her orders were being obeyed, she bustled out again in a swirl of black skirts.

The next few days were a blur of activity, meals reduced to hastily consumed slices of bread and cheese, as preparations for Father Peter's visit went ahead apace. The carcasses of the pigs were reduced to joints and roasts, the blood caught in huge basins to be turned into humbler black puddings. The long trails of guts were emptied, laid in the stream to be cleansed by the running water, then filled with minced meat and herbs to produce fat sausages. The kitchens smelt of blood, meat and smoke in equal proportions, filled with the red glow of the fires and sweating black-clad figures, like some anteroom to hell.

To Jane's portion fell all the filthiest jobs. Burning the bristles from the carcasses. Scraping the bloodstained fat from the skins, while plump black flies buzzed around her head and settled on her sweaty face. She stank from head to foot of smoke and grease, her shift was sodden with unmentionable liquids, and every bone in her body ached with effort. Still, all this was nothing compared with what she had already endured – and at least in the whirl of activity she could push her humiliation to the back of her mind and forget it in sheer physical exertion.

Even better was the fact that Mother Ursula seemed to have forgotten all about her. Without lifting so much as a lily-white finger, the woman supervised everything, chivvying the already harassed nuns into further effort. The guestrooms were scrubbed and polished, the mattresses lifted and laid in the sunshine to sweeten. The chapel brasses were polished to perfection and the altar cloths laundered to within an inch of their lives. Jane smiled ruefully. Anyone watching the frantic activity would have thought the Pope himself was coming to visit!

Finally all was done. In her comfortless cell at the end of the last busy day, Jane raised her arm to wipe the sweat from her forehead and recoiled in revulsion. She stank like a polecat. She looked down at her stained shift in disgust. The laundresses had been working overtime as well, but while everyone else had been issued with clean habits in honour of Father Peter's arrival, she had been conveniently forgotten. She pulled a wry face. No doubt this was all part of Mother Ursula's plan to keep her in her place: humble, downtrodden – and smelly into the bargain!

She grinned. Well, it wouldn't work. She might not be clad in velvet and ermine, but at least she could be clean. Before her courage deserted her again, she tiptoed to the door, eased it open and listened. Nothing but silence greeted her ears. The exhausted nuns had settled gratefully into their narrow cots, like a flock of plump chickens settling back into their nests after the fox has gone. Hardly daring to breathe, she stepped out into the corridor. There was a faint sound and she froze, then laughed softly as she realised it was nothing more than a ladylike snore from the adjoining cell. Barefoot, she crept along the corridor to the outer door, wincing as the huge iron key screeched in the rusty lock. Closing her eyes she waited, expecting Mother Ursula to sweep down on her in a fury at any moment. Nothing. Pulling the door open barely a crack, she slipped through.

She stopped on the threshold, breathing in the clean night air after the stench of the previous few days. Moonlight silvered the trees and the dew-pond gleamed like a dark mirror in the hollow between them. For a moment she stood there, savouring the beauty of the night, before running lightly down the hill towards the cool inviting water, her bare feet leaving dark prints in the soft damp grass.

Stripping off the stinking shift, she threw it into the shallows to soak, and stood there, a slim white statue in the moonlight. Then, bracing herself, she waded in, sending silvery ripples across the still surface of the pond. She shuddered as the water crept up her thighs, caressing her sweaty skin with cold fingers. When it reached her waist she flung herself forward, gasping as it enveloped her completely, her nipples shivering into tight buds with the shock of the icy embrace.

Laughing, she rolled on her back like an otter, kicking her legs to propel herself towards the centre of the pond. A few sleepy quacks protested this unexpected disturbance, only serving to make her laugh the more. Buoyed by the silky water, she lay there staring up at the starry sky as a feeling of peace washed over her.

All too soon more prosaic thoughts crept in. If she had not done this on impulse she could have planned it better, and stolen some lye soap from the laundry. As it was she would have to do the best she could without it. Using her hands she rubbed every inch of her body, to remove the last lingering traces of sweat and grime. Her skin tingled beneath her fingers and she could feel herself moisten in ready response, but briskly she pushed the tantalising feelings away. There was no time for that sort of thing when her absence could be discovered at any moment.

Ducking her head beneath the water she scrubbed her hair and scalp, hoping the itching she experienced there was due to sweat and not lice. When she re-emerged her wet hair clung to her in dark tendrils. Sighing regretfully, she swam back towards the edge. Time to wash her shift and get back to the convent before anyone noticed she was missing.

Despite its soaking and her feverish scrubbing, there were still faint stains on the threadbare garment. But she had done the best she could under the circumstances and at least it no longer stank. She wrung it out as much as possible and struggled back into it, the wet linen clinging to her equally wet body, outlining every curve and hollow, her nipples jutting against the harsh material. Shivering with the cold, she set off up the hill towards the dark hulk of the convent.

She breathed a sigh of relief when she found the door still open as she'd left it. Slipping through, she closed it carefully behind her. She'd got away with her little escapade...

'Dear, oh dear,' came the voice she hated more than any other. She whirled to find Mother Ursula standing behind her, tapping her foot, a mocking smile on her lips. Behind her, in the shadows, other figures stood, waiting. Gasping with shock, Jane pressed her back against the door as if she could force herself through it by sheer will alone.

Mother Ursula heaved a dramatic sigh. 'Such a headstrong girl,' she tutted, through pursed lips. 'It seems that one lesson was not enough. We shall have to teach you again.' She put a thoughtful finger to her lips and cocked her head to one side. 'I fear a harder lesson is needed this time, but what to use? The quirt? The rod? Yes, the rod, I think.' She clicked her fingers, motioning to the shadowy figures. 'Take her to my study.'

This time Jane did not even try to struggle. What was the point? The end result would be the same and why should she give Sister Michael the excuse she needed to fumble and grope her reluctant body? Besides, she would need all her strength for the ordeal to come. Meekly, she allowed herself to be led along the corridor.

Sister Ursula's study was a revelation. Even in her state of shock, Jane noticed the opulence of the Reverend Mother's private quarters. Carpets from Turkey decorated the polished floor. The chairs and settle were covered in soft brightly coloured cushions. A fire burned in the grate and tall white candles in silver candlesticks gleamed off a goblet of Venetian glass, filled with rich red wine, that sat on the small table beside it. Apparently the vow of poverty the nuns had sworn did not extend to Mother Ursula!

She did not have time to appreciate her surroundings. 'The prie-dieu,' snapped Mother Ursula.

Jane's eyes widened as the heavy prayer chair was dragged into the middle of the room and she was forced to kneel at it. Her hands were jerked above her head and fastened to the arms, leaving her helpless. Lingering over the task, Sister Michael peeled the damp shift up, revealing the soft white globes of Jane's buttocks, still beaded with droplets of water. She licked her lips and Jane cringed away as those grasping hands reached towards them.

'Not yet,' purred Mother Ursula. Sister Michael's hands dropped reluctantly to her sides. 'Later,' she promised. 'Punishment first and pleasure afterwards.' She pointed an imperious finger. 'The rod,' she snapped. Obediently, one of the others scuttled to a corner to fetch it, handing it reverently to her. Jane peered fearfully over her shoulder as Mother Ursula bent it between her hands, flexing it in anticipation. She tapped it lightly on her hand. 'For what you are about to receive, may the Lord make you truly grateful.' She smiled, raising her arm. 'And now we shall begin.'

Jane closed her eyes, clenching her muscles against the blow about to fall.

But it never came.

The sound of hasty footsteps broke the spell. Frantic

hands beat a tattoo on the study door. 'Reverend Mother, Reverend Mother,' called a voice. Mother Ursula's arm fell and she tossed the rod on to a chair before opening the door a crack.

'How dare you disturb me while I am at prayer?' she demanded.

'I am sorry, Reverend Mother,' came a breathless voice. 'But it is Father Peter and his company. They have arrived already.'

'What?' gasped Mother Ursula. 'But he is not due until tomorrow afternoon.' She regained her composure. 'Take them to the guest rooms and offer them refreshment,' she ordered. 'I shall be there immediately.'

As soon as the door was safely closed she whirled round. 'Do not think you have escaped,' she hissed at Jane. 'Your punishment is merely postponed. This will give you time to reflect upon what is to come.' She turned to the others. 'Release her and take her away. I must go and greet Father Peter.'

Back in her cell, Jane offered up a prayer of thanks. It was a sign from heaven. Father Peter's timely arrival had saved her – and he would save her again. Safe in the confessional she would tell him everything.

She smiled with relief. Mother Ursula's perverted reign of terror was about to come to an end.

Chapter Eleven

Next morning Jane hurried to the refectory, eager to see her saviour in the flesh. The early morning hum of conversation was subdued, in deference to the visitor and his entourage. Slipping unobtrusively into her place, she bent her head as Father Peter stood to say grace. A reverential hush fell and his deep voice echoed round the silent room as he intoned the blessing. Once he was seated again Jane lifted her spoon and surreptitiously examined him from the corner of her eye.

He was tall and lean, his plain black robe distinguished only by the richness of the cloth. As he sat at the high table his silver hair caught the sun from the stained glass window, creating a nimbus of light around his head, enhancing the almost saintly impression given by the narrow face and high cheekbones of a confirmed ascetic. Long fingers toyed with a morsel of white bread as if their owner was above mere mortal appetites. He sipped sparingly from a goblet of heavily watered wine.

She breathed a sigh of relief. He was everything she had imagined him to be. This was no complacent priest to tolerate sin in return for a rich table and comfortable life. This was a soldier of the Church Militant who would take up arms on her behalf, against Mother Ursula's hidden wickedness.

Her gaze drifted to his companions and a pang of uneasiness ran through her. The contrast between them was unsettling. The monk on his left was shovelling food into his mouth as if his very life depended on it, washing each greedy mouthful down with copious amounts of unwatered wine. His ruddy complexion, bulging belly and the stains on the front of his habit suggested that this self-indulgence was nothing new. As she watched a belch escaped his greasy lips and he grinned and wiped his soiled fingers down his robe before reaching again for his goblet. Jane's mouth twisted in a moue of distaste.

The one on his right was even worse. A parody of his master, he was scrawny where his superior was lean, and whereas Father Peter's thin face suggested aristocratic good breeding, his companion had the narrow skull and darting eyes of a rodent. His thin lips parted to reveal pointed teeth and Jane was unpleasantly reminded of a weasel or a ferret. She shivered. He was like some cheapjack imitation of his master – but she reminded herself that Father Peter was a priest, subject to the rules of the church, and as such, had no say in the choice of his companions. It was hardly his fault they were so repulsive.

She suppressed a smile. Despite Father Peter's unprepossessing companions, Mother Ursula fluttered round all three, dancing attendance on them as if they were the Holy Trinity itself. A wave of triumph lifted her spirits further. The Reverend Mother could dimple and defer as much as she liked, but once Father Peter knew the magnitude of her sins, no amount of cozening smiles would save her from retribution.

Jane's duties took her to the still room that morning, for which she was grateful. The air was heavily perfumed by the bunches of herbs hanging to dry, and there was something intensely satisfying about pulverising them to dust beneath her pestle – as if she was grinding Mother Ursula's smirking face. It was a chance to escape into a more ordered world, away from the hidden depravity lurking at the centre of the convent. Woundwort for cuts. Marigold for bruises. Poppies for sleep and to soothe pain. Each with its place and function.

She looked at the serried ranks of flasks and jars filled with unguents and tinctures, and sighed. Even here there was a dark side. Too generous a dose of poppy syrup could ease, not to sleep, but to death. Instead of aiding a failing heart, foxglove could force it to bursting point and still it forever. Pennyroyal could cleanse a womb of an unwilling burden. For a moment a vision of Mother Ursula raising a goblet, freighted with death, to her lips flashed through Jane's mind and she was horrified by her own wickedness. She sighed again. Yet another sin to confess.

A timid tap at the door interrupted her gloomy thoughts. She opened it to find an anxious woman, clutching a grey-faced child in her thin arms. A yawning cut gaped from the boy's knee to his ankle and the stench of decay hit Jane like a blow. Her own troubles were forgotten as she cleansed and stitched the wound, the child too listless even to protest.

By the time the woman had departed, thanking her profusely, there were others demanding her attention. As she busied herself about their ailments she blessed her mother and old Alice for schooling her so well. She smiled wryly. Not only could she prepare lavender water and pot pourri like a lady, she could cut and bind as well as any hard-swearing field surgeon. And a good job, too. What would these people do if there were no convent here to minister to their ills?

She was late for the midday meal, earning herself a glare from Mother Ursula. Hurriedly she bowed her head for Father Peter's blessing, then reached hungrily for the food. Her hard work in the still room had given her a fierce appetite. But her hand was stayed by Mother Ursula's next words.

'Father Peter will hear confession this afternoon,' she announced, 'so that we may celebrate High Mass this evening.'

Jane's heart began to pound as she stood after the meal to help clear the refectory table. Her chance had come at last. Lost in her thoughts, she barely noticed the sting of the lye soap on her split and coarsened hands as she scrubbed and cleaned the greasy pile of pots and pans – another unpleasant duty forced on her by Mother Ursula. When at last they were finished and the cook grudgingly gave her permission to leave, she hurried to the pump in the yard, sluiced the smell of the kitchens from her skin and tried to tidy herself the best she could. But disappointment washed over her when she reached the chapel. It seemed as if every nun in the convent was there before her. Chattering like magpies, they sat waiting for their turn to confess. With a sigh she crept into the back of the chapel and knelt out of sight behind a pillar, to wait until they had gone.

She must have fallen asleep, because when she came to the chapel was empty and the shadows were creeping across the grey stone floor. She groaned. Had exhaustion and stupidity cheated her of her one opportunity? But then she saw the red curtains of the confessional part and the tall figure of Father Peter emerge. She wasn't too late after all! Leaping to her feet, she hurried up the aisle towards him.

'I'm sorry, Father,' she panted. 'Have I missed confession?' Her eyes mutely implored him to say no.

He smiled, and again she was reminded of a saint from her mother's Book of Hours. 'Of course not,' he said kindly. 'God always has time for His children. Come.' He replaced the stole around his neck and parted the curtains for her to enter, then took his place again.

'Bless me, Father, for I have sinned,' she whispered. 'It is three months since my last confession.' She crossed herself and bowed her head, as she began the litany of her petty failings. Pride. Vanity. Unkindness. When she paused for breath, his voice interrupted.

'*Ego te absolvo*,' he said. 'Three Hail Marys. Now, go your way and sin no more, my child.'

'No! No, Father!' she gasped, panic-stricken that he would leave her with her soul only half unburdened. 'Those are only venial sins. There's more.' A sob caught in her throat. 'Much, much more.'

She bit her lip and a tear trickled down her cheek as it all spilt out. Ralph's death and his father's outrageous proposal that she wed him instead. Her dalliance with sweet Robin and the bitter aftermath of her stepfather's abuse. The scene in the stable on her journey to the convent. Mother Ursula's beatings and the perverted attentions of Sister Michael. Like poison from an infection it all poured out in a stream of vileness – even her passing thought about Mother Ursula's murder.

She could hear Father Peter's sharp intake of breath and his breathing becoming heavier with shock and disbelief. At last she fell silent and the question she had been dreading finally came.

'And did you enjoy any of this wickedness, my child?' he asked softly. 'Did their male members pleasure you? And when Sister Michael thrust the candle into your privy place, did it engender the sin of lustfulness in your loins?'

Her cheeks flushed scarlet and she hung her head in shame as she remembered the evil feelings that had flooded her body. Even the thought of it sent an unwelcome heat stirring between her thighs and she shifted uncomfortably on the hard seat of the confessional. 'Yes, Father,' she whispered.

'Have you entertained lewd thoughts since, my daughter?' he asked, his breath coming faster with outrage. 'Has the devil tempted you into the sin of Onan? Touching yourself intimately while you imagine some mighty organ thrusting into you?'

'Yes, Father,' she muttered, her voice barely audible.

She heard him groan in dismay and, even with the wall of the confessional between them, felt him shudder with revulsion. There was a pause as his breath slowed and he composed himself again.

'The matter of Mother Ursula is a grave one, my child,' he said. 'You must leave it with me to deal with.' His voice became serious. 'As for your own sins, they too must be expiated. You will fast for the rest of the day and spend the night on your knees in the chapel, praying for forgiveness. *Ego te absolvo*,' he repeated and, at his words, she felt the burden of sin falling from her shoulders.

At mealtime she drank only water and, when mass began, she watched Father Peter adoringly. When he placed the host to her lips her heart soared with relief and thankfulness. As the last pure note of the choir sank away and the nuns began to file out, she conccaled herself in the shadows, to begin her night of prayer.

As she knelt, head bowed, the light gradually died from the windows, leaving only the flickering altar candles and the vigil light burning redly. Darkness crept slowly from the corners and, despite herself, she remembered the last time she had been here, stretched naked on the altar like some pagan sacrifice. She shivered and shook her head to dislodge the unsettling memory. The silence suddenly became oppressive and she became uncomfortably aware that she was totally alone.

The sound of quiet footsteps made her leap to her feet and whirl round in fear, then she sagged with relief. 'Father Peter!' she gasped. 'You frightened me.' She smiled at him. How kind he was to give up his own sleep to accompany her in her vigil.

There was no answering smile. His eyes glittered in the candlelight as his eyes wandered over her body in the thin shift. His lips twisted in a strange expression of lust and contempt and horror ran through her. It was as if he had removed the mask of saintliness to reveal a hungry beast beneath. Unconsciously, she began to back away.

A high-pitched giggle stopped her in her tracks and her eyes darted frantically round the dark chapel to find its source. The weaselly monk stepped from the shadows, sharp teeth gleaming in a predatory grin. Behind him stood his fat companion. His tongue flicked out to lick his thick greasy lips, and Jane shuddered.

For a moment she stood as frozen as a startled doe, then fear lent wings to her feet. Ducking the restraining arm Father Peter held out to stop her, she fled down the aisle towards the open door. If only she could reach it in time she would be safe!

Freedom was almost within her grasp when Mother Ursula stepped out and pushed the heavy door shut, turning the iron key in the lock. She leaned against it, smiling in triumph at the terrified girl. Jane halted, her eyes searching frantically for another escape.

There was none. As she stared into Mother Ursula's cold eyes hands gripped her and she was hauled backwards towards the altar rails, her heels trailing helplessly. Once there she was jolted upright in front of Father Peter. Smiling, her reached out and ripped her shift from neck to hem, revealing the quivering body beneath. He took in the pert breasts, the soft curve of belly and hip and the smooth white thighs, then his expression became almost vicious as his elegant fingers explored her body, twisting her nipples until she gasped, then thrusting their way between her tightly clenched thighs.

'Strip her and bind her,' he ordered, indicating the altar rail. The last pitiful remnants of her shift were torn away and she was bent over the hard wood, her wrists lashed to the balustrade. Pinioned in place, she knelt in a parody of devotion, her breasts thrust upward by the pressure of the rail, the soft globes of her buttocks jutting invitingly behind. Giggling lasciviously, the ferret-faced monk used this opportunity to fondle her breasts, gripping and squeezing them in his bony hands. Her skin crawled and, to her horror, she realised that his fat companion had reached beneath the bulge of his belly and was fumbling at himself through the heavy folds of his habit as he stood and watched.

Terrified, she craned over her shoulder to see Mother Ursula, standing with a quirt in her hand, while Father Peter smiled on approvingly.

'So,' she purred, tapping the short length of plaited leather in her hand, 'you sought to oust me, did you?' Her arm rose and the quirt descended on Jane's naked bottom, leaving a white weal across the creamy skin. 'You told Father Peter of my wickedness?' Jane's buttocks jerked as another blow reddened the shrinking flesh. 'You even wished to murder me?'

This time Jane screamed as the third blow landed. 'Forgive me, Reverend Mother, forgive me!' she wailed. She struggled against her bonds, but the cords merely bit the tighter into her aching wrists and her writhings served only to inflame Mother Ursula further. Her arm rose and fell in a paroxysm of rage, until Jane's bottom was scarlet and incandescent with pain.

Exhausted at last, Mother Ursula's arm fell to her side and the beating stopped. The only sounds were those of Jane's frantic sobbing, Mother Ursula's pants of exertion and the heavy breathing of the watchers.

And it was the latter that frightened Jane the most.

Closing her eyes, she offered up a prayer that her ordeal was at an end – but with little hope that it would be answered.

An icy hand touched her aching bottom and she flinched, waiting for the pain to begin again. It wasn't long in coming as long fingers trailed down the cleft of her buttocks to the vulnerable opening of her vulva, parted the soft lips and thrust themselves rudely inside. She groaned and writhed, but this only served to plunge the invading fingers deeper into her private place.

She groaned again, this time in despair, as the scolding pain from her beaten bottom radiated through her lower body, wakening a different kind of heat. As the fingers continued their invidious invasion she felt herself moisten in response, and there was a grunt of satisfaction from behind her. The hand withdrew and she was unsure whether she felt relief or disappointment.

In two quick strides Father Peter was standing in front of her. She looked up at him, her eyes begging for mercy, but he was relentless. With a cruel smile he traced the sign of the cross on her forehead with a finger coated in her own juices, and she shuddered at the blasphemy.

He clapped his hands and the two monks hurried forward with a heavy chair, placing it at the foot of the chancel steps. Unhurriedly, he took a seat and Mother Ursula joined him, sinking to her knees beside his chair in abject obedience. Flanked by his minions, he sat for several moments, staring at his helpless victim over steepled fingers as he decided what to do next. Jane waited in horrified expectation.

Finally he turned to the two animals beside him. 'Well done, thou good and faithful servants,' he said, in a twisted parody of the parables. He waved an elegant hand towards her. 'Now you may take your reward.'

Jane gasped as the implications of his words hit her. Her struggles redoubled as they eagerly divested themselves of their robes and advanced upon her. Her eyes flickered from one to the other, hardly believing what was about to happen. Their nakedness was obscene. The weaselly monk's skinny body seemed hardly strong enough to support the massive organ that sprouted from between his thighs, its swollen length bobbing as he walked towards her, while his companion's gross wobbling belly practically concealed his member. It peeked out from beneath the folds of flesh like a small pink mouse.

'No...' she pleaded desperately. 'Please, leave me alone!'

With a grunt the fat one sank to his knees in front of her, engulfing her in a wave of sweat and stale wine. One hand reached greedily for her pert young breasts, his fat fingers kneading and twisting the soft pink crests of her nipples until, despite herself, they rose, hot and hard in response. The other slid lower, between the rods of the altar rail, to tease the rising bud of her clitoris.

Behind her the scrawny one was kneeling too, as he fondled her nether regions. She whimpered and squirmed as one bony finger pushed its way into the tight pucker of her anus, but a sharp slap on her already tender bottom made her freeze obediently in place, fearful that resistance would bring more pain. He withdrew and bent his head and she could feel a wet tongue probing its way between her labia. She shivered in unwilling reaction, the tendrils of wicked lust spiralling out as she was lapped and fingered to meet the maddening sensations coming from her swollen nipples. The groan that broke from her lips was a mixture of pleasure and dismay.

His eyes hooded, Father Peter watched as the two monks fondled Jane's body. He had pulled his cassock up above his waist and his own member rose, thick and stiff, its head red and swollen, engorged with blood. His long fingers toyed with his shaft as Mother Ursula looked on in anticipation. He nodded at her and she knelt and reached for him, her mouth opening as she sucked him in. Her coif was dislodged by the movement and Jane watched in horrified fascination as her shaven, skull-like head bobbed up and down, one hand thrust frantically between her own thighs as she serviced her master.

A movement behind her brought her back to awareness of her own predicament. The skinny monk had finished his lapping and, taking his hard prick in one hand, he pushed it against the soft opening of Jane's body. She whimpered as her body tried to resist the invasion. There was a brief flash of pain, then his mighty member slid smoothly inside her and she groaned as he began to move, his skinny buttocks tensing as he thrust into her tight wetness.

The fat monk redoubled his efforts, bending to suck first one swollen nipple then the other into his greedy mouth as he continued to finger her. A scream began to build in her throat as she gave herself up to the lust that washed through her. She was no longer Lady Jane. She was no longer the unwilling novice. She was merely a bitch in heat being serviced by whichever hot cock presented itself to satisfy her needs.

Panting and gasping, the skinny monk heaved himself against her and she met every thrust with one of her own, taking every inch of him eagerly. A whine of disappointment escaped her as he groaned and fell away, his viscous come spurting before she could reach her own release.

Leaping to his feet with a lightness that defied his bulk, the fat monk hurried round to take his place and Jane grunted with satisfaction as another urgent prick slid inside her. Her breasts quivered and bounced as he jerked and pounded, his heavy body almost crushing her beneath its weight.

It was too much for Father Peter. He grasped Mother Ursula's neck and pulled her away, his cock leaving her mouth with an almost audible pop. She sprawled on the floor, bewildered, her habit round her waist, exposing her gaping cleft. She stared at him in dismay as he strode towards Jane.

He thrust his cock towards Jane's mouth, its swollen head still glistening with Mother Ursula's saliva, but she was beyond caring. Her lips peeled open and she sucked it in, secretly relishing the feel of the throbbing flesh stretching her mouth. He moaned as her tongue ran teasingly round the rim. One hand placed on the back of her head in a grotesque imitation of the blessing, he forced himself deeper into the velvet softness as she whimpered in a paroxysm of tormented lust.

The fat monk gave one final desperate thrust and pumped his seed inside her. Father Peter's prick swelled and jerked too, the salt taste of his juices filling her mouth, and Jane screamed in mindless pleasure as her own climax exploded forth.

She sagged back, only the bonds holding her in place. It was the sound of her own voice echoing from the roof of the chapel that brought her back to her senses. Sick comprehension swamped her. What was she becoming when her own body could betray her into wickedness and corruption? And how could there be any escape when even those who swore to uphold goodness were tainted with evil? Tears of despair trickled down cheeks still flushed from unholy lust, and darkness swept her soul.

There was no hope.

No hope at all.

Chapter Twelve

The next few weeks passed in a mist of misery. When Mother Ursula bid Father Peter and his minions farewell, the nuns fluttering and giggling round them like a flock of giddy geese, Jane hid herself away, too shamed to show her face. Tormented by memories of that hideous evening she trudged about her menial duties without a word, head bowed lest any should see the guilt in her eyes. Even the arrival of the pedlar failed to shake her from the darkness that enveloped her.

Swaggering like a bantam cockerel, his face as brown and weather-beaten as the leather pack on his back, he strode into the courtyard as if he owned it. 'What d'ye lack, ladies?' he asked, grinning, as he shrugged his pack from his shoulders and spread it out on the ground. 'Pins? Needles?' He held up a few skeins of coarsely dyed thread. 'Fine silks to embroider a new altar cloth?'

His wares were as shabby as himself, but the others gathered round as if he carried all the treasures of the Orient, glad of anything that broke the monotony of the convent routine. Even Mother Ursula hurried down, eager not for his cheap gewgaws but for the most precious commodity any pedlar carried – news of the outside world. The snippets of gossip he brought would provide fuel for the long winter months ahead, as it was hashed and rehashed, gaining savour with every telling.

And what news, too!

The money for the pins and needles safely tucked away in his greasy purse, and fortified by bread, cheese and ale, he settled down to tell his tale. Eyes widened and mouths fell open as it unfolded, as compelling as a fairytale. Lust and deception; the true queen locked away while a usurper took her place; betrayal and death – and all laced with tantalising whispers of witchcraft. It was better than any mummers' play.

Despite herself, Jane listened. She could not prevent a bitter smile. What difference did it make to her if Good King Henry put away his lawful wife and married the Great Whore? He was a man, wasn't he? And no different from the village bully who beat his wife if she burned the porridge, or used her till she was a raddled husk worn out by work and childbearing, then turned his attentions to someone younger and prettier. Her smile became cynical. This Anne Boleyn might be riding high just now, but what a man could do once he could do again – and if she lost his favour, what would happen to her then? For a moment a dark shadow seemed to block out the sun and she shivered as if a goose had walked over her grave. There would be no happiness for Mistress Boleyn. She shook off the unwanted premonition, smiled ruefully and went back to scraping plates into the slop bucket for the pigs that had replaced their unfortunate predecessors. What did the fate of this unknown woman matter to her? She had troubles enough of her own to contend with. She snorted. As for King Henry's making himself head of the church in order to wed her – it was ridiculous! The Pope was the head of the church and always would be. She looked round at the grey stones of the convent, timeless and immovable as the landscape it sat on, and heaved a miserable sigh. Nothing had changed in over a hundred years – and nothing ever would.

A few weeks later she was proved wrong. She was on her hands and knees, scrubbing the worn slate floor of the chapel when she heard the sound of hoof beats on the cobbled yard. Her first thought was that Father Peter and his cohorts had returned and she shrank inwardly, crouching down over her scrubbing brush as if to make herself invisible.

However, instead of a murmur of welcome, there came the sounds of argument. The dull rumble of a male voice was interrupted by Mother Ursula's lighter one, which rapidly rose in tones of dismayed dissent. Jane sat back on her heels in surprise. Who would dare argue with Mother Ursula? The woman's word was law. Throwing her brush into the bucket of dirty water she pushed herself to her feet and tiptoed to the door to listen.

The scene before her was totally unexpected. Mother Ursula, her face as scarlet as the crest of a cockerel, was standing, arms akimbo, in front of a group of half-a-dozen horsemen. Their leader, an expression of amused contempt on his lips, stared down at her.

'How dare you force your way in here?' snarled Ursula. 'This is a house of religion.' She drew herself up to full height and pointed towards the gate with a shaking arm. 'Take yourselves off, bag and baggage, or it will be the worse for you.'

'A fine Christian welcome, madam,' drawled the leader of the horsemen. 'But I think not. I have business here – and here I shall remain until it is finished to my satisfaction.'

'What business?' Mother Ursula demanded. 'This land belongs to the church. You have no right here.'

The man's face darkened. 'His Majesty is head of the church now,' he snarled. 'And as his representative I have every right.' He fumbled in his pouch and produced a scroll, which he flung at her feet, forcing her to bend to pick it up. Even from her vantage point in the dimness of the church porch, Jane could see the heavy seal at the bottom – and the expression of dismay on Mother Ursula's face as she read it.

Still, all credit to her, she recovered swiftly, thought Jane with grudging admiration. Pasting a smile on her face, Mother Ursula dropped a low curtsey. 'Welcome, Master Horner,' she said, though the words must have been sour on her tongue. 'Our humble guest quarters are yours until your inventory is complete. Please make yourselves at home.'

Master Horner smiled. 'Oh, we shall, madam, have no fear of that. And here we shall remain until we have reckoned up every last item, to the last grain of corn in your granary.' Turning, he began to bark orders at his men. They dismounted, and three of them produced quills, ink and parchment from the dusty bags that hung from the pommels.

Mother Ursula gasped. 'Surely you do not mean to begin at once?' She remembered herself, and forced another smile. 'You must be weary from your journey. Come. A glass of wine and some refreshment before you start your task?'

Master Horner's expression became icy. 'I think not, mistress,' he said curtly. He raised a cynical eyebrow. 'I have found that less – honest – houses have used the time to try and hide their treasures. I would not wish to put temptation in your path.'

Jane never knew what prompted her next action – the foresight that had warned her of the fate of Mistress Boleyn, or sheer madness. Scurrying back to her work she seized the filthy wash cloth and wrung it out. Glancing over her shoulder to check she was still alone, she hurried towards the altar. What should she take? It must be small enough to hide, but valuable enough to be worth risking her neck for.

Heart beating, she crossed herself and offered a quick prayer for forgiveness, before grabbing the tiny jewel-studded reliquary, that was said to contain the finger bone of their patroness, Saint Ursula – from whom Ursula had taken her name. A gold filigree cross with a huge ruby at its centre was next, followed by a magnificent gold-chased chalice. Wrapping them in the slimy cloth, she bundled them under her shift and fled through the side door.

Thankfully the gardens were deserted. Head down she scuttled towards the pigsty, heart pounding. Climbing over the low wall she nudged aside the grunting animals that rushed to her, demanding food, and made her way to the darkest corner at the back of the sty. Ignoring the stench, she dug a hole in the soft muck, threw in her bundle, covered it up and stamped down the surface.

She nodded in satisfaction. There! In the sea of trampled earth no one would ever know the ground had been disturbed. Just pray to God the pigs didn't root her treasure out again!

By the time the first clerk entered the chapel, quill and paper in hand, she was back on her knees, scrubbing industriously. Apart from a fastidious wrinkling of his nostrils as he passed, he ignored her. He was still writing as she gathered up her brush and bucket and tiptoed away.

The next few days were uncomfortable, to say the least. Meals were eaten in resentful silence. Master Horner's men were everywhere with their poking and prying, turning out even the most remote, spider-infested corners of the convent, noting down every detail.

Wouldn't surprise me if they *was* counting every grain of corn,' grumbled the cook, irritated beyond belief by an unwelcome scrivener under her feet while she was trying to prepare the meals. 'Here you, wash them plates again,' she ordered Jane. 'That nosy parker's stirred up the dust something dreadful. Wass the point of it all, thass what I want to know. My great-grammer told me about some old king – wossisname?' She wrinkled her brow in thought, then brightened again. 'William, thass it! Him that came over from Normandy. He did the very same thing with the land. Put it down in some old book or other.' She shook her head over the stupidity of kings. 'Now what difference did that make to the price of corn? None!' She glared at the unfortunate clerk, thumped her dough vigorously and dismissed the whole subject with a snort of derision.

Eventually it was over. Bearing their parchments, now covered with lists of everything from the bed linen down to the very last horn spoon, they clattered out of the courtyard again, leaving peace and quiet in their wake.

Until Mother Ursula discovered the missing treasures.

'Scurvy rogues,' she raved, clenching her fists in furious impotence. 'Using His Majesty's orders to line their own greasy pockets.' Her eyes narrowed and she lost her veneer of gentility, spitting on the ground like a cheated peasant. 'Well, God's curse upon the thief. May a thousand devils plague him as he rots in hell.'

Jane's lip curled in a cynical smile as she remembered Father Peter's sweating face, twisted with lust as he thrust his rampant member between her reluctant lips. Mother Ursula's curse held no fears for her. Trapped in this godforsaken place, she was in hell already.

Chapter Thirteen

The brief flurry of excitement was soon over and forgotten and Jane's life sank back into its usual dreary routine. Day followed miserable day and she felt as if her youth was slipping away. She would be nineteen soon, almost an old maid.

Head bent over the greasy plates, she thought wistfully of Ralph. If he had lived she would be married now, mistress of her own household, and probably a mother by this time. Instead she was incarcerated in this glorified gaol, treated worse than any kitchen slut.

Light footsteps made her start, the plate she was holding slipping from her fingers with a clatter. 'Wh-what do you want?' she stuttered, regarding Mother Ursula with frightened eyes. She bit her lip and cringed inwardly, terrified that her question would be regarded as insolence and bring another punishment down on her head.

'Why, only your spiritual welfare, my daughter,' gushed Mother Ursula, seeming to delight in Jane's obvious fear. 'How long have you been here now?'

Jane remained silent. It seemed an eternity. Shut away from the world, she had lost all track of time.

It didn't matter. Mother Ursula had the answer at her fingertips. 'Six months,' she smiled. 'And still a novice. I have been remiss in my duties. It is time you made your final vows and joined our little community properly.'

Jane swayed, her eyes closing in horror at the thought. Once she had taken those vows she would be shut away in this place, subject to Mother Ursula's perverted whims, forever. She envisioned her future and a sob caught in her throat. No hope. No love. Nothing but an endless stretch of empty days, broken only by moments of pain and terror. It was unbearable. She'd rather be dead!

Her lips tightened. She refused to give the bitch the satisfaction of seeing her beg. Pulling herself together she forced a smile back into Mother Ursula's taunting eyes. 'But Reverend Mother,' she said smoothly, 'I am unworthy of the honour you do me.' She lowered her head humbly. 'You must give me more time. You have said yourself that I am proud and wilful. How can I become a holy sister when I am stained with sin? It would rest heavy on my conscience if I came to God when I am still so full of wickedness.'

Mother Ursula's voice was gentle, belying the wickedness beneath. 'Fear not, my child,' she replied softly, her narrow tongue flicking lasciviously over her lips, as she eyed Jane the way a snake eyes a plump rabbit. 'Your sins may be many, but I warrant they will be well purged before you take your vows.' She chuckled softly and the blood froze in Jane's veins. 'Sister Michael and I will see to that.'

'Wh-what do you mean?' stammered Jane.

'Why, if the devil is in you, then he must be beaten out, must he not?' said Mother Ursula 'You will hold your vigil in the chapel the night after next,' she ordered. Her tongue flickered over her lips again. 'Sister Michael and I will accompany you, and by the time it is over your sins will be washed away – in blood. Don't think I didn't see the way Father Peter rejected me in favour of you, pushing me aside so he could pleasure himself in your pretty mouth. Well, when I have finished with you no man will look at you twice. When you limp down the aisle to make your final vows, you'll be glad of that nun's habit to hide your scars.'

Jane stared after her in horror, her knees threatening to give way. There had been murder in those pale grey eyes. Murder – and a cold, gloating enjoyment at the prospect. She swallowed, and her mind flew unbidden to the day she had walked in the graveyard beside the church, idly noting the inscriptions on the gravestones and wondering why so many nuns died young, when they were well-housed and fed compared to many another.

At the time she had shrugged it off and thought no more about it. Life was precarious at the best of times, when the plague or sweating sickness could carry off whole families in a matter of days – but now she shivered as a darker thought struck her. How many other young girls, like herself, had entered this evil building and disappeared forever? The grave was a dark forbidding place capable of concealing many a sin. She swallowed again, her mouth dry with nameless fear.

The night that followed was not a pleasant one. Lying wakeful on her narrow cot, she stared into the darkness as the minutes ticked away, carrying her closer to her unknown fate. Even when she finally fell into a leaden sleep, it was only to be tormented by dreams filled with blood and pain.

Next day she woke dull and heavy-headed. She dragged herself through the day with a feeling of sick apprehension lodged in the pit of her stomach, and at meals in the refectory she pushed away her plate untouched, sickened at the thought of food. If Mother Ursula had intended her to suffer with her threat of terrible punishment, she could not have done a better job.

Another sleepless night followed the first. Time was running out and her feverish brain could come up with no escape from what was to come, no matter how often she went over her predicament. One last day and then she must face her vigil – and Mother Ursula. Bitterly, she remembered thinking that she'd rather be dead than spend her life here. It seemed as though that wish might yet be granted.

She shuddered beneath the threadbare sheet, her skin dimpling into gooseflesh despite the heavy closeness of the cell. There was a storm coming; she could feel the thunder gathering in the air. As if her thought had called it up, the first dull rumble split the skies. She could feel the vibration even through the thick walls.

She sat up, sudden excitement coursing through her. That wasn't thunder, it was the sound of hooves!

Scarcely daring to believe it in case she had been mistaken, she held her breath and listened. She had been right. It *was* hoof beats – and they were getting closer! Flinging a swift grateful prayer towards heaven she leaped from her cot, dragged on her shift and, still binding her hair, ran barefoot along the passage.

As she reached the outside door the first peal of thunder broke. A flash of lightning split the dawn sky and heavy raindrops spattered down. Within seconds Jane's shift was soaking wet, clinging to her body in transparent folds. Lost in relief and exultation, she didn't even notice.

The other nuns were gathering too, muttering amongst themselves as they peered through the downpour at the approaching horsemen. Jane stared in amazement. No wonder she had mistaken the sound of their hooves for thunder. There were at least twenty of them and they must have ridden all night to get here. What on earth had brought such a company to this remote and unimportant convent?

That question was obviously uppermost in Mother Ursula's mind, too. Still in her night rail, she pushed her way through the chattering sisters and stood in the centre of the courtyard, arms folded as the leading horseman drew to a halt scant inches in front of her, spattering her with mud. His followers gathered behind him, silent except for the jingle of reins and the panting of their sweating horses.

Jane stared at him. He was without doubt the ugliest man she had ever seen. One eye had been lost in some battle, the empty socket covered by a black velvet patch that could not conceal the puckered flesh around it. The other eye glinted a wicked blue. Heavy lines bracketed a mouth slack with dissolution, and although his doublet was made of rich velvet and his cloak lined with silk, both were stained with travel. There was a brooding threat about him that made her shiver just to look at him.

Ursula was unimpressed. 'Who are you?' she demanded, her voice shrill with anger. 'To come breaking the peace of this holy place at such an ungodly hour?'

'Sir Edmund Spence at your service, my lady,' he replied, sweeping off his hat in a mocking bow. He looked round greedily. 'But this is no longer a holy place. This belongs to me now.' He stared coldly down at Mother Ursula. 'So you may pack your possessions and go. You are trespassing.'

The colour drained from Mother Ursula's face. 'That is impossible,' she hissed. 'This land belongs to God. No man can own it.'

He shook his head. 'This man can, courtesy of His Sovereign Majesty, King Henry VIII, Head of the Church – and I have the deeds to prove it!' His lips tightened. 'Now take your gaggle of prattling geese and shift yourselves, before I am tempted to do it for you.'

'We will not go,' said Mother Ursula coldly. 'Here we are and here we shall remain – under the Lord's protection.'

'The Lord's protection is a pretty chancy thing to rely on,' he said. 'And you cannot say you were not warned.' He turned in the saddle and grinned at his followers. 'Right, boys. Here's a fine covey of partridges to be flushed out. Let's show them what happens to trespassers on Sir Edmund Spence's lands.'

In an instant they were down from their horses and descending on the huddle of nuns like wolves on a flock of sheep. The sisters scattered, shrieking, but were captured one by one by the laughing, hullooing mob. Jane stared at the nightmare scene in horror.

As she watched two jeering men brought down Sister Michael. As one held her the other fell on his knees between her straddled legs, fumbled with his breeches, produced his swollen cock and rammed himself into her. Her screams echoed off the high stone walls as he ravaged her unmercifully.

Sister Ursula had been grabbed by a grizzled giant of a man who tore her night rail from her with one huge hand, bent her over like a rag doll and plunged himself savagely between her buttocks. Her mouth gaped in a silent howl as he pleasured himself in her helpless body.

Jane had only time to feel a flicker of satisfaction at her tormentors' fate before she was seized and satisfaction was replaced with terror. One man grabbed her breasts, hands squeezing and kneading the soft flesh, while another slipped his arm round her waist from behind and his rough fingers pushed between her thighs. Foul breath seared her neck and she struggled frantically, the linen binding falling from her head. Her long red hair spilled out and one of them grabbed it, pulling her head back as his companion's wet lips slobbered at her nipples. She closed her eyes and waited for the worst.

'Hold hard!' bellowed Sir Edmund, his voice cutting through the bedlam like a knife. Silence descended on the courtyard – and suddenly she was free, her captors standing sullenly beside her. Breasts heaving, she stared up into Edmund's amused face.

'Why, if it isn't the busy-fingered wood nymph,' he drawled. 'A juicy bird to find amongst these dried-up old hens.'

She gaped at him in total incomprehension. What was he talking about? Then realisation dawned. Her mind raced back to that long-ago spring morning when she'd lain on the cool grass, her skirts about her waist as she explored her budding body. The laugh she'd thought she'd heard, and put down to some bird calling in the woods, had been no figment of her imagination. He had been there – watching her! Her face flamed as brightly as her hair.

'This one's mine,' he announced, slipping from the saddle and reaching for her. She took a step back and spat at him like an angry kitten.

'Touch me at your peril,' she warned. 'I am no leman to be taken with impunity.' She glared at him haughtily. 'I am Lady Jane Montague. Lay one finger on me and my stepfather, Sir Thomas, will make you pay for it.' This was no lie – but not because her stepfather held her in any affection. She was his chattel as much as any of his other possessions and his pride would brook no interference with those. He might kick his dog, but heaven help any other man who did the same.

An uneasy expression crossed Sir Edmund's face. It was clear he wanted her – but not at the price of a feud with her stepfather. Temptation warred with prudence.

Watching him struggle with his indecision, Jane held her breath. A sudden movement distracted her. At the gates some of the villagers, alerted by the arrival of strangers, had gathered, staring aghast at the scene of devastation before them. At the front was the child whose leg she had stitched, clutching his mother's skirts. He was still thin and pale, but he was healthy – and standing unaided.

Her heart smote her. What would happen to these people if the convent was no longer there? Who would feed them? Who would tend to their ills? She made up her mind.

'I will be your whore,' she said boldly. 'On one condition.'

Sir Edmund stared at her in amusement. 'Oh, yes? And what might that condition be?'

'A whore receives payment in return for her services,' she said. 'And for my payment, I want this convent.'

His eyebrows rose and he whistled through his teeth. 'You put a high price on your favours, my lady,' he exclaimed. He ran his good eye over her shapely body and made up his mind. With all his acres of land, what were a pile of old stones and a couple of fields to him? 'Done,' he agreed. 'If you please me, you may have it, but not all at once. You may earn it piece by piece – and you may find the price is high.'

She ignored his warning. He was ugly, but not misshapen. He looked clean and not too old – and after all, she could always close her eyes. With all those innocent lives at stake she could force herself to bed with him. She shook her head ruefully. After all she had been through since that morning when he had watched her pleasure herself, what else could he do to her? 'Done,' she echoed, spitting on her hand and holding it out to shake on the bargain. He leaned from the saddle and, as his hand touched hers, she felt a strange pang of excitement run through her.

'Right, back into the saddle, lads,' he ordered. Reluctantly his men left their prey and mounted up. Sir

Edmund looked at the sisters huddled together again, whimpering and holding their ravaged bodies. A fat one caught his eye and he smiled to himself. Armed only with a ladle, she'd fought like a tigress. Two of his lads were nursing a fine set of bruises and regarding her with disgruntled respect.

He looked at Jane. 'Who's that?' he demanded, pointing at the nun.

'The convent cook,' she replied.

'We'll have her, too,' he said flatly. 'I'll need a decent cook for the castle kitchens – and she looks like a good recommendation for her talents.' Without further ado she was hauled on to the back of a packhorse, squawking with indignation.

'We'd better have a lady's maid for you, too,' he said thoughtfully. He looked speculatively over the timorous nuns. 'Pick one for yourself.'

Jane smiled wickedly. Revenge was indeed sweet. 'I'll have her,' she said, pointing at Mother Ursula, who glared back, hatred gleaming from her pale grey eyes.

'A good choice,' replied Sir Edmund approvingly. 'I think Oswald has taken a fancy to her.' He winked at the grizzled giant who grinned back, revealing a mouthful of rotten teeth. 'She can warm his bed as well as serving you.'

Oswald slid from his horse again, lumbered over and scooped up the struggling, shrieking Mother Superior and deposited her in front of him on his saddle. Holding her in place with one hand, he amused himself and his companions by groping between her skinny thighs with the other.

Sir Edmund held out a hand and Jane took it, leaping up lightly behind him. As the cavalcade trooped from the courtyard she waved gaily at the others she was leaving behind. Excitement welled up inside her. She had saved the convent and the villagers. She had escaped a stultifying existence as a nun, and she had seen her tormentor, Mother Ursula, humiliated and humbled.

A slight frown creased her brow. Of course, she still had to keep her bargain. She clicked her fingers and dismissed the thought with a merry laugh. Giving her body to Sir Edmund? In comparison to what she had undergone, it would be easy!

At long last she believed that nothing could go wrong...

Chapter Fourteen

As the small cavalcade trotted along euphoria cheered Jane. In her new-found freedom from the claustrophobic walls of the cloister the world seemed to be freshly minted. Even the crisp autumn air seemed fresher. It had been May when the heavy gates of the convent closed behind her, the fields just turning green with new growth. Now the harvest was over and they lay golden with stubble in the mellow October sunshine. Peasants, gathering the last gleanings, turned to watch as Sir Edmund's party passed and, in a fit of exuberance, she smiled and waved.

The journey was remarkably short. It seemed strange to think the castle lay only two miles away. She could have walked there in a morning. Yet, trapped within the convent, it might as well have been in a different country, a thousand miles away.

They passed through a small wood, the trees scarlet and russet in the sun, and the road began to grow steeper. As they trotted out from beneath the canopy of autumn leaves Jane got her first glimpse of the castle, and her fragile feeling of well-being dissipated as quickly as morning mist.

It sat on the hilltop like a dark stain on the golden landscape, a brooding nightmare of turrets and towers. The stone teeth of the castellations and battlements seemed to bite at the sky. She shivered. This was no comfortable country mansion. It was something older and more sinister.

'Almost there,' Sir Edmund called, spurring his horse forward. The sudden change of speed jolted Jane forward, and she was forced to grab on to him to prevent herself from falling. She grazed his codpiece, felt something stirring like a snake beneath a rock, and jerked her hand away as if it hand been burned. Through her humiliation she felt the vibration of his laughter.

Her breasts bobbed with the horse's rhythmic jogging, their tender nipples brushing against the rough material of his cloak. She was horrified to find herself becoming aroused, her nipples hardening and her vulva moistening in response to the unexpected stimulation. Heat began to radiate from her groin and her eyes half-closed as she gave herself up to the tantalising sensations.

The sound of their hooves clattering over the drawbridge brought her back to reality and, as they rode beneath the portcullis, her budding desire was quenched as effectively as if a bucket of icy water had been flung over her. The sun was blotted out and she shuddered, gritting her teeth to prevent them from chattering. The dark stones on either side seemed to reek with ancient blood and she had the horrible feeling that if she only concentrated hard enough she would be able to hear distant screams echoing from the past.

The feeling eased slightly as they rode out into the sunshine of the courtyard again. Eased, but did not entirely fade. The courtyard was a small oasis of light in a desert of darkness. Black stone walls rose sheer on all sides, arrow-slits peered down like narrowed eyes, and the doors which led off to different parts of the castle either gaped like half-open mouths or remained tightly shut as if concealing some evil secret. It was like being swallowed by some mythical monster.

Sir Edmund obviously felt nothing of this. Gazing round in satisfaction at his new possession, he gave the order to dismount. Sighing with relief his men did so and the silence of the courtyard was suddenly broken by the hubbub of a dozen different voices.

A shrill shriek of outrage rose above it all and Jane stared at the little drama unfolding before her. Oswald, to ribald cries, was hauling a struggling Mother Ursula from the back of his horse. Handling her like a sack of flour, he dumped her unceremoniously on her feet, so hard that her teeth rattled, then stood back in amusement. It was a mistake. Recovering instantly she flew at him like a fury, her fingers curved into claws, and the grin was wiped from his face as she sank her nails into his face, leaving four bleeding lines scored into his grizzled cheek.

For a moment he was frozen with astonishment, then with a roar of rage he seized her and flung her over his knee, pulling off the cloak she had been wrapped in to reveal the pale globes of her bottom. 'Scratch me, would you, you little wildcat?' he panted. 'Well, I'll draw your claws for you.'

As she wriggled and kicked he raised his hand and brought it down with a thwack on her exposed flesh, leaving a massive handprint on her buttocks – first in white then in red as the blood rushed back. She screamed again, this time in pain. His arm rose and fell again and again, until the cheeks of her backside were as scarlet as those of her face. Her writhings had obviously excited him. Still gripping her with one hand, in case she made a break for freedom, he pushed her from his lap and began to fumble with his codpiece. Jane gasped as he produced his male member; purple, swollen and almost two hands-breadth in length. Mother Ursula recoiled in horror, but he shoved her to her knees, gripped her by the scruff of the neck and pushed her face towards it.

'Here's the answer to your prayers,' he said, chuckling. 'Chew on that, instead of your holy bread.'

Mother Ursula's eyes watered with tears of humiliation and she gagged as he forced himself into her mouth, while his companions roared their encouragement. Jane watched with fascinated dread as the fat length of his cock slid in and out between the woman's reluctant lips. Grunting and pumping his hips he moved faster and faster until, with a groan, he withdrew at the last minute. There was a ragged cheer as his prick jerked and spasmed, splattering Mother Ursula's face with his seed.

Indifferent now, he pushed her aside, adjusted his clothing and strode off, barking orders. Still kneeling in the dust, Mother Ursula wiped the defilement from her mouth and cheeks and glared up at Jane. Only her eyes were alive in her bone-white face, and Jane shuddered inwardly at the expression of hatred in them. She was the one who had brought Mother Ursula to this place and this humiliation – and if the woman had hated her before, it must surely be nothing to what she felt now.

Entertainment over, Sir Edmund clicked his fingers and the audience broke up and set, grumbling, about the task of unsaddling. Beckoning to Jane, he strode through the half-open door of the main hall, only to stop in shock.

'God's teeth!' he exclaimed, wrinkling his nose in disgust. 'The place is foul!'

Jane stared around in dismay. Dust coated every surface and cobwebs hung in festoons from the corners. The rushes stank, and nothing remained of the furniture but a few items too heavy to carry or broken remains deemed too worthless to take. The previous owner might have died a traitor's death, but his family had taken everything they could carry before they fled. What little they'd left had obviously been scavenged or smashed.

'Someone will pay for this,' Sir Edmund snarled. Spinning on his heel he stalked out again. 'Oswald!' he bellowed. 'Oswald! Get your lazy carcass over here. Now!'

When Oswald appeared Sir Edmund began issuing his orders.

'Take five men and scour the village for what's been stolen,' he snapped. 'And round up every able-bodied villager you can find. I want this place scrubbed from top to bottom. They can pay for their thievery with hard labour. You!' he snarled, pointing to another of his men. 'Ride back to the convent and get the nuns.' He glared at Ursula. 'Those idle women of yours can earn their keep as well.'

Sir Edmund strode round, tapping his lips thoughtfully with one finger. 'We're going to need food. Didn't I hear pigs squealing in the convent yard?' Ursula nodded reluctantly. 'Good. That should keep us going until my baggage carts arrive.' He turned back to his man. 'And burn down the sty. A little fire is always a salutary lesson in obedience. Even the most unimaginative peasant can envision his own house being next.'

Jane flushed guiltily as she watched them ride away. What if Sir Edmund's men found the treasures she had buried there? He would punish them all. She closed her eyes and offered up a quick prayer to Saint Jude, the patron of lost causes. Pushing the unpleasant thought away, she rolled up her sleeves, found a broken broom and prepared to join Sir Edmund's remaining men in tackling the accumulated filth.

The hard work did not serve to dismiss Jane's niggling fear and her heart sank when she saw the plume of dark smoke rising on the horizon and smelt the faint tang of burning on the air. Even the arrival of the villagers and the brief flurry of organising them and ordering them about their tasks failed to distract her completely.

When the men returned, herding the reluctant nuns before them like a flock of frightened geese, she scanned their faces carefully, then sighed with relief. There was no sign of the excitement that surely would have followed the discovery of such bounty, and the only thing bundled on their saddles were the gutted carcasses of the pigs and what appeared to be the entire contents of the chicken coop, dangling from the pommel by their twisted necks. Her secret was safe.

Her mind at rest, she set to with a will, dispatching the nuns to aid the villagers. The castle soon seethed with activity as dust billowed from every door and window. Satisfied that her orders were being obeyed, she set out to deal with the more pressing problem of food.

'Thass a fine old mess,' complained Sister Martha, hands on hips as she surveying the kitchens. 'You there,' she ordered, pointing at one of the men who still sported the bruises from her earlier attentions, 'clear that hearth and start a fire if you want to be fed.' With an apprehensive glance over his shoulder he hastened to obey.

'I need water, too,' she snapped, once the fire was safely established. 'And bring me them chickens. There's not a pick of flour or a morsel of cheese. It'll have to be broth.'

The poor man staggered back in again, his neck festooned with dead chickens and carrying two overflowing buckets of water. Dumping them at her feet he attempted to make good his escape, but Sister Martha was clearly not satisfied.

'Thass not enough!' she exclaimed, forsaking Christian charity and giving him a swift box on the ears. 'I can't work miracles! Who do you think I am? Jesus Christ?' She crossed herself piously and followed the first box with another. 'You keeps bringing it till I tells you to stop. And fetch me down that cauldron while you're at it, you great stupid oaf. You can't expect a poor weak woman like me to lift a heavy lump of a thing like that!'

When Jane slipped out of the kitchen, ignoring the pleading looks cast at her by the unfortunate man, the 'poor weak woman' was standing over him, hefting her ladle menacingly while he plucked and gutted the chickens, his ears still scarlet from her tender ministrations. It was clear that Sister Martha was in her element. She had already thrown aside her wimple and, going by the coy smiles Jane had caught her exchanging with one of the archers, her vow of chastity would not be long in following. Having almost been trapped herself, Jane had nothing but sympathy for the woman. In her position she would have done exactly the same.

The week that followed was so busy Jane hardly had time to think of the bargain she had made. For the first two nights the entire company slept round the fire in the great hall, wrapped in whatever they could find. The fresh rushes, hastily brought and laid, barely cushioned the hard floor, but Jane was so exhausted she hardly felt the discomfort. Curled up in a spare cloak, she was asleep within minutes.

After that the baggage carts began to arrive, the horses, sweating from their heavy burdens, plodding wearily up the hill towards the castle. The courtyard was filled with shouting carters as beds and bedding, tables and chairs, wall-hangings, furniture, clothing and provisions were unloaded and carried to their appointed places. Bit by bit the place began to seem less like a bare stone prison and more like a habitation.

Finally the last plate and spoon were laid away, the last candlestick put in place and all was done. Jane stood in the middle of the room she had been allotted – thankfully to herself – and smiled with pleasure. With only a bed, a chest, one rickety chair and a small tapestry that barely covered the stone wall beneath, it might not be as comfortable and well-appointed as her room at home, but a fire flickered in the hearth and, compared to her bleak cell in the convent, it was paradise.

A tap on the door made her start. 'Enter,' she called nervously, then laughed in relief as one of the servants staggered in bearing something long and rectangular, swathed in coarse linen. He propped it against the wall and tugged his forelock.

'Sir Edmund sent you this, my lady,' he muttered. Jane flew across the room and eagerly began to peel off the wrapping.

'A mirror!' she gasped. She stared in pleasure as the ornate frame was revealed. What luxury!

But her pleasure quickly turned to horror at the reflection that stared back. Despite the hasty sluice she'd taken every day beneath the yard pump, she was absolutely filthy. She was still wearing her convent shift and it was torn, stained and smeared with dust. One hand flew to the tangled bird's nest of her hair, trying to tug it into some semblance of neatness. The movement released a wave of stale sweat and she wrinkled her nose in disgust. She looked – and smelt – like some beggar woman from the stews.

A flicker in the depths of the mirror made her whirl round. Mother Ursula was standing at the door, her lips curled in a sneer. Despite all she had undergone, she still managed to look untouched and Jane felt even worse in comparison.

Mother Ursula clicked her fingers and another two servants staggered in under the weight of another enormous chest. 'Put it there,' she ordered, glaring at them. 'Then get out, all of you!' One look at her expression and the hapless servants scurried to obey.

'What do you want?' demanded Jane, striving to conceal the quaver in her voice.

'Why, only to serve you, mistress,' said Mother Ursula, through gritted teeth. The word 'mistress' fell from her lips like a curse. 'Am I not to be your lady's maid?'

Jane straightened her back. Of course. She had the upper hand now. The woman who had so frightened and humiliated her could no longer touch her. She smiled. 'In that case you may begin your duties by opening that chest,' she ordered. 'I would see what Sir Edmund has sent me.'

Taking her own sweet time, Mother Ursula sauntered across the room and threw open the chest. For the second time that morning Jane gasped. Heaps of velvets, satins and lace in jewel colours glowed from within the chest like treasure. Excitedly, she lifted out the dresses and laid them on the bed.

'Where did they come from?' she asked in puzzlement. 'Surely Sir Edmund doesn't carry woman's clothing about with him?'

Mother Ursula shrugged indifferently. 'One of his men found the chest in the garderobe. It must have been left behind when the family fled.'

At the bottom was a dusty black dress. Jane held it up and pulled a face. It was plain and unflattering. A flicker of maliciousness ran through her and she flung it at Ursula. 'You may wear this,' she said.

For the first time Mother Ursula looked disconcerted, but she recovered quickly. 'I am perfectly happy as I am,' she demurred.

'You will do as you are told,' snapped Jane. 'As you pointed out, you are my maid now – and this is perfectly suitable for a maidservant.' Mother Ursula picked it up with her fingertips, as though afraid it was flea-ridden.

'You may change elsewhere,' Jane went on. 'And when you are suitably attired, you may attend upon me. I wish to take a bath. See to it. At once.'

Fuming, Mother Ursula left, the despised dress over her arm, and Jane smiled with satisfaction. After what the woman had put her through, it was a pleasure to see her brought low.

When Mother Ursula returned she was wearing the dress and Jane was delighted to see how badly it suited her. It hung loosely from her thin frame, and the colour drained her skin, making her look sallow. The proud Mother Superior had been transformed into a dowdy serving maid.

'Your bath, madam,' she hissed, as two sturdy men carried in a heavy wooden tub and placed it in the centre of the floor. A steady stream of serving wenches followed, bearing jugs of steaming water, which they tipped into the tub before returning to fetch more. Drying clothes were brought and hung in front of the fire to heat, while from somewhere a washball had been found. Jane sniffed at it, savouring the sweet smell.

Once the servants were gone, apart from Mother Ursula, Jane flung off the filthy shift and eased into the perfumed water, sighing with pleasure as it lapped her breasts. Eyes closed, she luxuriated in the warmth for a few moments, then set about the task of making herself presentable once more. Ducking her head beneath the water she scrubbed until she was satisfied that all the dust and grease was washed away.

'You may rinse my hair,' she ordered. With an expression which suggested she wished the clear water was lye, her new maid did as she was bidden. Once it was clean of soap Jane wrung as much water from it as she could, and twisted it in a thick knot on top of her head. 'Now you may scrub my back,' she commanded.

Gritting her teeth, Mother Ursula rolled up her sleeves and set to. Jane gave a small exclamation as sharp fingernails dug into her back. 'I'm sorry, madam,' Ursula apologised. 'Did I hurt you? My hand must have slipped.'

Jane glared at her smirking face. Accident? Hah! The woman had done it a-purpose.

'Fetch me the drying cloth,' she ordered. 'I am done now.' Face averted, Mother Ursula held it up as Jane stood and stepped from the tub. Well wrapped against the chill from the walls, she seated herself in front of the fire and shook out her hair. 'Brush it well,' she said. 'And do it gently, too.'

Ignoring the second part of Jane's order, Mother Ursula dragged the brush roughly through the tangled mass, almost jerking the hair from her head. Jane whirled round. 'I told you to be gentle,' she spat. 'Are you so stupid that you cannot understand a simple command?'

It was too much for the former Mother Superior. Goaded beyond endurance she lashed out and slapped Jane's face.

'You little bitch!' she hissed. 'Who are you to give me orders as if I were some kitchen slut? Once Sir Edmund has bedded you he will cast you out like the worthless whore you are – and then we shall see who has the last word.'

'You overstep yourself,' said Jane icily. 'How dare you raise your hand to your mistress? I shall have you whipped for that.' A cruel smile curved her lips. 'And I know just the one to administer the beating, too.'

When Oswald entered the chamber he was carrying a small dog-whip. Mother Ursula backed away, fear replacing her supercilious expression. 'Still not learned your place, eh?' he chuckled. 'Well, I'm the very man to teach you.'

As Jane watched he advanced on Mother Ursula. When

she lashed out at him he caught her wrists and spun her round. Holding her fast with one hand and ignoring her struggles, he fumbled in his pouch for a short length of leather twine. In a trice she was secured helplessly to the bedpost, her hands stretched above her head.

One massive paw reached out and grasped the neck of the ugly black dress. Jane could hear the seams rip as he tore it down about her waist, revealing the woman's skinny white back. Her hand flew to her mouth and she wished she could recall her order, then she tightened her lips. Mother Ursula had had no second thoughts when their positions were reversed, so why should she? Ignoring the tremor in the pit of her stomach, she watched as Oswald lifted the whip and brought it down. A thin red mark appeared on the pale flesh and Mother Ursula screeched. Again and again the hand holding the whip rose and fell, until Ursula's screeches became whimpers and her back was criss-crossed with scarlet lines.

'Enough! Enough!' said Jane, turning away, sickened. 'Take her away and salve her to ease the pain.' Oswald undid the bindings, caught Ursula as she crumpled and flung her over his shoulder as if she were no heavier than a pennyweight. He grinned lecherously as his free hand fumbled beneath her skirts.

'And I've got just the salve for her,' he leered, heading towards the door. 'One dose and she'll be on her feet again – or on her back!'

'A fine performance,' said Sir Edmund, chuckling, as he stepped aside to let Oswald pass. 'A pity we cannot see the next act.'

'Wh-what do you want?' stammered Jane, flushing guiltily as she realised he must have watched the entire sorry episode.

He raised an eyebrow. 'What do I want?' he asked in

mock hurt. 'Have you forgotten so soon, my lady? We have a bargain.' He gestured towards the door, through which Oswald had just carried Mother Ursula. 'And that little scene puts me in the notion to begin collecting on it.' He ran his one good eye over her, gleaming lustfully. 'I have been neglectful, my sweet,' he purred. 'But my affairs are almost settled. There is time now for a little dalliance.

'I shall attend upon you tonight, mistress,' he said, with a mocking bow. 'And I trust I shall find you waiting – ready and eager.' Turning, he sauntered off, leaving Jane staring fearfully after him.

His words had been a threat rather than a promise – and why should witnessing Mother Ursula's beating seem to excite him so? An icy finger touched her spine. Perhaps her 'bargain' would prove harder than she'd thought.

Chapter Fifteen

Once Sir Edmund had gone Jane turned away, fear gnawing at her stomach. The mirror caught her eye and she stared at her reflection, seeing only a terrified face. She smiled ruefully, a smile that was nearer a grimace. Hardly the vision of a girl awaiting her lover, was it? A thought struck her of a sudden, and she brightened. She might not be able to put off Sir Edmund's attentions indefinitely, but perhaps she could postpone them a little?

She looked wistfully at the dark green velvet gown already laid out on the bed. Green became her, intensifying the colour of her eyes and showing her auburn hair off to its best – and the snug fit of the gown would emphasise her tiny waist and high breasts to perfection. Still, her intention was to repel, not to attract. Sighing regretfully, she carefully folded and laid it aside.

Raking through the chest, she dug out a gown she had relegated to the bottom as never to be worn. Shuddering, she held it up. It was truly hideous. Who knew what had possessed its previous owner to choose such an unprepossessing colour – unless it was to conceal the dirt. Made of coarsely woven linen it was the same yellowish-brown as a diseased turd. Even a roll in the farmyard would be more likely to improve than detract from its appearance. As a final delightful touch, the cloth beneath the armpits was stained in wide circles with old sweat.

She sniffed cautiously. Thank goodness the dress was so old that the odour had dissipated long since – though perhaps it might have been better had it not. Surely Sir

Edmund would be less keen to touch her if she stank like a polecat?

Slipping the gown over her head, she regarded her reflection with satisfaction. She had never looked uglier in her life. The colour drained her complexion, making her appear sick of the jaundice – and the gown only fitted where it touched. In fact, it was so big that it concealed every curve and made her look positively scrawny.

Seizing her hair she drew it back from her forehead and twisted it into a bun, so tight that her eyebrows were pulled up, giving her a look of pained disapproval. She regarded the apparition in the mirror. God's teeth! She had seen better-dressed creatures set in the fields to scare crows! Her eyes sparkled and a dimple appeared beside her mouth. She could not wait to see whether Sir Edmund was so eager to bed her now. With a final mischievous glance in the mirror she swept out of the room to go and break her fast.

The word 'swept' was highly appropriate. The gown was so long that it trailed after her, the hem becoming grubbier with every step. Jane tossed her head, caring not a jot. A few more tasteful stains would simply add to the effect. Pausing dramatically at the door of the great hall, she made her grand entrance. Sir Edmund's eyes ran over her without recognition and, for a few moments he continued his conversation with Oswald between mouthfuls of bread and cheese. Then his gaze swung back, and he almost choked.

'God's blood, girl!' he spluttered as Oswald pounded his back. He stared at her in horrified disbelief. 'What have you done to yourself? I've seen better looking corpses dragged out of the Thames!'

Jane suppressed a gleeful smile at the success of her ruse. She stared at him with wide-eyed innocence and dropped into a deep curtsy, her gown pooling round her feet like a puddle of bile. 'I am sorry, my lord,' she said demurely. 'Do I not please you?'

For a moment he stared, his good eye narrowed to a slit, then he flung his head back and roared with laughter. 'I see your little ploy, my lady. Well, it won't work.' He gripped her chin and pushed his face into hers so that she felt his breath hot against her cheeks. 'Did you really think I would be put off by a shabby gown?' His expression became wolfish. 'You forget I have already seen the sweet body that lies beneath – and a treasure is worth more for a little digging.'

His mouth came down on hers, his tongue pushing its way between her reluctant lips. For a long moment he held her immovable, savouring her sweetness, then he thrust her away so violently that she staggered and almost fell. She stared at him, panting with a mixture of excitement and fear.

'A little something on account,' he sneered. 'I shall collect more of your debt tonight. Come, Oswald,' he ordered, and strode off without a backward glance.

She stared after him, rubbing at the white marks his cruel fingers had left on the soft skin of her face. He was like one of the great cats she'd seen at the Tower when she was small: bejewelled and chained – but with the threat of violence and death barely concealed beneath the tawny hide. She shivered. Why did she have the horrible suspicion that he would make her pay for her feeble attempt to deceive him?

Her appetite had shrivelled at the encounter and she sat alone at the high table, her nervous fingers reducing the soft white bread to crumbs, the small beer sour in her throat – and made the sourer by her grudging attendant. Mother Ursula, her cheek marred by a bruise about her left eye, waited on her silently, only her eyes revealing her true feelings. They glinted in her white face with hatred and resentment and she looked at Jane with the expression of a whipped cur who longs to bite, yet fears the consequences.

'Will there be anything else, my lady?' she muttered through gritted teeth. 'More beer, perhaps?'

The thought of poison laid an icy finger on Jane's spine and she pushed her tankard away. The woman would dose her with some deadly brew as soon as look at her. Aye, and stand smiling as she writhed away her last breath. She shook herself. She was jumping at shadows. 'No, thank you,' she replied coldly. 'You may clear away.'

Leaving Ursula to go about her menial job, she wandered from pillar to post, seeking something to distract her weary thoughts. There was nothing. Everyone had their allotted tasks, from sweeping the courtyard to washing the linen. At her approach they redoubled their efforts and she smiled wryly. It was the servants' creed in halls and mansions all over the land: 'here comes the mistress. Look busy!'

The smile vanished as quickly as it had come. She was mistress of the castle – and tonight she would become Sir Edmund's mistress in the bedchamber, too. It was not a prospcct shc was looking forward to.

Her aimless footsteps led her to the kitchen. The usual clattering and chatter masked her entrance and for a moment she stood unobserved. Martha's bowman was comfortably ensconced with his feet under the table and the remains of a handsome meal in front of him. As she watched he washed down his last mouthful, leaned back and rubbed his belly with satisfaction. 'A fine meal,' he grinned, giving Martha's buttocks a hearty slap. One eye closed in a wink. 'And a fine woman into the bargain. What more could a man ask?'

Martha fluttered her eyelashes at the compliment, like a village maiden at her first May dance. 'Get away with you, Gareth Jones,' she chuckled, her formidable bosom wobbling with amusement. 'You archers are all the same. I'll bet you says that to all the girls.' Still simpering, she hit him a friendly buffet that almost knocked him off his seat.

A pang of envy ran through Jane. Neither Martha or her swain were good-looking – or in the first flush of youth for that matter – but she would lay her last farthing that there would be more wholesome jollity between *their* coarse sheets than between her own silken ones. She sighed as she remembered Ralph, who'd never had the chance to share her bed – and Robin, who'd taken her gently, with only the green sward for a pillow. Damn the woman, but Ursula was right. Gild it how you would, she was nothing but a whore. How had she come to such a pretty pass as this?

She must have made some tiny movement, because Martha looked up, startled, and hurried towards her, her face becoming anxious. 'What ails thee, mistress?' she asked, taking in Jane's pale cheeks. Deference quickly evaporated, replaced by concern. 'God's teeth, girl, you're as white in the face as a baker's cuddy! Get your backside on that seat before you fall down.' She tugged Jane towards the settle that had been hastily vacated by her wooer, who now stood, clutching his hat uneasily between two large hands. Martha glared at him. 'What are you standing there for, you great sumph?' she demanded, shooing him away like a horsefly. 'Haven't you any work to do? Get about your business and leave me to mine.'

He stood, grinning like an idiot beneath her scolding, before ambling off.

Turning back to Jane, Martha regarded her, hands on

hips. 'Now then, my girl. Let's get something inside you. There's hardly enough meat on you for a sparrow. Here!' A chunk of roast meat, still dripping with juices, was thrust into one hand and a goblet of mulled wine into the other. Comfortingly reminded of old Alice, Jane did as she was told.

She was halfway through her impromptu meal when the kitchen door burst open. A dusty young man stood on the threshold, his clothes showing the evidence of a night's hard riding. Scanning the room, his gaze settled on Jane; he hurried forward and made a sketchy bow.

'Your pardon, my lady,' he said, 'but I bring grave news. Where is the master? His uncle lies at death's door, struck down by the sweating sickness. I have orders to bring him at once.'

Jane stared at him, hope bubbling up inside her. She had been reprieved! God must have heard her prayers! But remorse struck her immediately. How could she be grateful that a man lay dying? And yet...

'The last I saw of him he was in the stables,' she said. 'If you hurry you will catch him before he rides out.'

With another brief bow the young man hurried out. Jane stared after him, then smiled with guilty relief. With Sir Edmund safely out of the way she could forget her fears for just a little longer.

'See!' exclaimed Martha with satisfaction, taking in the fresh colour in Jane's cheeks and her renewed appetite. 'That's all you needed. A bit of decent food in your belly.' She folded her arms. 'And I was right, wasn't I?'

'Yes, Martha, and I thank you for your kindness,' said Jane, demurely knowing she could never explain the real reason for her sudden happiness.

Beaming with pleasure at her own cleverness and the vindication of her good food, Martha patted Jane's hand

and bustled off to order the kitchen staff about with renewed vigour. Jane laughed at the sound of a brisk slap and Martha's scolding voice echoing in her ears as she left the kitchens.

When she reached the courtyard Sir Edmund was already saddled and mounted, his face black with suppressed anger. Jane bobbed a curtsy and smiled up at him. 'My condolences upon your ill news, my lord. I wish you a safe and speedy journey.' And a slow and tedious return, she added mentally.

He wheeled his horse round and glared down at her. 'God rot my uncle. He picked a damned inconvenient time to go about his dying. But do not think you have escaped, madam,' he warned, his good eye glittering menacingly. 'This merely delays my pleasures. My time will come soon enough – and appetite grows with denial.' He hauled on the reins, dug his heels into his horse's sides, and clattered out of the courtyard with Oswald close behind.

Jane watched until the two figures disappeared over the horizon, then turned away, offering up a quick prayer that his unfortunate uncle would postpone his departure from this world – and delay Sir Edmund's inheritance – for as long as possible.

It was as if Sir Edmund had taken a huge black cloud with him. For the first time since she had clattered beneath the forbidding portcullis on the back of his horse, she felt totally unafraid. It might only be a brief reprieve, but she intended to make the most of it.

With a spring in her step she returned to her chamber, pulled off the horrible dun gown and dropped it in a hcap on the floor.

Dressed in the becoming green velvet she tugged her hair out of the tight bun and tossed her head, her auburn curls tumbling about her face. She smiled wickedly at the reflection of the bright-eyed girl who dimpled back, almost unable to believe the transformation in her appearance. She pulled a face of mock sympathy. What a shame Sir Edmund wasn't here to appreciate it.

The day passed in a whirl of pleasant activity. For the rest of the morning she supervised the gathering of rose petals from the neglected garden and set about making pot pourri in the still room. After a hearty midday meal she rode down to the convent and appropriated needles, linen and silks; luxuries she had been denied under Ursula's heavy hand. The afternoon she spent in the solar, happily planning out her embroidery.

In the evening she dined alone in her room, free from the lewd stares of Edmund's men. Yawning, she sat comfortably in front of the fire, sleepily watching the patterns in the flames, and when she finally crept into her bed, alone, she was soundly asleep within seconds.

She awoke with a scream as pain lashed through her. Terrified and disorientated, she groped for the covers to draw about her – and discovered that they had gone, leaving her unprotected, save for the thin material of her night rail. She stared at the shadowy figure looming over her in the semi-darkness. Had Edmund returned so quickly? Another tongue of pain lashed across her tender breasts and she writhed in agony against the crumpled sheets. As her sight adjusted to the dimness she saw her attacker clearly, and gasped in horror. Illuminated by a solitary candle, Mother Ursula's face glistened with the sweat of madness. Her coif was gone and flashing eyes glared down at Jane from her shaven skull. Her lips were pulled back in the grin of a rabid bitch and flecks of saliva gleamed on her chin.

Jane shuddered and recoiled. Mother Ursula's grin widened even further as the claw holding the short-handled dog-whip rose to deliver the next blow. The lash whistled through the air to cut a fine red line across Jane's quivering belly and she moaned and curled herself around the pain.

'Thought you'd got away with it, didn't you?' snarled Ursula. 'Well, you were wrong, my fine lady. How dare you humiliate me!' Her voice rose in a crescendo of self-pity and insanity. 'Me, your Mother Superior!' Reaching down she ripped the thin night rail from Jane's shrinking body, revealing the girl's creamy back and smooth pale buttocks.

The whip rose. The lash wrapped itself round the curve of Jane's hips and another tongue of fire licked her cringing body. Mother Ursula cackled with glee. The horrifying truth dawned on Jane. This was no ordinary whipping. The madwoman intended to beat her to death! She whimpered with fear, but self-preservation goaded her into action. Ignoring the pain she pushed herself to her knees, swayed for a moment, then lunged towards her attacker.

Mother Ursula easily evaded Jane's feeble hands, then lunged herself, knocking Jane backwards. Her head banged against the bedpost and everything went grey. Through the mist of semi-consciousness she barely felt the rain of blows or saw the madness in the other woman's face as she groped for something heavy to finish the job she had started.

Dreamily, Jane watched as the heavy iron candlestick rose in the air and began to descend in the final killing blow. She stared up in dull resignation and waited for it all to be over.

The blow never came. From out of nowhere it seemed, a hand grasped Mother Ursula's wrist. Hissing and spitting with frustrated fury she struggled to break free, but to no avail. The candlestick was wrenched from her fingers and dropped at her feet, the candle, which had miraculously stayed alight until now, finally flickering out. Jane's rescuer dragged Mother Ursula's arms behind her back and bundled her, still cursing and spitting, out into the corridor and the tender care of two men-at-arms.

Still dazed, she stared up in complete incomprehension. Sir Edmund appeared to be staring down at her.

She blinked and rubbed her eyes. When she opened them again, he was still there. 'But... but I thought you were attending your dying uncle?' she stammered.

'Stupid old fool,' he snorted in response. 'He was no more dying than I am.' He waved a dismissive hand. 'A surfeit of damned lampreys was all he suffered from. Half a day in the stool-room and he was as healthy as an ox. We were barely two hours on the road when we met the second messenger coming to inform me of his miraculous recovery.'

Jane closed her eyes. 'Thank God,' she said fervently. 'If he had not – and you had not returned when you did...' Her voice trailed off into silence as she realised that, for her, his uncle's recovery truly had been miraculous. Without it, she would have died as well.

She opened her eyes again and stared up at him in gratitude. 'And thank you, my lord. Still, at least my ordeal is over now.'

His cruel laugh startled her into fresh terror. 'Oh no, my pretty one,' he said, shaking his head. 'You're wrong there.'

'But I don't understand,' she whispered. 'Wh-what do you mean?'

'What do I mean, my lady?' he scoffed. 'I mean that your debt is due and that I intend to start collecting.' He smiled down into her horrified face and slowly began to unbuckle his belt. 'Your ordeal has only just begun.'

Chapter Sixteen

'Please, please, I beg you,' Jane whispered, backing as far away as the bed and her aching body would allow. 'Do not hurt me any more. I could not bear it.'

Sir Edmund stopped, a frown crossing his face, and strode to the door. 'Candles!' he bellowed. 'Now.'

There was the sound of hurried conversation, followed by that of scurrying feet, then light filled the doorway as two servants hurried in, carrying a brace of candlesticks each. 'Put them down there,' he ordered. Bobbing a hasty curtsy they hastened to obey, then stood waiting for further instructions.

He glared at them, tapping his foot impatiently. 'Well? What are you standing there for? Be about your business.' He paused. 'No, wait. Bring me clean cloths, salt water and some marigold salve.'

Once they had finally gone he turned back to the bed. 'Let me look at you,' he commanded. Clutching the remnants of her night rail to her in a vain attempt to conceal her private parts, Jane did as she was told, groaning as every movement set off fresh pain. She rolled on to her stomach and buried her head in the pillow, ashamed both of her weakness, and the fact that she was stretched out naked and helpless before him.

He stared down at her, his eye following the soft curve of her shoulders, half-hidden by the tangle of auburn hair, down to the indentation of her narrow waist, the voluptuous swell of her hips and her long smooth thighs. A soft whistle escaped from between his teeth as he saw the damage Mother Ursula had inflicted upon the slim young body.

A network of fine red lines criss-crossed the soft creaminess of her flesh. In places the skin was broken and angry purple bruises bloomed. But it could have been much worse. Had that demented bitch had a horsewhip instead of a dog-whip, he would be looking down at a stiffening corpse instead of a warm breathing body. He reached for the ewer, poured water into the basin and dipped the cloth into it.

Seeing the sudden movement from the corner of her eye, Jane stiffened in apprehension. 'What are you going to do?' she croaked through dry lips. 'Are you going to beat me, too?'

He gave a harsh bark of laughter. 'Don't be ridiculous, girl. Why should I beat you? Only a madman would ruin a mare he wishes to ride. And I intend to ride you well and long. No, girl, I'm only going to tend your wounds.' He lifted the dripping cloth from the basin. 'Prepare yourself,' he ordered. 'This is going to hurt.'

Jane winced and bit her lip at the first touch of the cloth, the salty water stinging the broken skin. Then she groaned with pleasure as the coolness soothed her throbbing flesh. Beads of water trickled slowly down her flanks, like an icy caress.

Once her wounds were washed he dabbed them dry with unexpected gentleness. Finally, he scooped up a generous helping of marigold salve and began to apply it.

Jane gasped again, this time with pleasure as his hard hands stroked and kneaded her from nape to ankle, lingering on the smooth curve of her buttocks. The pain was fading now, to be replaced by a warm tingling. His fingers dipped delicately between her thighs, grazing the soft lips of her sex, and she drew in a ragged breath, feeling herself moisten at his touch.

'Roll over,' he ordered, his voice husky with desire. Reluctantly she did so, holding the tattered remnants of her night rail against her, her face flushed with shame at the heat that pulsed through her. He plucked the thin material from her clutching hands and threw it to the floor. 'God's teeth, girl,' he muttered. 'How am I supposed to tend you if you try and hide yourself?'

He stopped, transfixed at the sight of her: the high round breasts with their enticing, unawakened nipples, and the triangle of flame-red hair that seemed to glow between her thighs like a beacon.

It had been her back that bore the brunt of Mother Ursula's punishment, but there were two ugly weals to show where her first blows had fallen. One lay across her belly and down the line of her hip, while the other had bitten viciously into the smooth flesh of her breasts, barely missing the tender nipples.

Sir Edmund traced the red line with his thumb and it was Jane's turn to gasp. Turning away, he dipped the cloth in the basin again and ran it over the soft curves of her body, watching in fascination as beads of moisture ran down her belly, disappearing into the brazen patch of pubic hair, and the tips of her breasts peaked and hardened as the cold water touched them. Swallowing audibly, he reached for the salve and began to apply it.

Jane moaned as his fingers strayed from their intended path. Taking each nipple in turn, he rolled them between finger and thumb till they stood out, hard and glistening against the soft white mounds of her breasts. Against her will, her thighs loosened and his other hand began to explore the wet warmth between them. Parting the flaming crest of hair, his fingers found the hot cleft of her sex, slid into it and began to move rhythmically. As he leaned over her his mouth replaced the fingers at her breast and he took first one and then the other between his lips, sucking eagerly as his tongue circled the tight buds. She moaned again, this time with pleasure.

Withdrawing, he stood up and began to fumble at his belt once more. Jane watched with heavy-lidded eyes as he dragged off his clothes and dropped them in a tumbled heap at his feet to stand before her naked.

She drew in her breath with astonishment. His broad shoulders and chest were covered with a thick pelt of dark hair, apart from a long thin line where the flesh twisted pink and gnarled. A sword cut – and one which had healed badly at that. But it wasn't this that made her gasp.

Her eyes followed the line of hair that bisected the muscular belly to where his manhood reared up as if it had a life of its own. Thick and swollen, it jutted from his groin like an iron bar, its purple tip so engorged with blood that the tight skin gleamed in the candlelight. She whimpered with a mixture of fear and excitement.

'Please don't hurt me,' she begged.

He was not listening to her. Overcome with desire he flung himself on her like a wild beast. Kneeling between her legs he pulled them apart until the soft lips of her sex parted to reveal the glistening pink opening inside. He was ruthless in his exploration, his fingers plundering the secrets of her body.

Seizing her wrists he held them above her head as his heavy body pressed down, immobilising her, his chest crushing her breasts. She groaned as the head of his cock pushed against her throbbing vulva, then yelped as the full length slid slowly and inexorably inside her.

For a moment he was still, then he began to move, slowly at first then faster as her juices lubricated him and eased his passage. At each thrust the whip marks on her back shrieked their protest, but the discomfort served only to increase the wild sensations running through her, until she could no longer tell pain from pleasure.

Despite herself her back arched and she wrapped her legs about his waist. Her hips rose to meet each new thrust, pushing his thick prick deeper inside her until she was sobbing with anguished delight. He groaned deep in the back of his throat and she felt his cock jerk and spasm as he spilt his seed. A scream escaped her own throat as it triggered her release. Gasping and juddering she clung to him as her vulva clenched and unclenched about him, milking the last few drops from his wilting member.

With a groan of satisfaction he rolled off her body and collapsed on the bed beside her, still panting. 'My God!' he rasped. 'For an innocent from the convent you fuck like an accomplished whore!'

Jane wasn't sure whether to be pleased or insulted, but his words brought back their bargain. 'I am delighted to have pleased you, sir,' she purred, rolling over and running a finger down the scar on his chest. 'Now what do you intend to give me for my services?'

He grinned at her lazily and reached over to tweak one subsiding nipple. 'The convent gardens, I think,' he said.

'Is that all?' She pouted. 'Am I not worth more than a few acres of ground?'

At her words his face hardened and he sprang from the bed as if he'd been stung. 'I might have known,' he snarled, staring down at her in disgust. 'You're like any other common whore – always looking for more.'

She gazed at him in dismay, regretting her hasty words as he reached for his clothes. With each garment he pulled on he became more distant until, by the time he was fully dressed, he was a stranger again. His face was set and hard. The gentleness with which he had tended her wounds might never have existed.

'I have broken you in gently,' he muttered as he stalked towards the door. His lip curled in a sneer as he stood on the threshold, his voice becoming grim. 'Next time it will not be quite so easy to earn your fee. As for that other bitch, Ursula, nobody damages my property and gets away with it. I shall deal with her tomorrow.'

The heavy oak door crashed shut behind him and Jane sagged back on the pillow, cursing her foolish tongue. He had been more than generous with his gift of the convent gardens in return for sharing her bed. Why had she asked for more? She blushed with shame. He was right. She had acted like a tavern whore, begging a few extra coppers for her favours. Her colour deepened as she remembered how willingly she had rutted with him, whimpering like a bitch in heat. In truth she was worse than a whore. No self-respecting tavern slut would have responded quite so eagerly to her customer's attentions.

The pain which had eased beneath his soothing fingers, and been forgotten entirely in the throes of passion, rushed back with a vengeance. She groaned again, this time with discomfort. Despite the soothing marigold salve every lash on her back stung and throbbed, the pain increased by her activities. Even the muscles between her thighs ached where she had wrapped her legs around Sir Edmund and held him to her.

Rolling over she buried her head in the pillow, praying for sleep – and oblivion.

It didn't come. As soon as she closed her eyes and began to drift off she jerked awake again, sure that Mother Ursula had returned to finish the job she had started. Even the light from the candles, still burning in their sconces, failed to dispel the shadows in the corners and she gazed at them fearfully, in case they hid the Mother Superior's avenging figure.

She must have slept eventually, for when she became conscious again sunlight was falling across the foot of the bed and the candles were nothing but waxen stumps. Dull and heavy-headed, she swung her legs to the floor and limped painfully across to the window.

The castle was already about its business. One of Martha's skivvies was scattering corn to the chickens that pecked around the kitchen door. A groom was leading a horse across the courtyard, stopping every now and again to check its left foreleg for injury. Two men-at-arms leaned against the wall, guffawing at some jest or other. In the corner three more were hammering away at a wooden structure. She turned away.

One of the maids must have entered while she slept, because her ewer was full of water that still held a trace of warmth. Pouring it into the basin she took a soft cloth and dabbed gingerly at her aching body. Standing naked in front of the mirror, she twisted her head to see her back, and sighed with relief. The network of fine lines was already fading and though the bruises remained, they looked worse than they actually were. For all her frenzied attack, Ursula had done no lasting damage.

She slipped into the green velvet gown, wincing as the material touched her welted skin. Sir Edmund had already enjoyed the pleasures of her body – and made it very clear that he fully intended to sample them again. There was no point now in trying to disguise her attractiveness. Walking slowly and with care, she made her way down to the great hall.

Sir Edmund was already there, seated at the high table with a dripping chunk of meat in his hand and a tankard of small ale at his elbow. At her entry he looked up and stared at her, unsmiling. A quiver of nervousness churned her stomach. With that black eye patch he looked like some ruthless corsair king; one whose word was law and who would order her keelhauled without a second thought.

'I am pleased to see you have recovered from the worst of your ills, my lady,' he grunted, and she breathed an inaudible sigh of relief. He waved a hand towards the seat beside him. 'Sit down and eat,' he ordered. 'You will need a full stomach for this morning's business.'

She stared at him blankly, barely aware of the kitchen maid who scurried to place food and drink in front of her. 'What do you mean?' she asked.

He chuckled. 'What a forgiving little creature you are. Perhaps the convent was the proper place for you after all.' His sharp teeth tore into the meat and once more she was reminded of a wolf. She watched, fascinated, as a trickle of meat juice, still blood red, ran down his chin. At last he stopped chewing for long enough to answer her question. 'Why, Mother Ursula's punishment, of course.'

She stared at him in dismay. God help the poor woman. Whatever she had done, she was surely going to rue it now. 'Wh-what are you going to do to her?' she blurted.

'Wait and see,' he replied simply. 'Now eat!'

Jane picked up her meat and took a tiny bite, the food turning to ashes in her mouth. She took a gulp of ale to wash it down, almost gagging at the bitter taste. Under his hawk-like gaze she forced herself to finish the meal.

'Good,' he muttered, wiping his greasy fingers on the front of his doublet. 'Now let us be about our business.' He stood up, made a mocking bow and held out his arm. Reluctantly she laid a hand upon it. He covered it with his other hand, masking his steely grip under the guise of courtesy, and led her through the arched doorway of the hall and out into the sunlit courtyard.

At first the light blinded her. But as her eyes adjusted

she drew a breath in a ragged gasp. In the corner where the three men had been hammering stood a set of stocks, and in the stocks, her head and wrists trapped, was Mother Ursula! She was already spattered with muck and kitchen refuse and there was a purple bruise swelling above one eye, where someone had thrown a stone. But her face was defiant as she watched their approach. Gathering her saliva, she spat at their feet.

Jane turned to flee, but Sir Edmund held her rigid. 'Oh no, my pretty one. I want you to see this.'

Frightened to move, Jane watched in horror as he strode across the remaining few paces and stared down at Mother Ursula. 'Well, madam,' he said. 'An eye for an eye and a tooth for a tooth, isn't that what the Good Book teaches?' Her head moved in a barely perceptible nod. 'Good,' he went on, 'perhaps you will learn that lesson better with a little help.'

He clicked his fingers and one of his men hurried forward. Jane gasped again as she recognised the object he was holding. It was the whip Mother Ursula had used on her the night before. The other woman recognised it too, and began to twist in a frantic effort to break free. Her struggles were useless. The top-piece of the stock held her in place as firmly as a bar of iron.

Sir Edmund took the whip and brought it down on the palm of his hand. Jane jumped as the crack echoed around the courtyard. The sound brought her out of her fearful trance and she hurried forward to grip his sleeve. 'Please,' she begged. 'Please don't do this.'

He brushed her off like a fly and she found herself being hustled back to her place. Smiling, he continued as calmly as if her protest had never occurred. Walking round behind Mother Ursula he reached out with one hand and ripped the gown from her back as if it had been made of paper. It fell in ragged tatters at her feet, revealing her scrawny white body, and her face flamed with rage as the men standing round the courtyard laughed and jeered.

'Touch my property, would you, you sullen bitch?' Sir Edmund snarled. 'I'll teach you!' His words were punctuated with the sound of leather on flesh as his arm rose and fell, scarlet weals blossoming on Mother Ursula's sallow skin. Jane closed her eyes and prayed it would soon be over, as the nun's shrieks filled the courtyard.

At last it was.

She relaxed and breathed a sigh of relief, but too soon.

'Right, lads,' Edmund announced. 'She's all yours. Do with her what you will.'

There was a whoop of glee as the first man hurried forward, his hands already scrabbling at the fastenings of his breeches. As Jane watched in horror he peeled them down to reveal a pair of skinny white buttocks, and an already rampant member jutting from beneath his homespun jerkin. Kicking Mother Ursula's legs apart he took his prick in one hand and spat on the other, rubbing the spittle over its swollen head till it gleamed in the sunlight. He spat again, thrust two fingers roughly into her gaping cleft and pushed them in and out until he was satisfied.

Grinning, he moved between her trembling legs, rubbed his cock against her, then thrust himself inside, his hands pinching and kneading her breasts as his buttocks jerked in a parody of the act of love, while his mates cheered him on and Mother Ursula screamed in outrage.

It was over in seconds and he pulled out, his seed dribbling down her thighs as the next man came to take his place, his prick already out and at the ready. Jane looked at the line of men, their faces filled with savage lust, eagerly awaiting their turn. There had to be ten of them, at least. She turned away, sickened, only to see that Sir Edmund was watching avidly, his expression mirroring theirs.

She turned and fled to the safety of her room, banging the door closed behind her and leaning against it, panting. It was no good. Through the open window she could still hear the woman's shrieks of pain and humiliation as the men took their pleasure of her helpless body.

Covering her ears to blot out Mother Ursula's cries, she flung herself on the bed, her stomach knotting with fear as she remembered the cruel lust on Sir Edmund's face.

Next time, it might be her!

Chapter Seventeen

Mercifully, the tortured sounds died away at last. Cautiously Jane rose from the bed, walked to the window and stared down. The courtyard was empty now, the jeering crowd dispersed. The stocks stood empty. Nothing at all remained to show the scene of depravity that had just been enacted. It might all have been a wild nightmare that disappeared at the first moment of waking.

The sound of movement startled her and she whirled round, her heart pounding in her chest. Sir Edmund was at the door, lounging idly against the frame, his arms folded. How long had he been standing there, watching her unobserved? And, more to the point, what did he want? She straightened her shoulders and summoned up her failing courage.

'What brings you to my chamber, my lord?' she asked, sketching a brief, mocking curtsy. 'Did seeing that poor woman abused put fire in your loins? Do you wish to collect another payment of my debt?' She indicated the bed with a wave of the hand. 'Perhaps I should lie down and spread my legs. Is that what you want?'

'That "poor woman" as you call her, tried to kill you,' he pointed out grimly. 'Had you forgotten so quickly? As to her punishment, she should count herself lucky she ended in the stocks instead of on the gallows. Servicing a few sturdy fellows is a small price to pay for one's life.'

He ran his eye over her flushed cheeks and heaving bosom and smiled slyly. 'Perhaps you are the one with the fire in your loins.' He glanced at the tumbled sheets and raised a quizzical eyebrow. 'May I point out that you were the one who suggested I bed you?'

'How – how dare you?' she spluttered, turning an even brighter crimson. 'What do you think I am? Some wanton slut?'

His grin widened. 'Madam, we have already established what you are. And an accomplished one at that.'

She bit her lip in shame, remembering the night before when she had writhed mindlessly beneath his body. Stung by the recollection she flung her head back and glared at him, her lip curled scornfully. 'And if I am a whore, who made me one? What does that make you? My whoremaster?' It was his turn to flush.

Delighted by his reaction, she hurried on. 'And what about my payment?' she demanded. 'How do I know you will keep your promise? For all I know you are some common cheapjack who will bilk me of my rightful dues.'

His face tightened. 'Madam, I am a gentleman. I have given you my word.'

'Hah! And how much is that worth? Talk is cheap. As far as I am concerned your promise is worth as little as the breath it took to utter it.'

Stiff with outraged pride, he drew himself up to full height and stalked towards her. Before she had a chance to move he had seized her shoulders and pulled her towards him. 'I warn you, my lady,' he hissed, his breath hot on her cheeks, 'don't push me too far. Just remember, between these walls I hold the power of life and death.'

She shivered in his grip. His mouth came down on hers, warm and wet, while one hand plunged into her neckline and roughly fondled her breasts, teasing her nipples into hardness. She could feel his manhood thrusting against her belly, even through the padded codpiece. She moaned deep in her throat as her lips opened in response and she sagged against him, her eyes flickering and closing.

With a cruel smile he flung her from him so hard she staggered and fell backwards on to the bed, her skirts tangled about her legs, one breast spilling from her dress. She stared up at him, wide-eyed in disappointment.

'See?' he sneered. 'Scratch a lady and find a whore. Why don't you admit it? You wanted me as much as I wanted you. Perhaps you didn't find this morning's little exhibition as distasteful as you claim.' With a final scornful glance he stalked from the chamber.

Groaning with humiliation, she rolled on to her belly and buried her head in her pillow. He was right. The vision of Mother Ursula's pale body jerking as it was ravaged by all those men, the swollen members thrusting between her parted thighs, came back uninvited into her mind. Sickening though it was to admit it to herself, beneath her horror ran a thin thread of shameful excitement.

She groaned again. Was she unique, or were all women the same? Did even the highest lady in the land secretly imagine what it would be like to be a tavern whore, fornicating with a dozen men a night?

The secret place between her own thighs throbbed demandingly, and she was tempted to lift her skirts and use her fingers to bring herself to blessèd relief. But the thought of Sir Edmund returning to catch her pleasuring herself was too much to bear. Scarlet-cheeked, she leapt from the bed, pulled down her skirts and adjusted the neck of her dress so that her exposed breast was discreetly covered once more.

Walking over to the mirror she checked her reflection to see that she was decent. Only her flushed face and glittering eyes revealed the confusion in her mind, but she could not stay here in her chamber, with only her tormenting thoughts for company. She had to find something to do. But what?

The answer came to her in a flash. Mother Ursula! For all she knew the woman was lying dead somewhere. She would find her and do what she could to ease her. Picking up the remains of the marigold salve Sir Edmund had used on her own weals she tucked it into the pouch that hung at her waist. But how to find her? The castle was huge. The woman could be anywhere.

The kitchen, that was it. If anyone knew where she was, it would be the servants. Gossip spread like wildfire through their ranks. She smiled ruefully. Many a fine lady, taking a lover to her bed, would be horrified to find out how much her maid and laundress knew about her so-called 'secret'. Martha would know what had happened to Ursula if anyone did.

The heat from the ovens hit her like a blow when she entered. For once Martha's swain was not hovering in attendance. As Jane entered, she was standing over a huge black pot, stirring the contents with her ladle. As soon as the cook saw her she nodded to a skivvy to take over, with strict instructions to continue until told otherwise, and hurried towards her.

'You'm looking better,' she said, eyeing Jane approvingly. 'Got a bit of colour in them cheeks of yours for a change. Come for some more of Martha's cooking, have you, lovey?'

'Thank you, Martha, but no,' smiled Jane. 'It is information I seek. Do you know where Mother Ursula is?'

Martha responded as if she had been asked to swallow poison. 'Her?' she said scathingly. 'What d'ye want to bother about that old cat for? Deserved everything she had coming to her, that one.' Her voice dropped confidentially. 'Mark my words. If you knew some of the tales about her, well...!' She shuddered dramatically, setting her plump body quivering with horrified delight. ''T'would freeze your blood, and no mistake.'

'I can well imagine,' said Jane grimly. 'But that doesn't matter now. I can't just leave her to crawl off and die in a corner.'

Martha's expression suggested that *she* could, without a second thought, but she shrugged and gave in to Jane's pleading glance. 'They do say,' she said slowly, 'as how she's in the old storeroom at the foot of the north tower. Best place for her if you ask me. Along o' the rest of the old rubbish.'

'Bless you, Martha,' Jane replied softly. 'You'll get your reward in heaven, for your good deed.'

'Humph.' She snorted. 'Like as not you're right – since it's certain I shan't get it here.'

Jane turned to go, then a thought struck her and she turned back again. 'Oh, just one last favour,' she said. 'May I beg a loaf of bread and a jug of wine?'

Martha's eyes narrowed. 'For that old bitch?' Jane nodded. 'Waste of good food, if you asks me. Let her live on her own poison.'

Despite this, she fetched the smallest loaf she could find and filled a dented mug with sour red wine.

'Thank you,' Jane said gratefully, taking them. Arms folded, shaking her head over the stupidity of soft-hearted fools, Martha turned back to her cooking, the matter at a close.

Ignoring the lewd comments from the lounging men-at-arms, Jane hurried across the courtyard to the north tower, careful not to spill the wine. As she approached her heart sank at the sight of the thick oaken door. If it was barred, then she had little chance of entry. It was, but the huge iron key was still in the lock. Grunting with effort she twisted it round, hearing the final click of the tumblers with relief. Her first attempts to push it open failed miserably, and she was forced to put her shoulder to it. Finally, it creaked open.

Coming from the sunlit courtyard to the darkness, she could see nothing at first. She wrinkled her nose at the stench of damp and must. The lower half of the north tower had obviously been used as a storeroom for time out of memory. Everything that was no longer useful, but was still 'too good' to throw away, had ended up in here, left behind when the previous owner of the castle had fled. Thick grey cobwebs festooned every nook and cranny and the dust, disturbed by her arrival, floated in the air like a miasma, catching at the back of her throat.

Then, as her eyes adjusted to the gloom, dim forms began to take shape. She scanned the dust-filled room. One corner was filled with broken arrow-chests, piled one on top of another in a mouldering heap. On rusting hooks hung ancient harnesses and an equally ancient saddle, their leather cracked and dried with age. Against the opposite wall there was even a dented suit of armour, lying in an agonised jumble of arms and legs. She shivered. It wouldn't have surprised her if the bones of the previous owner were still inside. A pile of black rags lay in the far corner. In the other—

She gasped, and her frightened eyes returned to the heap of rags. It was moving! Her first thought was that rats had built their nest amongst them, then a low groan revealed the truth. She had found Mother Ursula.

Oblivious to the clouds of dust stirred up as her skirts swept the floor, she hurried across and knelt down beside the huddled figure, placing the bread and wine at her side. Mother Ursula stared at her with unseeing eyes. 'No, please, no more!' she whimpered, rolling away and curling into a frightened ball.

The movement dislodged the remnants of the dress that covered her and Jane gasped again. Her back was a score of criss-crossing red lines and a bruise in the shape of a handprint curled round one bony hip. Tentatively she reached out and touched Mother Ursula's shoulder. The woman jumped as if she'd been scalded.

'Fear not,' said Jane gently. 'I have not come to harm you. I brought salve for your wounds.'

Instead of soothing Mother Ursula, her words had quite the opposite effect. Quick as a snake the woman twisted round and uncoiled, her clawed hand striking unerringly for Jane's eyes. If Jane had not jerked back at the last minute she would have been blinded. Spent by the effort she lay there panting, staring at Jane with hatred.

'Have you come to gloat?' she hissed, her voice malevolent despite her weakness. 'To enjoy the sight of me brought low?'

'N-no... of course not,' Jane stammered. 'I came to help.' She reached into her sleeve for the pot of salve and held it up. 'See, I came to ease your pain.'

'There is no salve in the world that can mend what you have done to me,' whispered Mother Ursula. She cackled softly. At the sound of the madness in the woman's voice, Jane's blood ran cold. 'But I shall have my revenge. You mark my words, my fine lady. Your paramour will soon tire of your niminy-piminy ways... and when he does, I shall be waiting.'

Jane rose to her feet, pretending a confidence she did not feel. 'Have it your own way,' she said, flinging the pot of marigold ointment down beside the food and drink. 'I have done with you.'

Head held high she stalked towards the door and the

blessed sunlight. Mother Ursula's laughter, venomous as a snake's hiss, followed her, and it took all her courage not to break into a run.

Once the heavy door was locked behind her she breathed a sigh of relief. She had done her best and been rejected. Whatever happened to the former Mother Superior now, her conscience was clear.

She made her way to the solar and the solace of her embroidery, but neither the weak October sun nor the fire crackling merrily in the grate seemed able to take the chill of the north tower from her bones, and the red thread against the white linen reminded her unpleasantly of the weals on Ursula's back. With a shudder she pushed her work away.

Unable to settle she walked across to the window seat, picked up the lute that lay there and attempted to play the latest song popularised by King Henry. Her nimble fingers plucked out the melody but the words 'Alas my love, you do me wrong' stuck in her throat. Rumour had it that the king had written it for the Great Whore herself. How ironic, when the wrong being done was to his faithful wife, Catherine. She threw the lute down and sighed. Was everything in the world tainted?

Wandering listlessly down to the great hall she picked at some food, then decided to return to her room. Lying on her back she stared at the ceiling and eventually drifted into a light doze. Even in sleep there was no escape. In her dreams she was trying to release a trapped hare, which twisted under her frantic fingers and, beneath her horrified gaze, turned into a black snake that sank its dripping fangs into her wrists. She awoke with a start, to find that she was not alone.

'Wh-what do you want?' she whispered, still dazed from sleep.

Sir Edmund stared down at her coolly. 'Not what I want, madam, but what you want,' he said. She noticed the figure standing behind him in priestly robes and her mouth dried.

Father Peter!

Was she to be subjected to yet another ordeal? But then relief washed over her as he stepped forward and she realised there was absolutely no resemblance at all between this priest and Father Peter.

A kind, elderly face peered out from beneath white curls and its owner cast anxious glances from Jane's face to Sir Edmund's. He cleared his throat nervously. 'May we get on, my lord?' he asked. 'I must be back at chapel in time for evening prayers.'

'Why certainly, Father Andrew,' gushed Edmund. 'This should not take us long.' He clicked his fingers and the priest held out a scroll. Edmund took it without a glance and flung it down on the bed beside Jane. She picked it up and began to unroll it.

'To whom it may concern,' it began. 'I, Edward Spence, Lord of the Manor of Edgeholme, do hereby deed and gift the following Properties in perpetuity, to Mistress Jane Montague and the issue of her body.' Beneath the heading the page was blank apart from the words 'Item One: the Gardens of the Convent of Saint Ursula at Edgeholme.'

She stared blankly from it to Sir Edmund. 'What is this?' she asked.

His lips curled scornfully. 'Do not pretend that you are stupid as well as grasping, madam. Since my word was not enough for you, here is the proof of it. Each of your "payments" will be added as you earn them.' His good eye sparkled icily. 'Will that satisfy you, lady? Or would you have me write it in my blood?'

Stung, she glared back. 'That will be unnecessary,' she retorted. 'Just one little detail, my lord. Who keeps this precious document? You, or I? I would hate it to have an "accident". After all, parchment burns so easily.' She laughed scornfully.

'God's blood, girl,' he snarled. 'Is there no end to your impudence?' He tore the scroll from her hands and pointed it at Father Andrew. 'The good priest will keep it in his charge. I trust you would not cavil with Holy Church?'

Jane opened her mouth to protest that Holy Church could be as venal as any innkeeper, then looked at Father Andrew and changed her mind. Not all priests were like Father Peter. This man had a transparent air of honesty and innocence about him. Obviously bewildered, he still had a quiet dignity that made her trust him instinctively.

'That will be perfectly satisfactory,' she agreed.

'Good,' snapped Edmund. 'We are in agreement at last.' He thrust the scroll into the priest's hands and waved a dismissive hand. Still bewildered, Father Andrew backed towards the door, sketched a brief sign of the cross in the air to give them his blessing, then disappeared, breathing a sigh of relief that his part in whatever was going on was at an end.

When they were alone, Sir Edmund stalked towards the bed and glared savagely down at her. Heart pounding, she cringed away. 'Well, my lady,' he hissed, 'now that matter is settled to your satisfaction perhaps you will be a little more eager to keep your side of the bargain, though whether you are or not, matters not one whit to me.' His face suffused with lust as his gaze raked her trembling body. 'I shall be coming to your chamber to exact payment tonight, madam.' He bowed mockingly. 'Whether you like it or not!'

Chapter Eighteen

Once Sir Edmund had gone, the heavy door slamming behind him, Jane got up and stared at herself in the mirror. She had haggled like a hardened whore, yet the face that looked back at her was still as fresh and innocent as it had always been. Or was there a new hardness round her eyes? She blinked away the thought. If there was, it was hardly her fault. She had not asked for any of this, and if she had to give an accounting of herself before the gates of heaven, at least she would be able to say that some good had come out of her wickedness.

Seizing her comb, she ran it through her tangled curls. If Sir Edmund thought she intended to cower in her room until he came to claim her, he had another think coming! Slipping off the green velvet gown, she lifted the lid of the heavy cedar chest and raked through its contents.

At last she pulled out what she was looking for, smiling with satisfaction. If he wanted a scarlet woman, then who was she to deny him? The gown she selected was a gaudy flame-red, the colour of autumn bonfires, matching her hair. The smooth satin caught the light from the hearth until the very room seemed to glow.

She slipped it over her head, and gasped as she struggled to pull it down. The waist was so tight she could hardly breathe and, without a corset, the neckline cupped and held her breasts, forcing them upwards until it seemed they would spill over. The soft material outlined the hard points of her nipples as they pressed against it, the effect somehow even more erotic than if she'd actually been naked.

She spun round in front of the mirror, laughing in delight. Armoured in youth and beauty she was dressed for battle, and it was time to slay the dragon. Straightening her shoulders, she marched across the room, flung the door open and set off for the great hall.

At the door she paused, her stomach fluttering. The evening meal was already in full progress. Servants scurried hither and thither, some carrying platters of meat and bread while others staggered beneath the weight of jugs of beer. There was the heavy rumble of male laughter interspersed with the occasional not entirely displeased shriek as one of the men-at-arms fumbled beneath the skirts of a serving-maid. Taking a deep breath, she entered.

There was an immediate stunned silence. Ignoring it, she walked the length of the hall, looking neither to right nor left. When she reached the high table she swept into a deep curtsy, her skirts spilling round her in a pool of flame. Sir Edmund stared, his food halfway to his lips.

She smiled up at him from beneath demurely lowered lashes. 'May I suggest you close your mouth, my lord,' she said, her cheeks dimpling. 'Otherwise the flies might get in.'

He flung down the chicken leg he was clutching, stood up, walked round and pulled her to her feet. Placing her hand on his arm, she was escorted gallantly to the seat on his left-hand side. Smiling graciously, she nodded her thanks. There was a low murmur from the hall, the men-at-arms staring at her enviously, nudging each other and winking lewdly. Jane flushed, then held her head higher. Let them chatter like washerwomen for all the good it did them. She might be their master's leman, but she was better born than any of them and nothing could change that.

A hand on her arm made her start. 'Some food, my lady?'

said Sir Edmund.

She nodded gratefully. Perhaps the master could behave like a gentleman even if his men could not. His next words shattered this pretty illusion.

'After all,' he continued, licking his lips and focusing his leering gaze on her half-exposed breasts, 'you must build up your strength for later. A good appetite at board means a good appetite in bed.'

She raised an eyebrow and stared back at him challengingly. 'Only when what is offered is tempting, my lord.' She smiled and ran her eyes over him, her expression disparaging. 'Even the healthiest appetite sickens and dies at the sight of maggoty meat.'

His blue eye narrowed. 'You did not find my meat quite so maggoty the other night, madam. 'In fact, if my memory serves me right, you swallowed it whole – and begged for more. In faith, it was like bedding a hungry cat. I still have the scratches on my back to prove it.'

Her face turned scarlet and she stared down at the food the harassed maid had just laid in front of her.

'What, my lady?' he went on. 'Cat got your tongue? Have you no witty riposte to put me in my place?'

Stung, she lifted her head and glared at him. 'I wouldn't waste my breath, you – you insufferable oaf! You have a hide like a donkey, and the brains to match.'

'And the other equipment as well,' he responded with a smirk. 'Don't forget to mention that. Particularly when you were so pleased to avail yourself of its services.'

She smiled sweetly. 'I think perhaps you overestimate yourself,' she replied. 'Did you truly think that I enjoyed your feeble attentions? As you have so kindly pointed out, I am your whore, remember? And a whore's most important job is to convince the man who pays her how marvellous he is – no matter how incompetent.' She lolled back in her chair, closed her eyes and began to pant in mock abandon. 'Oh! Oh! Oh!' she gasped, rolling her head back and clutching the edge of the table. 'Yes! Yes! Please! Now...' There was a stunned silence and many open mouths in the hall as every eye focused on her, writhing and moaning.

She sat up straight again in triumph. 'There! Was that not a pretty performance? And that's what you bought, my lord. Not love, not passion, not even lust – a performance. Something you could have had for pence from any cheap mummer.' Her mouth curved in mockery. 'And you were too much of an arrant fool to know the difference!'

A ripple of amusement ran through the hall, as those at the nearest table passed her words on to their neighbours. Sir Edmund glared from face to face until it died away.

His face was white with shock and fury. 'You're lying!' he snarled.

She picked up a morsel of meat, popped it between her lips and smiled. 'Am I, my lord? And how would you know?' She stared fixedly at his face until he shuffled uncomfortably in his seat. 'Have you looked in the mirror recently?' Do you honestly believe those features would inspire love in a maiden's heart? I think not. You have but one eye, and that scar... God's blood, sir, I have seen better looking jack-o'-lanterns! Small wonder you have to pay. No woman in her right mind would bed you willingly.'

His hand lashed out, catching her on the cheek with a loud retort and making her head spin.

She smiled through the pain, quoting his words back at him. 'What, my lord? Cat got your tongue? Have you no witty riposte to put me in my place?' She paused, her eyes flashing defiantly. 'Obviously not, when violence is your only answer. Where did you learn your wooing skills, sirrah? In the stables with the other beasts?'

'You will soon find out,' he promised grimly. 'And then I think you will regret your foolhardy words.'

She rose swiftly to her feet. 'In that case, my lord, in for a penny, in for a pound, as they say.' Lifting her manchet, she broke it over his head. Meat juices and bits of broken bread slid down his horrified face and dripped on to his satin doublet. 'There, my lord, your appearance is much improved.'

Head held high, she stalked through the stunned silence in the hall. As soon as she had left it she took to her heels, and as she fled along the corridor she could hear the laughter swelling in her wake. Laughter at Sir Edmund's expense.

Back in the safety of her room she banged the door shut and leaned against it, giggling. What a fool the man had looked with his hair plastered to his scalp and gobbets of meat dribbling down his ugly face. It had been worth a king's ransom just to see it.

Gradually her laughter died away to be replaced with apprehension. She must be mad to do what she had just done. She had humiliated him in front of his entire household. He would never forgive her for that, and as he had already pointed out, between these stone walls he held the power of life or death.

She shivered, suddenly cold despite the crackling fire. Every castle had its oubliette: a small hidden cell, where those who had displeased the lord of the manor could be imprisoned and conveniently forgotten about. Forever. Perhaps in centuries to come they would find her remains – a small heap of bones, mouldering to dust – and wonder what she had done to deserve such a fate.

She shook herself. Sir Edmund would never condemn her to death. He still lusted after her body far too much to deprive himself of it by shutting her away to rot. The thought was not a particularly comforting one. She had laughed at him, and impugned his manhood in front of his men. It was the worst thing a woman could do. What would he not do to punish her for that?

She shivered again, remembering a young whore she had seen once, when her family had visited nearby York. Her face had been hideously scarred and she had overheard the servants discussing her. 'Used to be a rich man's mistress,' they whispered, 'till he caught her putting the cuckold's horns on him with one of the grooms.' The poor creature had been in a terrible plight; gaunt, haggard and reduced to servicing all comers for a few farthings. Would that be her fate, too? She pushed the thought away. Even death would be preferable to that.

Hugging herself for comfort, she walked up and down her chamber. As the candles burned lower and the shadows in the corners lengthened, her natural optimism reasserted itself. Perhaps he would not come after all, and by the time he had slept on his anger he would have mellowed.

She stopped suddenly, her head cocked to one side like a frightened doe. Was that the sound of footsteps echoing along the corridor? Her mouth dried and her heart began to pound. It was! He was coming! All her fears rushed back and she stared towards the door in dread.

She gasped as it swung open and banged against the wall. Judging by his flushed face and the smell of wine that oozed from his pores, it was obvious Sir Edmund had drowned his humiliation in his glass. The smile on his face was ugly, and as he strode into the room he stumbled. She cringed inwardly. Had he been sober she might have had a chance to reason with him; high-flown with drink, there was no chance.

'Wh-what do you want?' she stuttered. Even as the

words left her mouth she realised how ridiculous they were. She knew exactly what he wanted. Her only hope was that it would be over quickly.

He leered at her drunkenly. 'Why, I am come a-courting, madam,' he announced, his tongue tripping on the words.

She stared at him blankly. 'A-courting?' she echoed, in disbelief.

'Yes.' He sat down heavily on the bed, his expression becoming crafty. 'I have brought you a gift.'

'A gift?' she echoed again. Was she run mad – or had he?

'Isn't that what one does,' he asked, hiccuping, 'to win a fair maiden? As you so kindly pointed out, madam, my face will never be my fortune so I must find another way into your heart.' He beckoned to her. 'Come, see what I have brought you.'

Was it some kind of a trick? Reluctantly, she walked towards him. He brought one hand from behind his back and proffered her a small package, wrapped in a scrap of linen. She accepted it, and stared at him suspiciously.

'It's not a dead toad, is it?' she demanded, remembering her sixth birthday and a cousin with an unpleasant sense of humour.

He blinked at her, then roared with drunken laughter. 'A toad? What put that notion in your head? Why would I give you a toad?' The laughter stopped and he eyed her lasciviously. 'No, it's something for you to wear. Go on, open it.'

Could it be jewellery? Her fingers picked the knots apart and the linen fell undone. She stared at the contents in bewilderment. What on earth were they? And how was she supposed to wear them? She held up the brief scraps of leather and suddenly everything became clear. She shook her head in shock and disgust.

'I will not wear those – those garments...' Words failed her for a moment. She flung the unwanted present back in his face and glared at him. 'They are indecent. No respectable woman would.'

'But you are not a "respectable woman", are you, my love?' he sneered. 'You are my whore.' His lips tightened and his drunkenness fell away as if it had never existed. His voice was chilling in its coldness. 'And as such, you will wear whatever I tell you to wear. Now put them on!'

Her own mouth set in equally stubborn lines. 'I won't!' she replied, tossing her head.

His hand snaked out so suddenly she didn't even see it coming. Grasping her wrist, he pulled her towards him and, with one quick movement, flipped her over his knees. She struggled furiously but he held her with one hand while the other reached down and scooped her skirts over her head, revealing her plump buttocks and long flailing legs.

Sir Edmund paused for a moment to admire the sight, then raised his hand and brought it down sharply on her bottom. The smack of hard hand on yielding flesh echoed round the chamber like the crack of a whip. She shrieked, but her scream of pain and outrage was muffled by the material of her gown and came out as a pathetic squeak. His hand was large and calloused – and it hurt!

The first blow was swiftly followed by another, and yet another. The creamy globes of her buttocks quivered, whitened, then turned scarlet beneath his cruel ministrations. She writhed in pain, but all that served to do was increase his excitement and she could feel his member growing beneath her, pressing hot and hard against her belly. Her shrieks turned to whimpers as the punishment continued and discomfort spread through her lower body. It felt as if she had been scalded, her bottom almost incandescent – and still he went on, until she would have promised anything if only he would stop.

Finally he did, pushing her from his knees to fall in a tumbled heap at his feet. Her face was almost as scarlet as the cheeks of her bottom and she stared up at him from tear-drenched eyes.

'Now,' he panted, 'do I have to repeat the punishment, or will you do as I have bidden you?'

She nodded, unable to speak.

'Good,' he said, unsmiling. He picked up the scraps of leather and cast them at her feet. 'Put these on and no more shilly-shallying. I am becoming impatient.'

Stiffly, she got to her feet and, modestly turning her back, began to disrobe.

He clicked his fingers in annoyance. 'Not like that, girl,' he snapped. 'Turn round. I want to see the merchandise I am buying.' Closing her eyes to shut out the sight of his leering face, she did as she was told. She winced as the flame-coloured gown slid down over her hips, hardly able to bear the touch even of the soft satin against her throbbing skin.

He let out a soft whistle of appreciation as she stood naked in front of him. Pert breasts, heaving with every ragged breath, stood proud against her ribcage and the tiny waist served only to emphasise the fullness of the swelling hips beneath. At the juncture of her slender thighs blazed the guardian fire to the secret temple of pleasure. He smiled with satisfaction. She might have driven a hard bargain, but he was going to get full value for his money!

Her breasts swayed softly as she bent to pick up the scraps of leather, making him harden even more. 'I hope you appreciate the trouble I've taken to acquire these,' he said. 'I had the garments made especially by the old crone who does the washing and mending. In her younger days she was like you. Provided other services, if you take my meaning. Mind, it would be a strong-stomached or desperate man who'd ask her for those favours now. She earns her living by sewing, now. You should have seen the pleasure she took in making those. Wouldn't surprise me if she'd once worn something like them herself.'

Jane was aware of him watching eagerly as she stepped into the tiny briefs, revealing a tantalising glimpse of her most secret place as she pulled them up her slender thighs. The leather cupped her buttocks like a second skin, outlining their firm contours – but it was not just that which excited him. Lacking a crotch, they framed her vulva, pulling the lips slightly apart to show the glistening pink between. She shuddered and tried to hide her shame. He glared at her, one fist raised, and her hand reluctantly dropped away.

Her breasts swung as she leaned to pick up the top from where he had flung it at her feet, then rose as she lifted her arms to slip into it. It was equally revealing. The cunningly stitched leather forced her breasts up until the soft flesh seemed on the verge of overflowing, and the peaks of her nipples thrust through strategically cut holes, forced into rigidity by the constricting material. The effect was deliciously wicked, somehow even more sinful than her nakedness alone would have been. He drew a ragged breath, his manhood swelling even further, pushing urgently against his codpiece. He unlaced himself and it sprang out, long and thick, its engorged head gleaming red in the firelight. Jane gasped, her first instinct to cower back, hunched up to conceal herself from his lustful gaze. Instead, she flung her head back defiantly and straightened her shoulders. The movement forced her breasts even more tightly against their constriction and she groaned inwardly as a familiar feeling of excitement coursed through her veins. Subduing it, she glared at him.

'Well,' she sneered, 'do you not wish to take possession of your property?' Her lip curled as she gazed contemptuously at his throbbing member. He seemed so close to spending his seed, at least it would be over quickly.

He leaned back and grinned. 'Oh no, my lady. You do not get off so lightly. Since I am such an appalling lover, then you must show me what pleases you.'

He raised one eyebrow. 'How else am I to learn?'

She stared at him in dismay. 'Wh-what do you mean?' she demanded.

His grin widened. 'Why, madam, is it not obvious? I wish to watch you pleasure yourself.'

'Oh, no!' she gasped. The very idea of it appalled her. The thought of him leering avidly while she fingered herself was so humiliating it was not to be borne.

'Oh, yes,' he sneered. He pointed at the chest. 'Sit there, whore, and part your legs for me.'

Shuddering, she did as she was told. The thin leather cut into the juncture of her thighs, forcing the lips of her vulva even wider. He licked his lips. She was fully exposed now, as juicy and glistening as a freshly opened fig. One hand went to his shaft, gripping it as he watched her.

'I am becoming impatient, my lady,' he warned as she sat there gazing at him, her eyes fixed on his. He ignored their mute plea. 'Begin… otherwise it will be the worse for you.'

Closing her eyes, she tentatively began to fondle her thrusting nipples, feeling their tips hard beneath her fingers. She drew her breath in as they tingled under her touch and she started to stroke them more firmly. In her mind she conjured up the picture of Robin, his head bent to her bosom, his eager mouth suckling her, his tongue teasing her flesh. Taking her nipples between finger and thumb she rolled and tugged them gently, imagining it was Robin's hands on her, not her own. Her breath came faster in her throat and she was no longer in her chamber but lying with her lover on the greensward beneath a canopy of leaves.

The heat of rising pleasure mingled with the heat from her beaten bottom, until pain and pleasure blended seamlessly to become one. She moaned, her mouth falling open as she lost herself in the sensations surging through her. Sir Edmund watched, rapt, as one hand continued to play with her erect nipples while the other strayed lower, down over the soft curve of her belly until it reached her waiting cleft. She parted the lips of her sex even further, deftly teasing the soft bud of her clitoris into hardness before slipping first one finger then another into the waiting wetness. Slowly at first, she began to slide them in and out, then her movements became faster as her excitement mounted. As she neared the peak she flung her head back and groaned rhythmically with every thrust. Beads of perspiration glistened on her flushed body like tiny jewels.

With a groan he leapt across the room, dragged her to her feet and pulled her against him, his rigid cock pressing into her belly like an iron bar. Her erotic dream shattered into a thousand pieces and she was back in her chamber with a man she despised. Rudely deprived of her climax one hand, the fingers still glistening with her own juices, reached out to claw his hated face. He grabbed her wrists and forced her arms behind her. The movement thrust her breasts against him and she groaned as the rough material of his doublet grazed their sensitive tips.

His expression was bestial. With a snarl he flung her face down on the bed, then flung himself after her. Kneeling behind her he slid one arm around her waist, pulling her up so that her bottom jutted in the air like that of a cat in heat, her wet opening offered to him.

With a groan he thrust his prick against it. There was a tiny moment of resistance, then he gasped as the swollen head was enveloped in her silken heat.

His hips jerked again and she whimpered as the whole shaft buried itself in her body. She closed her eyes and moaned again as he started to move, his cock filling her completely. Her pleasure began to mount once more and she pushed her hips backwards against him, matching each thrust until there was nothing else in the universe but his turgid prick inside her. One hand reached down to stroke her clitoris, moving in time with each shuddering breath until she could bear it no longer. With an animal howl she climaxed, her spasming vulva clamping down on him rhythmically until he groaned deep in his throat and spent himself in one last, monstrous thrust. Gasping, he collapsed on top of her, sweat cooling on his fevered skin.

He was the first to recover. Pulling away, he stood up and adjusted his clothing as he regained control of his breathing. He grinned down, his expression smug as she rolled over and glared up at him, his seed still glistening on her thighs.

'Well, madam, another portion of your bargain completed,' he said coolly. 'And what payment shall we say for this little bout?' He clicked his fingers. 'I have it. The dorter. Or do you not appreciate the irony of being given the celibate sisters' sleeping quarters in exchange for such hot and sleepless sin?'

She gritted her teeth as she stared at his exultant face. Damn her treacherous body! How could it respond so vilely to a man she loathed and detested? 'That will do very well,' she muttered. 'Pray tell Father Andrew to add it to his list.' She rolled on her side so that she did not have to look at him. Her passion spent, she could not bear to spend another minute in his company. 'Now go. You have taken what you wanted. Leave me be, before I vomit at the very sight of you.'

'Do not deceive yourself, madam,' he said, casting her earlier words back at her. 'That was no "performance". You writhed beneath me as eager as a bitch in heat. I did not take what was not offered freely.' He reached down and pulled her back round to face him again.

'You make a good whore, my fine lady,' he whispered tauntingly, 'but do not think you can rest upon your laurels. Next time we shall try something a little... different. And we shall see how you enjoy that.'

With that, he stalked from the room, leaving her staring after him in dismay. She shivered, the perspiration on her skin suddenly icy. 'Something different'? What could he possibly mean by that?

Chapter Nineteen

'What? Still abed, my lady?' came a mocking voice. 'And the morning already half-gone, too.' Footsteps crossed the room. Jane heard the rattle of rings along the wooden bed-pole and light spilled across her pillow.

It cut through her troubled dreams like a sword. She groaned, rolled over and opened her eyes, covering them with one arm to shut out the early morning sun. Even half-blinded she could recognise the dark figure, hands on hips and legs wide, silhouetted against the window. Just so had King Henry stood in a portrait she had seen once; the same male arrogance, the same knowledge that he was master. She was suddenly fully awake.

'What do you want?' she stammered fearfully, struggling into a sitting position and pulling the coverlet up to hide her naked breasts. 'Surely even you are not so lost to decency as to take me against my will, in broad daylight. Have you no shame?'

Sir Edmund gave her a hurt look. 'Why, mistress, you misjudge me,' he said. 'When my only intention was to please you.' He gestured towards the window. 'Look, the sun is up. The dew still lies upon the grass. It is a fine morning to go a-hunting. Do you not wish to join me?'

She glared at him suspiciously. Was this another trick? She took in his worn leather jerkin, the sturdy woollen hose and the scuffed riding boots. Perhaps not. Not even he would come to her bedchamber booted and spurred, surely? She became aware of voices rising from the courtyard below: the jingle of harness and the clatter and whinny of horses, fresh from the stable and eager for the chase.

Sudden excitement ran through her. It been so long since she had been on a proper ride, galloping with the wind in her hair, feeling the silken surge of powerful horseflesh between her thighs. For a moment she forgot how cruelly Sir Edmund had abused her and gave him a smile of genuine pleasure. 'I thank you for your kindness, my lord,' she replied. 'It would please me greatly.'

'Good,' he grunted. 'Then dress – and quickly, mind. I do not like to be kept waiting.'

As soon as he had left she leaped from her bed and rummaged through her faithful chest, finding a serviceable linsey-woolsey in a warm reddish-brown. The boots she discovered at the bottom of the chest were dry and cracked and far too big, but they would have to do. Lacking a hat, she scraped her hair back and pinned it firmly. She glanced at the rosy-cheeked girl in the mirror and winked approval at her reflection.

She ran down the stairs and out through the heavy door into the sunshine. Sir Edmund and his men were already horsed and waiting. With a smile of thanks to the groom who offered his linked palms, she mounted the bay mare and the small group cantered out through the gates.

The day was as cool and crisp as an autumn apple and she drew a deep breath, savouring the sweet taste of freedom. The horses left a trail of wet hoof prints through the long grass as they rode, the hounds sniffing the air for the scent of their quarry. It was like a scene from some ancient tapestry.

She was brought from her reverie by Sir Edmund drawing his horse alongside hers. 'I trust you are enjoying yourself, madam?' he enquired politely.

'I am, sir,' she replied. 'It is a pleasant morning.'

'Let us hope the hunting is good,' he went on. 'There is nothing like the chase to raise the heart and set the blood pounding in one's veins.' The scar on the side of his face twitched unpleasantly as his lips curled in a cruel smile. He leaned over and kneaded her thigh with one gloved hand. 'Or perhaps there is. We shall find that out tonight, shall we not, my lady?' He jerked the reins and his horse shied and pulled away, leaving her staring after him.

Why did he have to go and spoil things? For a few moments she had managed to forget her situation. Now he had brought it home again – and all the worse for her brief illusion of freedom. His words came back to her: 'We shall try something a little... different.' They pounded in her head, over and over, in time with her horse's hooves, and she felt the familiar sickness rising in her belly.

The view hulloo distracted her. On the edge of the woods stood a stag, its antlers gleaming in the sun. As the sound of the horn shattered the morning, it gave one startled glance and bounded off. The hounds raised their heads as one and set off baying, the men and horses in hot pursuit.

She felt her own mount tense beneath her, desperate to join the race, but she dragged on the reins, holding it back. Thoughtfully she watched as the hunt disappeared, leaving her behind in the clearing.

She was alone for the first time in months. No Mother Ursula. No Sir Edmund. No servants poking and prying and watching her every move. Her thoughts raced. If she fled now it would be at least two hours before they noticed she was gone. She could dig up her hidden treasures and be long away before they even noticed she was missing.

But what about her bargain with Sir Edmund? If she fled now it would be rendered null and void. Her hard-won property would revert to him and the local peasants would be left with nothing – to starve or ail without help or comfort.

Self-preservation won over conscience. What were they to her? And she had tried her best – she could hardly be blamed if she could not bear to carry on. She was no holy martyr, she was only an eighteen-year-old girl.

Guiltily, she dragged on the reins and pulled her horse round in the opposite direction from the one Sir Edmund and his men had taken. Taking a deep breath, she prepared to spur her mount to freedom, then paused as the bushes nearby rustled and two figures stepped out.

'Mistress,' called a low voice. Jane stared as an ill-dressed woman hurried towards her, tugging her child behind her. She stopped, bobbed a curtsy and stood looking up at Jane, her hands nervously twisting her ragged apron.

'Yes,' snapped Jane as each moment lessened her chances of escape, 'what is it, my good woman? Make haste. I have no time to tarry in idle chat.'

'I am sorry to detain you, mistress,' the woman said humbly. 'I only wished to thank you.'

'Thank me? Thank me for what?'

'My son's life,' she replied, her expression suddenly alive with happiness. For a moment Jane could see the carefree girl beneath the careworn face. The woman drew her reluctant son from behind her skirts and thrust him forward for Jane's inspection. He stood staring up at her, wide-eyed, one grubby finger stuck in his mouth. 'See?' the woman said eagerly. 'Thanks to you his leg has healed and scarce left a limp.'

It all came back to her now. This was the woman who had brought her bleeding child to the convent, what seemed a lifetime ago. She cast a professional eye over the skinny leg. The scar was still red and inflamed, but there was none of the oozing yellow pus or blackening flesh that anyone skilled in tending the wounded knew and dreaded. She smiled down at the woman.

'The scar will always remain,' she said, 'but it will fade a little with time. As for the limp, it will go as the child grows and his legs strengthen.' Provided of course he got enough to eat and did not fall prey to the myriad ills that lay in wait for rich and poor alike.

Seizing the hem of Jane's skirt, the woman brought it to her lips and kissed it reverently. 'A thousand blessings, my lady,' she said fervently. 'I will remember you in my prayers. God must have sent you to me in my hour of need.' With one last grateful glance, she scooped up her son and fled back the way she had come.

Jane stared after her in despair. Why had the woman turned up now, just as she was on the verge of fleeing herself? Without her skill and knowledge that child would be mouldering in a pauper's grave by now, and how many more like him were there who would die if there was no convent to rely on? She heaved a bitter sigh. There was no way she could leave now.

Wearily, she wheeled her horse round in the direction of the hunt and spurred its flanks. No doubt she would meet Sir Edmund and his men as they returned.

She had almost reached the rise over which they had disappeared when the sound of pounding hooves filled the air. She stared in surprise as they galloped over the ridge to meet her. How odd. She would have expected them to be miles away by this time. Had they run the stag down so soon? She looked, but there was no bloodied carcass. Had it escaped, and if so, why had they not followed it?

Sir Edmund drew up beside her, his horse's sides heaving with exertion. He leaned on the pommel, regarding her, his face inscrutable. 'What? Still here, madam? We thought we had lost you.'

She scanned his face, trying to read his expression, her skin prickling. Then horrified realisation dawned on her and her mouth dropped open. 'Oh,' she gasped and a hand flew to her lips. 'You... you planned this all, didn't you?' She shook her head in a vain attempt to rid herself of the knowledge of his treachery. 'I was *supposed* to run, wasn't I?' she said softly. She waited for his denial, but the truth was written on his face. '"A fine day for the hunt" you said,' she went on remorselessly. 'But it wasn't a deer you had in mind, was it? I was to be the quarry!'

She closed her eyes, seeing everything. Her panic-stricken flight. The hounds baying after her. Sir Edmund and his henchmen in hot pursuit, urging each other on as they hunted her down. And what of when they caught her? The vision of the carcass of a deer, lying gutted on the ground, sprang into her mind and she shuddered. Her fate would have been worse. She stared from one hard face to the other. With the bloodlust on them they would have torn the clothes from her back and fallen on her like snarling animals, fighting amongst themselves to possess her.

She swayed and would have fallen had Sir Edmund not caught her arm. His touch was enough to revive her. Revulsion surged and she snatched her arm away.

'Don't touch me, you bastard!' she snarled. 'You make me sick to my very stomach.' Her lips twisted in contempt. 'I am truly sorry to have disappointed you. How inconsiderate of me to have spoilt your sport.'

He shrugged. 'No matter, madam. I am sure I shall think of some other entertainment.' He grinned unrepentantly and something inside her snapped.

Her fingers hooked into claws, she dashed forward and, before he could stop her, she dragged them down the side of his face. Her nails caught the twisted scar on his cheek, tearing through the puckered skin as if it were paper. Blood welled up and ran in freshets down his face, dripping from his chin and staining the front of his leather jerkin. She stared in fright at what she had done.

He did not even flinch. Only his face changed. It became deathly white, the scar standing out angrily. His expression changed to one of furious rage, twice as terrifying because it was kept under such iron control. His blue eye flashed coldly.

'The man who gave me this scar died for the privilege, madam,' he said icily. 'Perhaps by the time I have finished, you will wish you had, too.' He turned to his men. 'Escort Lady Jane back to the castle. I have business elsewhere.'

The journey back was a miserable one. The little party rode in silence, even Sir Edmund's men seeming subdued. In the courtyard Jane dismounted and, without a backward glance, ran to the relative safety of her chamber.

When hours had passed without Sir Edmund's retribution descending upon her, she eventually ventured out. Tiptoeing along the corridors, she reached the hall. To her great relief it was empty. The servants were obviously at their own meal in the kitchens, because the remains of the last meal still lay scattered on the tables. Glancing nervously over her shoulder, she seized a broken chunk of bread, a lump of cheese and a half-full tankard of ale. Clutching the food she fled to the solar, opened the door and slipped inside.

A fire burnt low in the grate. She poked it into life, laid another log on it and seated herself beside it, grateful for the warmth. Despite the autumn sun spilling through the window she felt chilled to the bone. Fear had stolen her appetite, but she forced herself to eat regardless, and felt stronger once she had.

Dusting the crumbs from her lap, she put the tankard

down on the hearth and stared into the flames. What now? She couldn't bear the thought of sitting idle. With nothing to do but brood on what the night might bring she would run mad.

Her embroidery frame stood beside the window seat and she seized on it gratefully. Concentrating on her needle would help to shut out the frightening thoughts that threatened to overwhelm her.

It was easier said than done. No matter how hard she tried, Sir Edmund's face kept coming between her and the work in front of her, his threats echoing in her ears. She gritted her teeth and stabbed the needle viciously into the linen, wishing it was his eye. Ridiculous though it was, this relieved her feelings somewhat and she was finally able to lose herself in the mindless task of stitching.

When she looked up again, she was astonished to see that the sun was sinking behind the horizon and the room was darkening. A tap on the door made her jump. 'Who is it?' she called nervously, then berated herself for her stupidity. Of course it wasn't Sir Edmund. He wouldn't have bothered knocking. He'd probably have kicked the door down!

'Iss just me,' called a familiar voice.

'Martha!' she exclaimed in relief. 'Come in.'

When nothing happened she put down her silks and hurried across to open the door. It immediately became obvious why Martha hadn't entered. She was almost staggering beneath the weight of a laden tray. Delicious aromas wafted from beneath the covered dishes and Jane's stomach rumbled in response.

'Shouldn't you be in the kitchens?' she asked. 'Why didn't you send this with one of the maids?'

'What? Them empty-headed strumpets?' snorted Martha. 'By the time they'd finished making sheep's eyes at the men my good food would be stone cold. No, if you wants something doing proper, do it yourself, thass my motto.' She nodded in agreement with herself. 'Now you sit down like a good girl and get something inside you.'

Obediently Jane seated herself at the table while Martha laid the dishes in front of her. There was bread, kale soup, half a chicken, a bowl of apples – even a dish of marchpane sweetmeats and a dust-covered bottle of wine to go with it. 'I'll never manage all this,' exclaimed Jane. 'Why don't you join me?'

Martha looked shocked. 'Me? Eat with the mistress?' She shook her head. 'Thass not right. I knows my place.'

Jane smiled to herself at the cook's reaction. In her own way, Martha was far more of a lady than Sir Edmund was a gentleman. The stray thought brought him back to the forefront of her mind. 'Does Sir Edmund eat in the hall tonight?' she asked casually.

Martha shook her head. 'There's neither hide nor hair of him,' she said. 'Not since he rode off after the hunt this morning. And good riddance to bad rubbish, I says. Forever glaring at you with that one ol' eye of his! That ugly face is enough to put any good Christian off their meat.'

Jane could not help but wonder what Sir Edmund had said, had he been present to hear Martha's apt assessment of his looks. Perhaps he had ridden off to tend to his other estates? At that comforting thought, her appetite returned and she ate her meal with gusto as Martha stood by, watching with satisfaction.

'Thass a good girl,' Martha beamed, stacking the empty plates on the tray. She folded her arms on her ample bosom and looked thoughtfully at Jane. 'Now you get yourself off early to bed and get a decent night's rest. Put some roses back in your cheeks.' She nodded to the bottle and winked. 'Thass his lordship's best wine. Another couple of glasses of that and you'll sleep like a baby.'

'I thank you for your kindness, Martha,' Jane said sincerely. 'What would I do without you?'

'Hah!' scoffed Martha, trying to hide her pleasure. 'You don't need some fat old hen clucking round you. You'm got a stout heart, girl. Supposing you was cast adrift in nothing but your shift, you'd still manage fine.' She picked up the tray. 'Now, drink your wine by the fire, then off to bed with you.'

Once Martha had gone, Jane took her advice. Belly full, she sat dreamily watching the flames and sipping the sweet red wine. Sir Edmund was safely gone – to hell for all she cared – and she was free from her constant fear. When she caught herself dozing she roused herself, picked up a candle and wended her way to her bedchamber.

There was another fire burning in the grate and the sheets were still cosy from the maid's services with the copper bed-warmer. Yawning, she stripped, slipped on her night rail and slid gratefully between the warm sheets. Pulling them up round her shoulders, she snuggled down and was asleep in moments.

'Wake up, you little bitch!' snarled a familiar voice. The sheets were wrenched from her and Jane was catapulted from her dreams into shocked wakefulness. For a moment she did not know where she was; then it all rushed back. But what was Mother Ursula doing in her bedchamber?

The dying coals illuminated the woman's face in a hellish red glow, the saliva on her teeth glistening like blood. Jane shuddered. Mother Ursula looked like a gargoyle brought to life by some evil spell. She tried to hide her fear.

'Get out!' she hissed. 'If Sir Edmund finds out about

this you will rue the very day you were born.'

There was a chuckle from the darkness and Jane started, peering into the shadows. One hand flew to her breast as Sir Edmund stepped into the light and bowed. 'Good evening, madam,' he smiled. 'As to Mother Ursula, why, she is here at my own invitation.' He raised an eyebrow. 'Your manners are remiss. Should you not greet her?'

Jane ignored his taunt. 'Why have you brought her here?' she demanded.

He grinned. 'A little notion of mine. I thought tonight's payment for your favours should be the chapel. Who better then to join us in our revels than the erstwhile mistress of the convent? Besides,' he went on, 'I rather think she has a crow to pluck with you – which should add a little extra spice to this evening's entertainment.'

'No,' gasped Jane, gazing beseechingly at him. 'I beg of you, no!'

'Oh, yes,' he said with relish. He touched the scar on his cheek, still crusted with dried blood where she had clawed him. 'Did I not warn you that you would pay for this? Well, it is time to settle your reckoning.' He clicked his fingers. 'Seize her!'

Mother Ursula needed no second telling. Grasping hold of the night rail she ripped it from Jane's back and hauled her from the bed. Her bony fingers dug viciously into Jane's arms as she pulled them behind her back.

'Excellent,' purred Sir Edmund as he regarded Jane's naked, struggling body, admiring her heaving breasts and the way the firelight gilded her smooth flesh. 'And now, the *pièce de résistance*.' With a flourish he produced an object from behind his back. It gleamed dully, and Jane froze.

'Wh-what is that?' she quavered. He shook it tauntingly before her eyes and it produced a musical jingling sound.

'It is a hood, madam,' he explained. 'If a falcon or a kestrel strikes out of turn, what do we do? We hood it, lest it strike again. Your claws drew blood today, my little bird, but I do not think they will again.' He glared at Ursula. 'Hold her!'

She struggled even more frantically, but Ursula held her in a grip of steel as he slipped the hood over her head, plunging her into suffocating darkness. She gasped for breath, then sighed with relief as she found the mouth-hole and drew blessed air into her grateful lungs. At least they did not mean to kill her. With the grotesque beaked hood, she looked like some mythical creature, half bird and half woman. Totally disorientated as she was, every sensation was magnified. Jane was aware of each individual nail on Ursula's fingers as they dug into her, could feel each diseased breath on the back of her neck, feel even the firelight as it danced across her skin. She shivered, her nipples tightening.

The next thing she was aware of was Sir Edmund's husky voice. 'Tie her to the bed. I would take my pleasure.' Within her confines, Jane relaxed. Perhaps her ordeal would be over sooner than she thought.

'You said I could punish her,' whined Mother Ursula. 'You promised!' The woman sounded like a bad-tempered child denied a sweetmeat. Jane tensed again, offering up a quick prayer that his lust would overcome him.

It was not answered. 'I did, didn't I?' he purred in reply. 'And a gentleman never breaks his word.' Jane could hear the twisted amusement in his voice as he used the same words to Mother Ursula as he had used to her. And her heart sank as she heard his next words. 'Do with her as you will.'

The world exploded into pain as Mother Ursula pushed her face down across the bed, wrenched her arms above her head and bound her wrists cruelly tight, fastening them to the bed-pole. Her legs were still free and she kicked desperately, but to no avail. Blinded as she was, her flailing legs met nothing but empty air. A sharp fingernail ran the length of her spine, almost breaking the skin, and she tensed in fear, dreading what must be coming next.

She did not have long to wait. Mother Ursula's gloating laugh was followed by a high-pitched, whistling noise and Jane shrieked as the lash met her quivering flesh in a burning kiss.

Sir Edmund drew in his breath as a thin red line appeared across the trembling globes of her buttocks. Mother Ursula cackled and raised her arm again.

Jane jerked and screamed as another red line appeared, lower this time, as the lash licked the soft skin just below where the sweet curves of her bottom met the smooth thighs. Sir Edmund's mouth was dry and his prick throbbed within its confines.

Another blow and another. Jane's bottom and thighs gleamed rosily where the blood had rushed to the surface. The chamber was silent now, except for Jane's muffled moaning, the slap of leather on flesh and Mother Ursula's grunts of pleasure. The nun raised her arm again, then snarled with thwarted rage as Sir Edmund seized her wrist before the blow could fall.

'Enough,' he ordered, pushing her away. 'Do you wish to mar the girl for life? Or worse?' He grunted as he fumbled at his hose. 'I do not wish to slake my lust upon a corpse.'

Jane whimpered again as he pulled her unresisting body round until she was lying face upwards. The movement had loosened her bonds a little, but they still bit into her wrists. There was no escape, no matter how hard she wrenched to free herself. She lay blind and helpless as his eager hands explored her body, wincing as he pinched her nipples until they began to rise. There was a pause, then she gasped as each teat in turn was enveloped in warm wetness. She moaned again, this time with reluctant pleasure, as his tongue circled one tight bud and his thumb stroked the other, teasing both into full hardness.

Bony hands seized Jane's ankles and pulled her legs apart. She tensed with fear as sharp fingernails scratched the soft insides of her thighs, creeping higher, towards her most privy place. What was Mother Ursula doing now? She braced herself for more agony.

It didn't come. Instead, she felt the soft lips of her vulva being parted and an eager tongue thrusting its way in, probing at first, then lapping at the hard nub at the centre of her being. The heat from her beaten bottom melded into the heat from her loins and she bit her lip, trying to suppress the wicked sensations. This was sin upon sin! Another woman licking at her private parts – and she was responding! Ursula slipped two fingers into the silky wetness and began to move them in time to her lapping tongue. Jane groaned and shuddered as waves of wicked pleasure washed through her, her hips rising to meet each new thrust.

Sir Edmund watched as Mother Ursula's tongue and fingers darted in and out of Jane's sweet cunny, her other hand plunging between her own thighs. He groaned aloud, his cock rigid with lust. Seizing the pillow he stuffed it beneath Jane's head, then straddled her upper body. Gripping her breasts he moulded them together and thrust himself between them, his thumbs still stroking their rampant crests as he rocked backwards and forwards.

Beneath her hood, Jane moaned again, no longer aware of who was doing what to her, but only of her own mounting pleasure. Sir Edmund gasped as he released her breasts and moved higher up the bed until his straining prick was pressed against the mouth-hole of the hood. She obediently opened her lips and drew him in, accepting the feel of the swollen head. She traced its smooth rim, then flicked its blind eye with her tongue, and it was Sir Edmund's turn to groan. His hips quickened as he plunged in and out of her snug, moist mouth.

Jane felt him swell, his loins shuddering, and groaned with satisfaction. The feel of the stiff prick thrusting into her mouth and Mother Ursula's eager tonguing had brought her to the peak of ecstasy. She no longer cared whether this was a sin, she only wanted it to go on until she exploded with pleasure.

His cock jerked and spasmed and she felt the sweet rush of his seed against the roof of her mouth. She swallowed greedily as her own climax took her, bringing her to shuddering release, and she sagged against the pillows as he withdrew, ignoring Mother Ursula's high-pitched moans as she, too, spent her solitary lust.

Sir Edmund was the first to recover and Jane blinked in dazed bewilderment as he pulled the hood from her head and smirked down at her. 'It seems you found this more pleasure than punishment, madam.' His lips twisted in a sneer. 'What a rampant little strumpet you are.'

He walked to the foot of the bed, kicked Mother Ursula and hauled her to her feet, her thin lips still glistening with Jane's juices. 'As for you, bitch, back to the kennels with you.' He pushed her towards the door, then paused on the threshold, turning back to Jane. 'They say that appetite grows by feeding. Perhaps next time we will find something more substantial to satisfy it.'

She stared after him in dismay, humiliation sweeping over her in a hot tide as she remembered how eagerly she had responded to him and, even worse, to Ursula. She groaned and tears of shame trickled down her cheeks. How much lower could she sink?

Chapter Twenty

As Sir Edmund loomed over her, whip in hand, Jane started awake with a shriek of terror. Then stared round her room, blinking in bewilderment. It was empty. No whip-wielding monster. No Mother Ursula leering down at her as she prepared to abuse the helpless body before her. Nothing but the late morning sunlight gilding the wooden panelling. She sighed with relief and sagged back against her pillows. It wasn't real. It had only been a nightmare.

The discarded dress, still lying in a crumpled heap on the floor, brought the previous night's events flooding back to her and she groaned in despair. Reality was worse than any nightmare.

Her back still hurt from Mother Ursula's beating, but worst of all was the shame that scalded her as she recalled how she had responded to their attentions. Even now her nipples were hardening in response to the memory and the secret place between her thighs throbbed demandingly, aching to be filled again by his thrusting prick. She groaned out loud and leaped from her bed. The water in the basin and ewer was icy, despite the sun shining through the window, and she fell on it gratefully, shuddering as she splashed it over her overheated body as if she could wash the sin of lust away. Cold and shivering, but blessedly free now of her tormenting urges, she wrapped herself in the drying-cloth and opened the cedar chest.

The dress she chose was as ugly as it was practical. Dark, loose and high-necked, it enveloped her from head to toe, hiding her hips and breasts like a nun's habit. She sighed, reached for her girdle and encircled her waist, then picked up her comb. Wincing, she tugged it through the tangles until her long hair fell into loose curls that hung softly over her shoulders. What was the point of scraping it back in an attempt to make herself undesirable? She'd tried that once already and it had failed to work, but at least in this voluminous gown she felt, in some strange way, safe.

The day lay before her emptily; nothing but another stretch of tedious hours to be filled before Sir Edmund came again to claim his rights upon her terrified body.

Her head came up as a horrible thought struck her. The deed! What if he had not fulfilled his side of the bargain? Even worse, what if he had taken it back from Father Andrew and destroyed it? Nothing was beyond him. She shook her head to clear it. She was worrying about nothing. He had given her his word.

But, once lodged in her consciousness, the worm of worry gnawed away at her certainty. How could she truly trust a man who abused her so? He would no doubt find it amusing to lead her on, take his pleasure upon her, then cast her out with nothing. She bit her lip. She could not settle until her mind was put at ease. After a moment's thought the solution to the problem presented itself. She would visit Father Andrew and see for herself, thus easing her mind and filling in the empty hours at the same time. Two birds killed with one stone.

The decision made, she was instantly more cheerful – then her face fell. What if Sir Edmund refused to let her leave the confines of the castle? Her lips set in resolution. What the mind didn't know, the heart didn't grieve over. She would visit the priest, but not as Lady Jane. The enveloping gown already hid a multitude of sins, and with the hood of her cloak pulled up to hide her distinctive hair, who would notice a serving-maid about her master's business? She set about pulling on the worn old boots, grateful now for their cracks and scuffs. Maidservants did not wear fine Moroccan leather slippers.

Head bowed, she scurried along the corridors and out into the courtyard. The sun had disappeared behind lowering grey clouds and heavy rain had begun to fall. By the time she came to the door of the kitchen her hair was plastered darkly against her scalp and her skirts were spattered with mud. She looked like any other draggle-tailed skivvy.

The kitchens were the usual seething mass of bodies and it was the work of a moment to pull a shabby cloak from the pegs at the door and wrap herself in it, tugging the hood up about her ears.

A familiar voice stopped her in her tracks. Martha! Her disguise had been penetrated already; her adventure stopped before it had even begun.

'Yes, you girl!' Jane turned and Martha glared at her without recognition. 'And just where d'ye think you're going?' she demanded, hands on hips. 'There's work to be done.'

'The privy, ma'am,' mumbled Jane meekly, head still bowed. 'I've got the bellyache.'

'Well, be quick about it,' ordered Martha. She thrust a large basket into Jane's hands. 'Here, do something useful while you're at it and gather them eggs on your way back.' She wagged a warning finger under Jane's nose. 'And if I finds out you been hanging about talking to them men instead of getting on with your work, there's going to be trouble. Now get on with it.'

A large hand propelled her firmly out of the door and into the rain again. Jane scarcely dared to believe her good luck. If Martha didn't recognise her, no one would. And the basket would add to her disguise. Poor Martha; she would have a long wait for her eggs. Jane could only hope she did not choose to take her disappointment out on some other poor unfortunate.

At the gate the guard did not even give her a second glance as she trudged through. She blessed the rain again. Had the sun still been out, no doubt he would have broken the boredom of his watch by chaffing any maid who crossed his path. As it was, he was far too busy trying to keep warm and dry to pay her any heed.

Outside she straightened her shoulders and took a deep breath. The air seemed cleaner away from the forbidding shadow of the castle. Resisting the urge to take to her heels and run, she plodded on, the veritable picture of a dutiful servant, resigned to an unpleasant task.

After half a mile it was no longer a pretence. Despite the cloak she was soaked to the skin, and the cracked boots had raised a blister on both heels. Thankfully, the church was only a mile away, on the outskirts of the village. As she crested the last hill it stood amongst the huddle of poor hovels, like a dowager duchess amongst a crowd of beggars.

The closer she got, the more she realised this was an illusion. This was nothing like the richly decorated chapel of the convent, with its polished wood and brass. The wall surrounding the graveyard was crumbling in several places and the stones had obviously been carried away long since, to be used elsewhere. As for the walls of the church itself, they were stained and cracked where ivy had grown wild and rank. Even the bell-tower looked distinctly precarious.

Inside, it was even worse. A puddle of water from the leaky roof sat in the centre of the aisle. The whitewashed walls were peeling and the mural of Christ on the cross behind the altar was so badly damaged by damp that the

Saviour had almost lost his face. Only one eye remained, to stare at her accusingly. The image reminded her unpleasantly of Sir Edmund. The solitary tallow light, flickering wildly in its battered pewter candlestick, barely impinged on the darkness and Jane's nose wrinkled at the stench of burning fat that filled the church. She shivered and pulled her wet cloak even more tightly round her. It was colder in here than it was outside.

A movement startled her as one of the shadows detached itself from the surrounding darkness and moved towards her. Her stomach clenched with fear, until she realised it was only Father Andrew.

She had not noticed before, but the priest was as shabby as his church. The hem of his cassock was frayed and the elbows had been clumsily darned. Despite this, he possessed a quiet dignity, at odds with his obvious poverty. 'How may I help you, my child?' he asked gently.

In response, she flung back her hood and his demeanour changed. 'My lady!' he gasped, bowing stiffly. 'My apologies. I did not know you.'

'No matter, Father,' she replied, smiling. 'We are all God's children, no matter how high or low our estate. I merely come to seek information.' She stared at him anxiously. 'Do you still have the deed Lord Edmund put into your safekeeping?'

'Of course, my lady. It is in the chest in my study. Do you wish to see it?' She nodded eagerly. 'Then come with me. There is a fire there. Please, you must dry yourself and allow me to offer you some refreshment.'

Gratefully, she followed him out of the church and into the priest's house that stood beside it. Peeling off her cloak, she held her hands to the feeble coals and looked round. His 'study' was a poor room, with only a rough chest beneath the window, a rickety table, a chair and a stool.

He dragged the chair towards the fire. 'Please rest, my lady, while I bring you some refreshment.' Once she had seated herself, he hurried out.

When he returned he had a bowl of thin broth and a hunk of bread in one hand and a horn cup of thin wine in the other. Only after she had greedily consumed both did the guilty realisation dawn on her that she had probably just devoured the poor man's meagre dinner.

'You must allow me to return the favour,' she said. 'I shall have a basket of provisions sent down from the castle to thank you for your generosity.' And she would stand over Martha herself to make sure she didn't skimp on it, either. 'Now, to business. May I see the deed?'

'Certainly,' he replied. He got stiffly to his feet, walked over to the window and raised the lid of the rough chest. 'Here we are,' he said, pulling out the scroll of parchment and proffering it to her. 'Sir Edmund rode over here himself, first thing this morning to amend it.'

She took it, unrolling it carefully and smoothing down the coarse parchment. Her eyes ran over the thick black ink and she sighed with relief. There it was, neatly added beneath the earlier script: 'The Chapel of the Convent of Saint Ursula'. She rolled it up again and handed it back.

'Thank you, Father,' she said. 'You have been most kind.'

'Not I,' he protested. 'It is Sir Edmund who is kind.' She gaped at him in disbelief. 'He explained it all to me,' he went on happily. 'How he is generously giving you the convent and its grounds for the benefit of the poor, in return for a few small services. Indeed, he is a truly Christian gentleman.'

Jane's disbelief turned to rage and she fumed inwardly. How dare he, the two-faced bastard? Exploiting her was bad enough, but to disguise his wickedness as good and pass himself off as a benefactor of the poor was beyond redemption. And he would hardly have bothered to enlighten the good Father as to the exact nature of the 'small services' he was claiming in return for all his so-called 'generosity'!

She opened her mouth to tell Father Andrew the truth about Sir Edmund, then stopped. He was still smiling over the supposed benevolence of his master, an expression of unworldly happiness on his face. Sir Edmund had already destroyed her innocence. Could she, in turn, now destroy that of this good old man? With a sigh, she nodded her head. 'A truly Christian gentleman,' she agreed, through gritted teeth. *And may his black soul rot in hell*! she added silently.

'I must go now,' she said, rising. 'My thanks again for your help – and your hospitality.'

Father Andrew beamed. 'You are welcome, my child. Is there no other service I may offer you, before you leave? Do you wish me to hear your confession, perhaps?'

She shook her head. 'Thank you, Father, but I must return to the castle. Mayhap another day, when there is more time.' Her confession? If she started on that they would be here till the trump of doom!

At the door he sketched the sign of the cross in the air and said a quick blessing. She bent her head and crossed herself in turn. Turning away from the brief moment of comfort, she set her face towards the castle again, and to the weary path ahead of her and whatever lay at its end.

If she had hoped to slip back into the castle as easily as she had left, she was very much mistaken. Instead of huddling out of the rain, the guard at the gate was standing rigidly to attention. At her approach his face broke into a relieved grin and he strode forward and gripped her arm as if to prevent her suddenly taking flight. Despite her struggles, he dragged her into the courtyard by brute force. 'I have her, sir,' he announced, hauling her up to his master.

'Unhand me, knave,' she snarled, shaking him off and glaring at Sir Edmund.

He was wearing his riding gear and was almost as bespattered with mud as she was. Stepping forward, he grabbed her shoulders and shook her till her teeth rattled. 'Just where the hell have you been, you treacherous little bitch?' he demanded. 'I've had this place turned upside down looking for you.'

'I merely walked out to see Father Andrew,' she retorted, wrenching herself free. 'Is visiting the church a crime, now?' She stared at him coolly. 'If so, perhaps you should shackle me and have done with it.'

'Don't tempt me,' he snarled. 'You'd not stray far with a set of leg irons round those delicate ankles.'

'Pretty sentiments for such a noble benefactor of the church,' she mocked. 'What a fine Christian gentleman you are!' He stared at her, taken aback by her response. 'Oh, yes,' she continued with a sneer. 'Father Andrew told me all about your "generosity"! Hedging your bets, are you? Hoping he will pray you into heaven?' She spat at his feet. 'I think not. It will take the hottest fire in hell to burn away your sins.'

'And yours, my lady,' he said softly. 'Or are you forgetting how eagerly you joined me in the sinning?' It was her turn to flush and he grinned in satisfaction. 'But I digress,' he went on. 'We have not finished discussing this morning's escapade.'

She opened her mouth to protest, but he stopped her. 'Don't waste your breath proclaiming your innocence,' he advised. 'That pretty story will not wash. Look at yourself!' His good eye raked her from head to foot, taking in the shabby gown and cloak and the egg-basket still clutched in one hand. 'What lady pays a visit to church dressed like a scarecrow? Do you think I am stupid? You knew exactly what you were doing, madam. Defying me yet again.' His lips set grimly. 'And for that you must be punished.'

He leaned forward until his face was almost touching hers. 'Perhaps you will be more anxious to obey your master after twenty-four hours with only bread and water for sustenance. Oh, and one last word on the subject of my sins, sweet lady.' He ran one finger teasingly over her lips. 'What I have done already is nothing to what I intend to do next. So, if confinement bores you, think on that. Anticipation should help to while away the weary hours.' He stepped back, clicked his fingers and two men-at-arms leaped to his command.

'Take her away,' he ordered. 'And lock her in the turret room.'

Chapter Twenty-One

Kicking and struggling, Jane was hustled across the courtyard to the east tower. The heavy door was unlocked and she was thrust over the threshold towards the narrow winding stairs. One guard pulled her upwards while the other, the erstwhile gatekeeper, followed behind to bar her escape.

'Little bitch,' he muttered, smacking her viciously on the rump. 'Cost me a week's wages, you did, sneaking out like that. Know what the sergeant said?' He mimicked his commanding officer. '"What kind of a guard are you, when you let a slip of a girl get past you?"' His voice became self-pitying. 'Then he docked my pay to "teach me a lesson".' Jane closed her ears to the string of curses that followed.

His companion grinned at him over her head. 'That little black-haired whore won't be so welcoming this week then, if you can't pay her. Poor Dickon. I'll think about you going without when I'm buried between her plump thighs.'

'Seems to me her ladyship here should make it up to me,' grumbled Dickon. Jane shuddered as his hand fumbled beneath her skirts and thrust its way upwards. He prodded crudely at her sex, seeking entrance, and his breath came heavy in his throat.

'Who's to know?' he panted, fingering her excitedly until, despite herself, her juices began to flow. 'There's only us here. We could take turns.'

'Fair enough,' agreed his companion. 'If you fancy singing soprano, that is. Old One-Eye'll have your balls on a plate if you so much as lay a finger on his doxy – let alone anything else!'

Dickon's hand withdrew abruptly. Jane breathed a sigh of relief, then squealed as he hit her bottom again, harder this time as he took his disappointment out on her. She stumbled as they reached the top of the steps and would have fallen if the other one hadn't hauled her to her feet, almost wrenching her arm from its socket in the process.

'In there, bitch, and I hope he leaves you to rot,' muttered Dickon as he shoved her into the small room, sending her flat on her face. The door banged shut and she was alone.

Sitting up and rubbing her shoulder gingerly, she looked around. The room was circular and completely empty. There wasn't even a pallet to sit on.

Light fell from an arrow-slit in the wall. Getting shakily to her feet, she walked over to it, then sighed. It was too high to look out from, even when she stood on tiptoe. Grimacing at the pain from her fall, she limped over to the wall opposite the door and sat down on the cold stone floor, with her back to it. She would give no one the advantage of taking her by surprise.

It soon became apparent no one was going to. The thin shaft of light from the arrow-slit had crept all the way across the floor, but time had crawled past so slowly she had lost track of how long she had been in there. Self-pity made her feel sad. She was hungry, and so cold that her teeth chattered. Perhaps Sir Edmund did intend to forget all about her?

The sound of footsteps on the steps made her freeze. Was it Sir Edmund, come to gloat at her downfall? Using the wall to brace herself, she got stiffly to her feet and stared defiantly at the slowly opening door.

She sagged with relief as the guard entered, clutching half a loaf of bread and a large jug of what was obviously water. Without a word he laid it at the door and walked out again. She went across and examined her meagre fare. At least the bread was fresh and free of weevils and, thankfully, it hadn't been Dickon who brought it. He would probably have spat in the water, or worse, on his journey to the little room. Still, she didn't know if more would be forthcoming, and she would have to make it last. There were no facilities in the room, though, so the empty jug would have to serve a more basic purpose. She was damned if she was going to squat in the corner and piss like one of Sir Edmund's bitches.

Her brief flicker of amusement passed. She was freezing already and it wasn't even nightfall. The wind keened through the arrow-slit, striking through her damp clothing like a knife. Despite her aching limbs she made herself walk up and down the room as she ate, flapping the cloak to try and rid it of the worst of its wetness.

She was not particularly successful in her attempts, but at least the exercise set her blood moving again and the bread stilled the worst of the hunger pangs. She forced herself to continue, pacing back and forth like a caged lioness until she could walk no more. Exhausted, she rolled the still-damp cloak around her as best she could and huddled down to try and sleep.

It was useless. As soon as she stopped moving the chill crept back, eating its way bone-deep into her body. Worse still, her mind too seemed beyond her control. Light-headed from hunger and cold, she was no longer in the turret room, she was being plunged once more into the barrel of freezing water by Mother Ursula and Sister Michael. She shivered uncontrollably, sure now that Sir Edmund had left her to perish.

When the door opened again she didn't even hear it. Sir Edmund stood on the threshold, looking down on the whimpering bundle, his lips twisted in a cruel smile. He nudged her with his toe and she stared up at him with frightened eyes.

'Not quite so defiant now, are you?' he sneered.

She tried to frame a suitable retort, but her quivering lips refused to obey her. He must have noticed the blue tinge to her skin, for a hint of concern crossed his face and hope flickered in her. Perhaps he did not intend her to die, merely to subdue her.

Bending, he scooped her up as if she weighed nothing. She huddled against him, grateful for the warmth no matter what its source.

Bellowing for servants he kicked the door back on its hinges and carried her down the winding steps and across the courtyard.

Within minutes she was back in her own room. Depositing her beside the fire, he peeled the damp clothes from her shivering body and chafed her numb limbs with a coarse cloth until the blueness began to disappear. Pulling the coverlet from the bed, he wrapped it round her, glaring impatiently at the door.

The first servant arrived with a steaming posset. Glancing nervously at her master, the girl laid it on the hearth. He picked it up and held it to Jane's lips. At first she coughed and spluttered as the hot wine trickled the wrong way down her throat, then she drank greedily, feeling the reviving warmth all the way through.

'Thank you,' she gasped, when she had finished. Another shudder racked her and she could feel her stomach rebelling against its contents. She swallowed convulsively. Sir Edmund would not take it too kindly if she vomited over him!

'Get into bed,' he ordered, then took in her apprehensive expression and snorted in exasperation. 'Not for that reason, you stupid girl. Do you think I wish to swive you now, like this? Don't be ridiculous. I like my women with a bit of fight left in them, not lying under me like a dead fish.'

The burgeoning smile of gratitude died on her lips. So much for his vaunted concern. She might have known. All he was concerned about was his own damned pleasure. She was only a convenient body to spend in, and he wanted that body in good condition.

Tugging the coverlet about her, she got to her feet, drew herself to full height and glared at him. Unfortunately, the effect she hoped to create was spoiled when she swayed and almost fell. Swearing under his breath, he caught her arm and helped her over to the bed.

'I can manage,' she complained weakly, pushing his hands away. Ignoring her, he lifted her legs, swung them on to the bed and roughly pulled the covers up over her.

Her ordeal and the posset, drunk so quickly on an empty stomach, caught up with her at once. Her eyes were closing even before her head hit the pillow. She snuggled into the warmth like a contented kitten, whimpering with pleasure. 'Goodnight, Alice,' she murmured, just as sleep claimed her.

Sir Edmund stared down at her in puzzled amusement. He'd been called many a thing in his life, but never 'Alice'. Was the girl delirious?

As he looked down on her sleeping figure, with her hair spread out on the pillow, her lips slightly parted and her breasts rising and falling softly as she breathed, he felt a sudden affection for her. He caught himself just in time and his lips tightened. No slip of a girl was going to trap him in her nets! She was nothing to him; just a plaything to be toyed with and then discarded.

How dare she worm her way into his affections? He

would stamp out this unmanly sentiment. He would stamp *her* out! He would use her and abuse her until she was nothing but the dust beneath his feet. He strode out, slamming the door behind him while, unaware of the fate he had planned for her, Jane slept peacefully on.

When Jane awoke it was still dark. She stretched and yawned, then sat up and looked around. How long had she slept? Surely not just for a few hours? She felt wonderful.

There was a perfunctory rap on the door, followed immediately by Martha's bustling entry. The cook bore a tray, which she deposited briskly in front of Jane. A bowl of broth slopped dangerously.

'About time, too,' she sniffed. 'I thought you was going to sleep forever.'

'What day is this?' asked Jane in dismay.

'Day?' snorted Martha. 'It ain't day no more. It's night. You been lying there snoring like a pig for more'n twenty-four hours. I seen folks in their winding sheets with more life in 'em.'

'I don't snore,' protested Jane.

'Well, mebbe not,' Martha conceded graciously, 'but you been out cold for long enough. Get that food down you quick. His majesty's getting impatient.'

Spooning up her broth obediently, Jane stared at Martha. 'Impatient for what?' she inquired anxiously.

'How should I know?' demanded Martha. 'He don't confide in me, do he? I'm just one of his skivvies.' She mimicked Sir Edmund's aristocratic tones. '"Tell madam I shall wait upon her this evening," he said. Thass all I know. Bad-tempered sod, I wouldn't fancy him "waiting on" me, I can tell you.' She shivered theatrically. 'That one ol' eye of his gives me the collywobbles, and no mistake. Looks at you as if you was something nasty he'd trod in.'

It was Jane's turn to shiver. She agreed with every one of Martha's words. 'Thank you,' she said. 'And once I have finished my repast, you may tell Sir Edmund he has my permission to wait upon me when he will.' Her fine words meant nothing; they were merely a sop to her self-esteem. Sir Edmund would come to her chamber whether she willed it or not.

She supped her broth as slowly as she dared, taking tiny sips from the spoon while Martha stood over her, impatiently watching every mouthful. All too soon the bowl was empty. Taking the goblet of wine, she gulped it down and poured herself another – and another – until the jug was drained. She needed all the help she could get to steel herself for Sir Edmund's visit.

Banging down the goblet, she smiled tipsily up at Martha. 'There,' she announced. 'Let him do his worst. I am ready.'

Martha picked up the tray and, shaking her head, bustled out as noisily as she had come, closing the door behind her.

Once she had gone Jane eased herself out of bed and, staggering slightly, walked across to the mirror, with the coverlet still around her shoulders. Now what should she wear to greet her master? She giggled drunkenly and spread it wide so that it framed her naked body like a pair of wings. Turning this way and that, she admired her slender figure, her pert breasts bobbing as she moved. Why bother wearing anything? He was only going to rip it off and there was no point spoiling another good gown. She would greet him as nature intended.

The door banged open again and she whirled round, almost falling again. Sir Edmund stood scowling on the threshold. She smiled at him, spread the coverlet and dipped into an unsteady curtsy. Her breasts swung forward as she bent so that her left nipple almost grazed her knee.

For a moment he gazed at her in astonishment, then his usual sardonic expression returned. 'I see you have dressed for the occasion, my lady,' he said dryly. 'How appropriate, seeing that we have company.'

She gaped at him for a moment, then her gaze shifted over his shoulder.

Behind Sir Edmund stood the hateful Dickon, who had already made his lustful intentions towards her clear. And beside *him* some grinning ruffian she'd never seen in her life. As they entered the room she was shocked back to sobriety. With a whimper she pulled the coverlet about her and began to back away, looking from one hard face to the other.

'What? Suddenly modest, my dear?' Sir Edmund asked sarcastically. 'How touching. But I fear your gesture is sadly wasted on our guests. I rather think they preferred you as you were.' He strode across the room and ripped the coverlet from her, leaving her exposed to the men's lecherous gaze.

Her hands flew instinctively to cover herself, but he wrenched them away too, pulling them behind her back so that her soft young breasts rose proudly. She closed her eyes, but she could not shut out the vision of Dickon's leering expression, nor the sight of the unknown man beside him. A filthy ragged beggar, he was propped on a crutch, because one leg was missing from the thigh. She opened her eyes again and stared at Sir Edmund in a mute plea for mercy.

He ignored it. 'Come now, why so shy? Let me introduce you.' He waved a hand at the other two. 'Dickon you already know, but I don't believe you've had the pleasure of meeting Arthur here.' The cripple nodded and grinned at her, revealing stained brown teeth. Sir Edmund quirked an eyebrow. 'But you will, my dear. In fact, you'll get to know him intimately.'

'Why are you doing this?' Jane asked softly. 'What have I done to you that I deserve such treatment?'

Sir Edmund flung his head back and guffawed. 'Why nothing, my lady. That's the beauty of it, don't you see? It's a cruel world. An evil man lives richly while a good one dies in poverty, and at the end of the day it doesn't make a penny's-worth of difference. Don't you find it all amusingly ironic? Well, perhaps not.

'It amuses me, though,' he continued. 'For tonight's amusement I intend to give you the hospice and the kitchens, so who most appropriate to benefit from your favours but a sick man and a crippled beggar? I'm sure our Lord would approve.'

'There's nothing wrong with Dickon,' she protested.

'Oh, but there is,' Sir Edmund assured her. 'He has a rather nasty swelling I think he'd like you to deal with.'

Dickon waggled his tongue at her and rubbed the front of his breeches suggestively. Even from across the room, Jane could see the bulge beneath the coarse material.

'But I must apologise,' Sir Edmund went on. 'I am keeping our friends waiting. They are impatient, and I believe young Dickon here has a bone to pick with you.' He nodded, and Dickon stepped forward, unbuckling his belt.

'Lose me a week's pay, would you, you snooty little bitch?' he snarled. 'Well, you're the one who's going to pay now. I'm going to tan the arse off you first, and when I've finished that, I'm going to fuck the arse off you, too.' He grabbed her arm, hauled her across the room and flung her face down on the bed. Wrapping his belt round his fist he raised the loose end and brought it down on her rump. The broad leather strap slapped against her bottom, making the plump globes quiver with the shock, while Sir Edmund and the crippled beggar watched avidly.

She shrieked with pain and tried to wriggle away, but he caught her ankle and dragged her back again. 'Oh no you don't,' he said. 'You'll take what's coming to you, and like it.' His arm rose and the thick belt smacked against her bottom again, two great swathes of scarlet staining the white skin where the blows had landed.

She writhed on the bed, whimpering. 'Please,' she sobbed, lifting a tearstained face. 'I beg of you, please stop.'

'I'll stop when I'm good and ready,' he panted, lifting the belt again. It leathered her bottom for a third time, and then a fourth, until finally she lost count as her world was reduced to the burning agony that encompassed her.

Finally he stopped, his breath coming hard in his throat, and she lay splayed on the bed looking up at him helplessly. The bulge in his breeches was massive now, and he fumbled at it eagerly, his cock springing free of its restraints, thick and swollen.

He wrenched her legs apart and knelt between them, hauling her rump up. The lips of her vulva parted and he gripped his prick in one hand, while the other forced it wider. He ran the head slowly up and down the gaping cleft, relishing the feel of the silken flesh. She whimpered as he lunged forward, pushing himself roughly against her. There was a moment's resistance, then the full length of his member rammed home.

He groaned as he was enveloped in the hot wetness, then slowly withdrew, only to plunge in deeper than before. He watched in fascination as his cock slid in and out of her, purple and glistening, then moaned in dismay as he felt himself losing control. He pulled himself out in a vain attempt to prevent the inevitable, but even as he withdrew his spasm came upon him. His member jerked and his seed spurted out, beading the flushed globes of her bottom with iridescent pearls. His organ began to droop, its last few drops dribbling on to his thigh. Biting his lip with disappointment, he stepped back from the bed.

Sir Edmund had watched it all without a word, his own cock stirring in response to every jerk and thrust until it pushed like iron against his codpiece. Moaning, Jane rolled over on to her back, her legs still parted to reveal the lips of her sex, red and swollen from Dickon's attentions. He licked his lips, his hands itching to explore her inner secrets, to caress those soft breasts and feel their nipples harden against his palms.

But there was more entertainment to come. One more humiliation to heap upon her head before he gave way to his own lusts. Grinning savagely he nodded to the crippled beggar, who hobbled eagerly forward to take his turn. Jane's eyes widened in horror and she gripped the sheets, her knuckles turning white as she tried to pull herself up the bed and as far away from him as possible. Dickon, still smarting from his over-quick performance, seized her ankles again and dragged her back.

'You're a pretty one, and no mistake,' leered the beggar, cunning eyes glinting lewdly from beneath the matted black curls that hung over his low forehead. He flung his crutch away and crawled on to the bed, straddling her right leg so that his stump was between her thighs. She was powerless to resist as he reached out to fondle her breasts. She shuddered as his dirty fingers found her nipples, twisting and pulling until they stood up hard and stiff. He leaned forward, delightedly, sucking first one then the other into his slobbering mouth, as one hand searched lower and the other kept his balance.

Jane held her breath against his stench, groaning as her body responded no matter how she tried to control it. His filthy hand had found her vulva, still throbbing from Dickon's cock, and he thrust two fingers deep inside, his thumb toying with the hard bud of her clitoris. Biting her lip she tossed her head from side to side, moaning denial of the blood that pounded through her, greedily demanding more.

'You likes that, don't you, my fine lady?' he chuckled. 'What about this then, eh?' He shuffled forwards so that his amputated leg was pressed to her gaping cleft and began to rock backwards and forwards, the stump pushing against her with every movement. 'How does that feel?'

She groaned in horrified revulsion, both at his filth and her own reaction. It felt vile... *deliciously* vile. It rubbed rhythmically, faster and faster, like some huge blunt cock, while his real member bobbed and swayed above her lower belly like a one-eyed snake. Despite her disgust her eyelids flickered shut and her hips began to move in time with his movements, forcing him harder against her.

Panting, he slid down so that his prick replaced his stump and, with one convulsive movement, pushed his cock deep inside her. It slid in easily, greased by the hot juices oozing from her and, for a few moments before he too shot his bolt, the beggar and the highborn lady groaned in mutual pleasure.

Jane groaned again, this time in dismay as he withdrew all too soon. Like Dickon before him, he had left her unsatisfied. Her sex ached for more, her nipples rigid with need. She whimpered with mindless frustration, arching her back as if swiving an invisible lover. How could she find pleasure in acts that should repulse her? The truth was that beneath the innocent face she presented to the world lay a whirlpool of dark desire.

Sir Edmund watched with a mixture of lust and grudging admiration, his cock so hard it felt as if it would explode. 'Get out!' he snarled at Dickon and the beggar, not even taking his gaze from Jane's writhing body. 'Keep your mouths shut and you'll be rewarded, but speak one word of it and I'll have your balls.' Exchanging frightened glances, they sidled from the room.

He leaned over her and ran one finger down her belly to her cleft where the nub of her lust jutted between the pouting lips. She jerked and moaned as if she had been scalded, raising her hips and parting her legs even further to allow him easier access.

'You want it, don't you?' he hissed. She stared at him wide-eyed and nodded dumbly. His lip curled. 'Then let me hear you beg,' he ordered.

'Please, please,' she moaned, her head tossing on the pillow, her red hair sticking to her face in sweaty strands. One of her hands went to her breasts, urgently stroking her own swollen nipples, while the other reached between her legs. 'Come into me now,' she whined.

'Oh, I will, my pretty,' he said. His nose wrinkled in distaste at the sight of the beggar's seed still trickling down her thigh. 'But I have never ploughed another man's furrow. I prefer virgin land.' Ignoring her protest, he rolled her back on her stomach and parted the still inflamed cheeks of her beaten bottom to reveal her tight, rosy anus.

Realising his intention, she squealed in outrage and tried to wriggle from his grasp. He brought his hand down sharply on her quivering buttocks and she subsided into muffled sobs. Ignoring those too, he spat on his hand, wet his throbbing cock and pushed it against the softly puckered opening. Slowly it gave way and he eased the swollen head inside, gasping at the tightness and the dark heat that seemed to radiate from her forbidden centre. Slowly, remorselessly, he sank inside until his shaft was buried to the hilt in her arse.

Her groans of pain turned again to moans of pleasure. Thrusting her fingers inside herself, she could feel the huge length of his cock against them. As he began to move so did she, pushing herself back until she was impaled on his thrusting prick, her fingers working busily, feeling the unbearable sensations mounting until she stiffened and screamed her release.

Her clenching muscles gripped him like a vice, and he groaned out his own pleasure as she milked the seed from him. He half fell across her and lay there, motionless, his skin sticking to hers with the sweat of their exertions.

Trapped beneath his heavy body, she closed her eyes and bit her lip. Once again he had brought her to her knees in shame, and she could see no end to the torment that lay ahead.

Chapter Twenty-Two

When Jane woke, she was alone – and the day already well past, judging by the failing sunlight stretched across the floor. She was soul-weary, aching in both mind and body. Snippets of the night before threatened to force themselves into her consciousness, but she dismissed them to some dark closet in her mind, and closed the door firmly on them. All she wanted was to sleep – and forget.

She rolled over, burrowing beneath the sweaty sheets and closing her eyes against the world.

Rough hands shook her out of her drowsiness and she batted them peevishly away. 'Leave me alone,' she moaned. 'What do you want now?' The hands continued their shaking and, reluctantly, she opened her eyes.

Martha's broad face scowled down disapprovingly. 'Are you ill, mistress?' she demanded. 'You have lain abed all day.'

'Yes,' Jane muttered. 'I am sick at heart.'

'Hah!' snapped Martha, folding her arms. 'Is that all? If we all lay abed when we felt sorry for ourselves the world would go to rack and ruin. Anyway, you must get up and dress.' Her already ample bosom puffed up with the pleasure of being the harbinger of exciting news. 'We have a guest.'

Jane groaned, burying her face in the pillow. 'The king himself could come a-visiting, for all it matters to me. Go away, Martha, and let me be.'

'Oh, I think you'll want to see this guest,' said Martha slyly, one eye closing in a lecherous wink. 'Any maiden would. As pretty a young gentleman as I've seen in many a long day. And he's keen enough to see you. Practically champing at the bit, he is!'

Despite herself a flicker of interest stirred in Jane. 'Oh yes, and did this "pretty young gentleman" give his name?'

'Robin Attwood,' announced Martha triumphantly. 'Your mother's steward.'

Jane sat bolt upright in bed. 'Robin?' she gasped, staring at Martha closely. 'What brings him here? And are you sure he said steward?'

'As sure as I'm standing here,' said Martha, smugly.

Jane's mind raced. Robin her mother's steward? He had been a mere groom when she left. Admittedly, he had some education. He had been a bright child and their local priest had made it his business to encourage him in his learning. He could read and write and reckon almost as well as she could. In fact, had his family not been so poor, he might even have gone into the church himself – but a steward? What had happened to her stepfather? He would not lightly have relinquished control of her mother's estates.

'Lay out my blue gown,' she ordered, swinging her legs out of bed. 'The one with the gold embroidery round the neck. And hot water to wash with.'

'Certainly, madam,' Martha replied. She took the gown from the chest, shook out the silken folds and laid it neatly at the foot of the bed, then dropped into a curtsey. 'I shall send a maid with water, immediately.' She was grinning as she left, delighted that her titbit of news had produced such a gratifying affect.

Half an hour later Jane had washed, dressed, and was sitting impatiently as the maid dressed her unruly hair into a sleek mass of ringlets that cascaded down her back beneath her head-dress. She gazed into the mirror, then pinched her cheeks and bit her lips to heighten their colour.

She hurried down to the great hall as quickly as her dignity would allow. At the door she paused, her eyes searching for Robin's familiar figure. They lit on the tall man seated beside Sir Edmund, carried on for a moment – then stopped and returned. It *was* Robin! But how he had changed in such a few short months!

He was taller than she remembered and his shoulders had broadened. But those were not the only changes. He carried himself with the confidence and surety of a man who knew his own worth, and this was reflected in his dress. His clothing was subdued but rich, his boots of fine leather. Though no one else would know, Jane's keen eyes detected her stepfather's hand-me-downs. Again that merely served to raise the puzzling question of what had happened. Her stepfather would no more hand over his good clothing to a groom than he would fly through the air!

Robin raised his head, caught her eye and his face was suddenly younger as it broke into the open smile she remembered so fondly. As she approached, for one heart-stopping moment she thought he was going to rush to take her in his arms, but he controlled himself visibly and bowed stiffly instead. 'My lady,' he murmured formally, taking her hand. 'I am pleased to see you again. I trust you are well?'

Unaware of the black expression on Sir Edmund's face, she dimpled up at him. 'All the better for seeing you, Robin.' Her welcoming smile disappeared, to be replaced by anxiety. 'But what brings you here? Is something wrong at home?'

A frown creased his brow. 'I am afraid so, my lady. I bring grave news—'

'My mother!' she exclaimed, an icy hand gripping her bowels. 'Something has happened to my mother!' Rage overwhelmed her. No doubt that bastard, her stepfather, had taken his beatings one step too far. She had always known it would happen someday.

He hastened to reassure her. 'No, not your mother, my lady. It is Sir Thomas...'

For a moment she stared at him, uncomprehending. Her stepfather, filling the house with his loud voice, his furious temper and gargantuan appetites, had always seemed so indestructible. Like some unpleasant and uncontrollable force of nature.

'What has happened to him?' she demanded. 'A fall from his horse? Some knife cut? What?'

'Leprosy.'

A ghastly hush fell throughout the hall as the word dropped from his lips, like a stone into a still pool. Ripples of horror spread as even the men-at-arms, veterans of bloody battles, blenched and crossed themselves.

Leprosy.

The very word was a curse, its bearers forced to dwell apart as their living bodies rotted. They would endure a miserable half-life, living on scraps in the lazar houses attached to the convents and monasteries, if they were lucky. If they were not, they were forced to beg out their miserable existence on the roads, ringing their bells to warn the populace of their presence, their call of 'Unclean! Unclean!' going before them, everywhere they went.

Jane was unable to believe what Robin had told her. An icy finger touched her spine as she remembered Sir Edmund's sweaty, heaving body as he rammed himself into her. Had he been tainted even then? A wave of faintness washed over her. She steadied herself, remembering how seldom the nuns who tended these unfortunates fell to the dreaded sickness. Her body was as smooth and unmarred as ever. The plague had passed her by.

'Where is he?' she asked, her voice steady.

'Why, at the convent of St Ursula,' answered Robin. 'In the care of the good nuns there.'

A bitter smile twisted Jane's lips. The Good Lord must have a sense of humour after all – and an unpleasant one at that. What a fitting act of justice that the man who had so corrupted her should end up in the very convent she was debauching herself to preserve.

She turned towards Sir Edmund. 'May I go and visit him?' she asked.

'Of course,' he nodded, a glimmer of pity in his eyes. 'It is only natural you would wish to show your devotion. You have my sympathies, madam.'

She would hardly have described her motives as springing from devotion to a man she so despised. Sir Thomas could rot for all she cared, but some dark force inside her needed to see how low he had been brought before she could dismiss him from her life forever.

'Thank you,' she murmured. 'I shall ride out first thing tomorrow, after I have broken my fast.'

Robin interrupted. 'I would not eat beforehand, if I were you, my lady,' he advised, his face twisting in revulsion. 'He is not the prettiest of sights to see on a full stomach.'

'Then I shall ride out at first light,' she said. 'I trust you will accompany me, Master Attwood?'

'It would be an honour,' he replied, bowing. Sir Edmund scowled again, but neither of them noticed, and he had concealed his displeasure by the time Jane turned back to him.

'If I may have your permission, sir, I would dine alone this evening, and pray for my unfortunate stepfather.' She lowered her eyes demurely. A triumphant smile touched her lips and she hid it quickly. It was no lie. She *would* pray for him. Pray that he lived long – and suffered as much as he had made her suffer!

Back in her chamber she found herself ravenously hungry. She waited impatiently for her food and fell upon it as soon as it was brought. It was only when she had half-devoured a chicken leg that she realised Martha was not her usual exuberant self. No scolding. No unasked-for advice. What was wrong? Was her friend ill? Guiltily, she put down her food and stared at the cook. Were those tearstains on her cheeks?

'Martha!' she exclaimed. 'What ails you? Has that archer of yours been dallying elsewhere? Shall I have him beaten?'

'No, mistress,' Martha sniffed. 'It's nothing to do with 'im.'

'Then what is it?' Jane demanded. 'You look as if you'd lost a crown and found a farthing.'

'It's ol' one-eye,' Martha burst out.

Jane stared at her in astonishment, wondering how Sir Edmund could have upset Martha so terribly. 'What's he done?' she asked.

'He's only bringing in a fancy new cook, thass what,' she wailed. 'Seems I ain't good enough any more. He's got to have some Frog he's brung over from foreign parts. Calls himself a sheff, whatever that is. As if good English cooking ain't good enough for 'is lordship. Snooty bastard!'

'But aren't you glad?' asked Jane. 'It means you won't have to work so hard any more.'

Martha stared at Jane as if she was mad. 'But I'm the cook!' she exclaimed indignantly, in the same tones of injured pride a better-born woman would have used to declare that she was a lady. Jane supposed she was perfectly right. In her own way, Martha was queen of her domain – even if it was only the castle kitchen – and she was about to be deposed by some foreign upstart.

Martha's voice wavered and she sniffed back more tears. 'What'll I be once he comes? Nothing but another one of the kitchen skivvies. It ain't fair!' She gave into her grief, plonked herself down and burst into noisy tears.

Jane patted the woman's heaving back, trying to console her. 'There, there, it's not as bad as that. I'll think of something. Just you wait and see.'

Martha raised her head and smiled at her tearfully. 'Thass a kind thought, girl, even if it comes to nought.' She got to her feet. 'Well,' she muttered, 'best get on. I wants that kitchen scoured from top to bottom. No fancy foreign sheff's going to say I keeps things mucky.'

Fuelled by new determination, Martha bustled out, leaving Jane to finish her meal and creep into bed.

She was up before cockcrow, dressed and ready by the time Robin came into the hall. Despite her brave words her stomach churned at the thought of seeing her stepfather again but, apart from the way her hands nervously twisted the folds of her riding skirts, she hid it well.

'Good morrow, Robin,' she said. 'I am ready. Are the horses saddled?'

'Waiting in the courtyard,' he replied. He gazed at her, his eyes serious. 'But are you sure you wish to do this? I warned you already that he is not a pretty sight.'

'And not one that will improve with time,' she said tartly. 'Now, do you accompany me, or shall I go alone?'

'I will accompany you,' he replied in resignation.

Out of sight of the castle Robin slowed his horse and leaned towards Jane. 'There is one other thing, my lady. I did not wish to speak of it in front of Sir Edmund, but your mother's estate is in a sorry state. When Sir Thomas first found out what ailed him he spent money like water on any charlatan who held promise of a cure. Wise-women. Amulets. Holy relics. Much good has it done him. He has Saint Stephen's knucklebone – and by the look of it, Saint Stephen must have been a pig! It will be a long hard winter for your mother, my lady. He has squandered everything.'

'What a surprise!' exclaimed Jane cynically, as the convent came into view. 'When did the bastard ever care for anyone but himself? Well, he is paying for it now.'

How high a price, she did not realise until she entered the darkened room where he lay. The stench met her first; a cloying smell of decay that caught in her throat and almost made her gag. As her eyes adjusted to the gloom her hand flew to her mouth and she gasped in horror as she saw his face.

Her stepfather's nose was nothing but a festering cavity, leaking noxious fluids; one ear was missing and the other was only a gnarled knob of raw flesh. His lips were half-eaten away, revealing the brown teeth behind them in a perpetual skeletal grin. She shuddered. He no longer looked human. It was the face of a rotting corpse – yet the worst horror was that it still lived. And this *thing* had once touched her! Vomit rose in her throat.

The scabrous lips parted in a sardonic rictus. 'Well,' he rasped. 'Have you come to gloat?' He turned his head this way and that. 'Take a good look, Jane. It's a handsome picture, is it not? One to bring a maiden sweet dreams.' He began to laugh, but it ended in a choking fit and he lay back on his stained pillow, gasping. His bandaged hands plucked convulsively at the coverlet and, with fresh nausea, Jane realised that half his fingers had rotted away.

'But I shall have the last laugh,' he spat viciously. 'I may be dying in this cesspool, but I shall have the picture of your sainted mother sitting hungry beside an empty hearth to keep me company.' His mad, cracked laughter followed her as she fled.

Robin was waiting where she had left him, but she managed to ride only half a mile before the sickness overwhelmed her. Dragging her horse to a halt, she swung down and scrambled into the bushes, where she bent over and retched until her empty stomach ached. Finally she stood upright, wiping her mouth.

A warm hand touched her shoulder. 'Are you all right?' asked Robin anxiously. Whirling round she flung herself into his arms, clinging to him like a child, feeling his strong body against hers.

Against all reason she could feel a warm stirring in her loins. Unconsciously, she ground her hips sensuously against him, rejoicing in his instant response. Perhaps this was no madness, but merely the reaffirmation of life in the face of death and horror.

He bent his head to kiss her, but she turned her face away. 'My breath must be foul,' she protested.

'Nothing about you could ever be foul to me,' he breathed, his mouth seeking hers, his warm tongue sliding between her lips. One hand stroked her breast while the other sought to lift her heavy skirts and he groaned as he felt her nipple grow hard against his palm. His fingers found the lacing at her bodice and he groaned again as the warm globes spilt out into his eager grasp.

It was her turn to groan as his lips left hers and his hot mouth traced a path down her throat and breast; then she gasped as he found her rigid nipples and took first one then the other between his lips, teasing the rosy tips with his tongue.

She was dizzy with lust, and had it not been for the tree behind her she would have fallen. Leaning back against it she hauled her skirts to her waist and parted her legs, allowing him free access to her cunny. His fingers stroked the soft flesh of her inner thighs, sending shivers of pleasure through her, then crept higher, sliding smoothly into her. She moaned again as they plunged in and out of her silken wetness.

Panting, he fell on his knees before her, lowered his head and parted the lips of her vulva. His tongue pierced her as he lapped at her sweet juices; then he found the hard bud of her womanhood and ran his tongue gently round it. She whimpered and ground her hips against his face, enveloping him in its musky scent.

Getting to his feet again he fumbled at his belt. His member jutted forth, thick and hard, then she closed her eyes as the swollen head butted against her. She whimpered as his cock slid inside, slowly and deliciously. Bracing herself against the tree trunk she met each thrust with one of her own until they shuddered out their mutual release.

Decent again, they cantered once more towards the castle, the picture of respectability. The only evidence that anything had happened was the feel of Robin's seed trickling between Jane's thighs as she rode. Despite what had happened, she felt strangely unsatisfied. There was no denying that their little dalliance had been pleasurable, and yet, like food without salt, his respectful advances had lacked savour compared to Sir Edmund's animal rutting.

Her lips parted and her heart beat faster as she remembered the hot sting of the lash, followed by Sir Edmund cruelly, ruthlessly slaking his lust on her body. She could not deny the dark passion he seemed able to rouse in her, until she debased herself at his feet, her debauchery matching his own.

She groaned inwardly as she felt herself stir again at the very thought. With one man's seed still inside her, she was already lusting after another. Had she finally run mad?

Chapter Twenty-Three

It was not she who ran mad, however – it was Sir Edmund.

'Bitch! Slut!' he snarled, banging open the door of her chamber so hard it hit the wall. In two brief strides he was across the room and had seized her by the hair, dragging her face close to his. 'How dare you? You could not wait two minutes before bedding him, could you?'

'Wh-what do you mean?' she quavered.

He flung her from him in disgust. Staggering, she fell sprawling across the bed and gazed up at him with frightened eyes as he paced backwards and forwards like a caged lion. 'You know exactly what I mean,' he retorted. 'Did you think I would let you go riding alone with that pretty boy and not have you followed? My man saw everything. Everything!'

Shame burned her cheeks at the thought of what he must have seen, but she rallied defiantly. 'And if he did, what business is it of yours? Your scruples come a trifle late in the day, my lord. You gave me to a beggar and watched while he swived me. It hardly becomes you to quibble should I choose to take my pleasure with Robin. And it was pleasure, believe me.'

The sound of a slap echoed through the chamber and she shrieked, a protective hand flying to her reddening cheek.

'It matters because I say it matters,' he hissed. 'And I did not give you permission to dally with that young upstart.' He gripped her chin, his cruel fingers digging into the soft flesh as he held her immobile. 'You are mine, to do with as I will. Remember that!'

She stared after him in dismay as he stalked from the chamber without another word, and a dreadful thought struck her. What might he not do to Robin in his rage?

Relief washed over her when she finally steeled herself to venture down to the great hall that evening. Far from punishing Robin, Sir Edmund appeared to be on the best of terms with her mother's steward. Seated at Robin's right hand, he was laughing uproariously and slapping him on the back, insisting that he be offered the best cuts of meat and filling his goblet almost before it was emptied.

Her relief turned to confusion as he caught sight of her and smiled. He rose to his feet and greeted her with a bow. 'Ah, Lady Jane. How kind of you to join us. Come, sit down, my dear, and grace our table with your presence.'

The little scene in her chamber might never have occurred. She stared at him suspiciously. What evil plan was hatching in that devious skull of his?

Despite her fears, he was gallantry itself, deferring to her every wish. Was she too hot? Too cold? Would she like more wine? Another helping of meat? By the end of the evening her suspicions had been utterly allayed. Back in her chamber she smiled at her reflection in the mirror. Perhaps he was prepared to let bygones be bygones after all?

How wrong she was.

A scuffling in the passage outside made her whirl round as the door was pushed rudely open and Sir Edmund strode in. Behind him, struggling between two of his henchmen, was Robin. As she watched in horror he was thrust into the heavy chair beside the fire and his arms and legs tied to it. He strained helplessly against his bonds as a rough gag was forced into his mouth.

'Turn him towards the bed,' ordered Sir Edmund.

Obediently, his men manhandled the chair until it faced the four-poster. 'Good, good...' He walked slowly round his victim. 'We would not wish to fail in our duties to our visitor, now would we?' He waved dismissively. 'You may go now.' Silently, the two men left the room.

Once they were gone Jane stared at him. 'What are you going to do?' she asked fearfully.

Sir Edmund grinned wolfishly. 'Why, entertain our guest, my dear. What else? Now take your clothes off,' he ordered. 'Or do I have to do it for you?'

She backed away, her hands protectively at her bosom, but he was on her in a trice. He grasped the neck of her bodice and tore it away. The remains of the gown slithered to her feet, leaving her standing naked to his lustful gaze.

She cowered away, but he seized her, twisting her arms behind her so she was forced to arch her back, her quivering breasts thrust into prominence. Trapping both her wrists in one hand he fondled them with the other, luxuriating in the feel of the soft flesh. Robin's eyes widened as she groaned and the delicate pink tips hardened beneath the touch.

'A pretty whore, is she not?' Sir Edmund asked conversationally. His hand strayed lower, toying with the auburn curls of her pubic hair. 'And one who enjoys her work.'

Jane shuddered as his fingers parted the lips of her vulva and plunged into the softness between. 'See?' he commented, removing them. They glistened in the firelight. 'One touch and she is hot for it. But then, you know that, don't you? You have sampled her wares already. Which reminds me, I have not yet punished her for that transgression.'

Dragging Jane after him, he seated himself on the bed in front of Robin and hauled her across his lap. She writhed and tried to free herself from his grasp, her slim legs flailing uselessly as the first blow landed on her clenched buttocks, making the flesh jump. She squealed as the pain erupted. Robin struggled fruitlessly against his bonds as he watched Sir Edmund's hand rise and fall, Jane's breasts bouncing with every slap. His outraged grunts and Sir Edmund's heavy breathing mingled with Jane's shrieks of terror and agony as the sound of flesh on flesh echoed through the chamber.

The soft white skin of her bottom gradually turned scarlet, the shape of his hand imprinted on her flesh like a brand of ownership. Sobs tore their way from her throat as each blow brought a fresh wave of pain, mingled with shameful excitement. Heat radiated through her lower body as she felt his member swell and push against her belly and she closed her eyes in humiliation that Robin should see her brought so low.

Finally, he was done. He pushed her from his lap, then stood over her as he unbuckled his belt and let it fall, tugging at his hose, releasing his erect cock. 'First the punishment – then the reward,' he murmured as he bent and hauled her on to the bed. He glanced over his shoulder at Robin. 'Watch well, boy, and see how a *real* man swives a woman.'

In front of Robin's horrified eyes, he pulled Jane's thighs apart and knelt between them with his prick in hand. She closed her eyes and groaned with pleasure as he rubbed its swollen head tantalisingly up and down her soft cleft as the other toyed with her breasts, pinching and squeezing their soft tips until they stood rigidly to attention beneath his fingers.

Tiring of this amusement, Sir Edmund gripped the plump globes of her bottom, pulled her upwards and thrust himself home. Jane whimpered as she was impaled on his member, like a butterfly on a pin. Savouring every moment of Robin's torment and his own pleasure, Sir Edmund moved slowly and sensuously in and out of the buttery softness as Jane writhed beneath him, her moans rising in crescendo as each stroke stoked the fire within.

He was moving faster now, withdrawing the full length of his prick then plunging back harder than before. Jane's control broke and she wound her legs round his waist to pull him even closer. Her nails dug into his buttocks as she urged him on, her breasts jiggling as his body pounded into hers. Finally, her back arched and she screamed as her climax exploded. Sir Edmund's hips jerked as he, too, spent his lust and he collapsed against her sweating body.

He raised his head and grinned at Robin. 'There boy, did you enjoy my lady's performance?'

A sob of shame escaped Jane's lips at his mockery. Still panting, Sir Edmund got to his feet and sauntered over to where Robin still struggled against his bonds. 'I hope so,' he goaded, 'because now it's time to deal with you.'

Stooping, he pulled the dagger from his fallen belt and held it poised over the other man's groin. Robin froze, his eyes fixed on the wickedly glittering blade as it descended. With two swift movements Sir Edmund sliced away the fabric and Robin's rampant cock sprang free, its head so purple and engorged that the skin shone taut in the firelight.

'What a compliment to your charms, my dear,' murmured Sir Edmund. 'Even the threat of cold steel has done nothing to diminish your admirer's ardour.' He snapped his fingers. 'Well, my love – to your duties. Our guest is waiting.'

Jane stared at him in total incomprehension, not daring to move. Sir Edmund strode across to the bed, seized her by the arm and dragged her to her feet. Pulling her bodily across the room he flung her down on her knees between

Robin's bound legs. She looked up at him imploringly, but he was adamant. 'Well, whore,' he sneered, 'be about your business!'

Stifling a sob, she lowered her head and took the swollen head of Robin's cock between her lips. His eyes closed in tortured pleasure as her soft mouth enveloped him. Jerking his hips involuntarily he uttered a stifled groan through the gag as her tongue ran round the rim of his swollen member, exciting him even more.

Sir Edmund seized the back of her neck and forced Jane's face even further into Robin's groin. She gagged as his prick slid deeper into her mouth, almost choking her. She withdrew instinctively and Robin groaned again at the movement.

Roused again by the scene before him, Sir Edmund's own member rose in response. Quickly he knelt behind Jane, his finger parting the lips of her vulva, still wet from his earlier attentions. With one jerk he thrust himself inside her again.

Despite herself, Jane felt the familiar quickening of her own desire. Her mouth engulfed Robin's cock again, eagerly this time. Her tongue laved the surface of his knob, her head bobbing in time as Sir Edmund thrust in and out of her sex. A moan escaped Robin's lips and Jane felt his member swell and spasm as his hot seed spurted down her throat. Sir Edmund's fingers kneaded her breasts and clitoris as he rogered her roughly from behind, and as he came her own climax exploded. With a groan of despair she bowed her head and sank back on her heels, wrapping her arms about her trembling body.

Sir Edmund was the first to recover. Getting to his feet he adjusted his clothing, then reached into the pouch that dangled from his belt. 'Here,' he sneered, taking out the scroll and flinging it down beside her. 'Your final payment, my dear. And worth every single penny.'

At the door of the chamber he paused and looked back, taking in the sight of her total humiliation. 'I'll leave you to set young Robin free. I'm sure you have sweet nothings to whisper in each other's ears.'

'Oh Robin, I'm so sorry,' Jane wept, her tears dropping on his bonds as she untied him. 'Can you ever forgive me?'

He said nothing, but he could not meet her eyes. As soon as he was free he strode from her chamber without a word or backward glance, leaving her sobbing in despair.

Sleep came late and bitter that night, but in the morning she woke with new resolution. It might have been dearly bought, but she had her freedom again.

'I shall be leaving soon,' she informed Sir Edmund coldly. 'The convent is mine. Our bargain is done.'

His response astonished her. Instead of looking dismayed, he burst into raucous laughter. 'Oh yes, my dear, and where would you go? Back to your poverty-stricken estate? I'm sure your dear mother would be delighted to welcome home her prodigal daughter. One more mouth to feed? I hardly think so. And who else would want you after what you have shown yourself to be? No decent man takes a whore to be his wife. Even your sweet Robin loathes you now.'

He stood over her, his good eye glittering savagely as he picked up his cloak. 'You are mine now, whatever you may say. I must ride to London for a sennight, but when I return you will be waiting for me. Ready and willing as always.' He blew her a mocking kiss. 'Not goodbye, my sweet Jane. Merely adieu.'

She stared after him in dismay, but she was determined not to let him win. If he thought she would be waiting on his return, then he had sadly misjudged her.

The following morning found her at the castle gates. 'Where do you think you're going?' demanded the guard, mindful of his colleague's previous failure of duty. She smiled at him sweetly and indicated the large wicker basket on her saddle.

'Why, merely to take a few provisions to Father Andrew and my ailing stepfather,' she simpered, indicating the basket.

Suspiciously, he pulled back the linen cover and inspected the contents. Discovering nothing more threatening than eggs, meat and calves' foot jelly, he waved her on her way.

On her return she called Martha to the solar. 'I have a proposition for you,' she began without preamble. 'You know that the convent is now mine?' Martha nodded; kitchen gossip had told her that almost as soon as Sir Edmund had handed over the charter. 'Good,' she continued. 'Well, I want you to run it.'

Martha gawped at her, then sat down abruptly. 'Me?' she demanded, when she had recovered from her initial shock. 'Are you mad, girl? I ain't no Mother Superior. And what of Mother Ursula?'

'I don't think you need worry about her,' said Jane. 'Oswald is far too smitten to ever let her go.' It was true: the former Mother Superior was but a shadow of her former self, and rumour had it she was with child. She was no longer a threat to anyone. 'So, Martha? What do you say to it?'

Martha shook her head. 'I couldn't,' she muttered. 'I got no schooling in such things. All that readin' and writin's a mystery to me.'

'Father Andrew will do all that,' said Jane. 'And see to the spiritual side of things. I spoke to him this morning when I left the charter in his keeping. It's all arranged. Come, keeping a few nuns in order would be simple for a woman who can feed an entire household on a few scrawny chickens.'

'It ain't no use you wheedling,' muttered Martha. 'I ain't doing it. I'm a cook, plain and simple – and thass an end of it.'

'But you won't be the cook for much longer,' said Jane slyly. 'Not when Sir Edmund's French chef arrives. If you're lucky, perhaps he'll let you prepare the vegetables.' She sighed and got to her feet. 'Still, if you're happy with that...' She let her voice trail away and waited expectantly.

'I'll do it,' snapped Martha. She folded her arms and glared at Jane mutinously. 'But I ain't being no Mother Superior, mind. I ain't giving up that man of mine, even if he is a useless big lump.' She nodded as she worked things out in her mind. 'I'll just sorta be in charge of things, thass all. Keep them in order.'

'Wonderful!' Jane exclaimed, bestowing an impulsive kiss on the plump cheek. 'You're a treasure. I knew I could rely on you.'

Blushing with pleasure, Martha left to set about organising things to her own satisfaction.

Jane's good mood lasted until the door had closed behind her. Persuading Martha to oversee the other nuns had been easy, but she was dreading what she had to do next. Robin had not even looked at her, let alone spoken to her, since last night. Still, if she wanted to escape from Sir Edmund, it had to be done. Gritting her teeth, she went in search of him.

Old habits died hard, and she found him grooming his horse in the stable. When she entered he turned away and pretended to be engrossed in his task. Straightening her shoulders, she marched up to him.

'I know you despise me,' she said bitterly. 'But no matter. I need your help.'

He avoided her eyes, gripping the curry-comb so hard his knuckles turned white. 'Despise you?' he said. 'I don't despise you. I despise myself.' He dropped his eyes and gazed at his feet. 'I know why you did what you did – but what excuse did I have? I watched that bastard abuse you, and then… and then…' His voice faltered to a stop and he turned scarlet with shame as he remembered his reaction.

Jane laughed with relief, then took his hand. 'What could you have done?' she asked softly. 'You were bound and gagged – as much a victim as I. As for what came next...' She shrugged. 'You are a man with a man's appetites. I shall forgive you, Robin… if you forgive me.'

Robin looked at her fully for the first time. 'Forgive you—?' he began, but she stopped him with a kiss.

'Enough,' she declared. 'We shall put it behind us. There are more important matters to discuss.' Pulling his head down she began to whisper in his ear, and a slow smile crossed his face.

For the next week the sight of her riding with Robin to visit her stepfather with her basket of food became so common that the guard no longer even bothered to challenge her. On the eighth day she was ready. The basket still contained food, but this time it was for their journey.

The visit was brief. 'Farewell, dear stepfather,' she smiled, gazing down at the ghastly living corpse, 'and long life.' Turning on her heel, she nodded to the attending nun. 'The air is foetid here. I shall take a walk around the convent grounds to clear my head. See that I am not disturbed.'

The pigsty was as she had left it so long ago, and it was the work of a moment to push the snorting animals out of the way and find the corner where she had buried the treasures from the altar. She sighed with relief as she unearthed them. Gold and jewels glinted from the filthy linen. Her stepfather had been wrong; there would be no hunger and no empty hearth. Once sold, these would bring enough to feed her household until the estate was on its feet again – and God would surely not begrudge her them.

Robin was waiting for her. Tucking the precious bundle into her basket she swung herself into the saddle. At the top of the hill she paused. From here she could see both the convent and the castle. She had survived them both, and if Sir Edmund wished her back again, why, then he must come a-courting like any honest gentleman! She smiled wickedly at the thought of his reaction to *that*.

Her horse shied suddenly as a small figure broke from the bushes, ran up to them and stopped, gazing shyly up at her. From behind his back he produced a posy of wild flowers, offered them, then took to his heels and fled. Her eyes misted as she recognised the boy whose leg she had healed. He, and all those like him, were safe now. Her ordeal was over, and all was well.

With a joyous laugh she turned her horse's head towards the sunrise and spurred it towards home and freedom. Just for once the Bible had been wrong. The wages of sin was not death. It was life!

Exciting titles available from Chimera

1-901388-20-4	The Instruction of Olivia	*Allen*
1-901388-01-8	Olivia and the Dulcinites	*Allen*
1-901388-12-3	Sold into Service	*Tanner*
1-901388-13-1	All for Her Master	*O'Connor*
1-901388-14-X	Stranger in Venice	*Beaufort*
1-901388-16-6	Innocent Corinna	*Eden*
1-901388-17-4	Out of Control	*Miller*
1-901388-18-2	Hall of Infamy	*Virosa*
1-901388-23-9	Latin Submission	*Barton*
1-901388-19-0	Destroying Angel	*Hastings*
1-901388-21-2	Dr Casswell's Student	*Fisher*
1-901388-22-0	Annabelle	*Aire*
1-901388-24-7	Total Abandon	*Anderssen*
1-901388-26-3	Selina's Submission	*Lewis*
1-901388-27-1	A Strict Seduction	*Del Rey*
1-901388-28-X	Assignment for Alison	*Pope*
1-901388-29-8	Betty Serves the Master	*Tanner*
1-901388-30-1	Perfect Slave	*Bell*
1-901388-31-X	A Kept Woman	*Grayson*
1-901388-32-8	Milady's Quest	*Beaufort*
1-901388-33-6	Slave Hunt	*Shannon*
1-901388-34-4*	Shadows of Torment	*McLachlan*
1-901388-35-2*	Star Slave	*Dere*
1-901388-37-9*	Punishment Exercise	*Benedict*
1-901388-38-7*	The CP Sex Files	*Asquith*
1-901388-39-5*	Susie Learns the Hard Way	*Quine*
1-901388-40-9*	Domination Inc.	*Leather*
1-901388-42-5*	Sophie & the Circle of Slavery	*Culber*
1-901388-11-5*	Space Captive	*Hughes*
1-901388-41-7*	Bride of the Revolution	*Amber*
1-901388-44-1*	Vesta – Painworld	*Pope*
1-901388-45-X*	The Slaves of New York	*Hughes*
1-901388-46-8*	Rough Justice	*Hastings*
1-901388-47-6*	Perfect Slave Abroad	*Bell*
1-901388-48-4*	Whip Hands	*Hazel*
1-901388-50-6*	Slave of Darkness	*Lewis*
1-901388-49-2*	Rectory of Correction	*Virosa*
1-901388-51-4*	Savage Bonds	*Beaufort*
1-901388-55-2*	Darkest Fantasies	*Raines*
1-901388-54-9*	Love Slave	*Wakelin*
1-901388-55-7*	Slave to Cabal *(April)*	*McLachlan*
1-901388-56-5*	Susie Follows Orders *(April)*	*Quine*
1-901388-57-3*	Forbidden Fantasies *(May)*	*Gerrard*
1-901388-58-1*	Chain Reaction *(May)*	*Pope*